2008

MW00945597

SINGER LANE

a novel

by

Janet Purcell

authorHOUSE®

AuthorHouse™
1663 Liberty Drive, Suite 200
Bloomington, IN 47403
www.authorhouse.com
Phone: 1-800-839-8640

First published by AuthorHouse 10/6/2008

ISBN: 978-1-4343-7408-0 (sc)

Library of Congress Control Number: 2008903711

Cover Art by Janet Purcell

Printed in the United States of America
Bloomington, Indiana

This book is printed on acid-free paper.

In memory of my parents

Lois Purcell and William Knock

This book is dedicated with love and admiration to my daughter, my friend, Jill Piggott.
I taught her to read,
She taught me to write.

To my son, John, who, though distance separates us, is always in my heart.
To my son, Jamey, who brightens my life continually with love and laughter.

And to my late husband, John Piggott, who always believed in me.

— *Author's Note of Thanks* —

Many thanks to all those who read parts of this book or all of it as it was coming into being, with special thanks to Jill Piggott for her valued input, Jessica Fuller Piggott for her insightful suggestions, and to my partner, Bob Cary, without whom I would never have come to know Cape Cod.

And to my writing pals, Dennis O'Neill and Nicholas Sant Foster, I say this book would never have been written without your encouragement, support and, most of all, the deep friendships we've shared all these years.

— *Chapter 1* —

THE LOCALS WONDERED ABOUT HIM. Joggers and dog walkers slowed their pace each day as they passed him on the lonely stretch of beach. The dogs felt a tug on their leashes if they tried to venture too close to him to get a sniff.

He was there every day walking along the water's edge. Sometimes he'd pick up a shell and turn it over in his hand to study it before he tossed it back onto the sand with an air of rejecting something more than a mollusk or a scallop shell. No matter what the weather, blustery or calm, rain, or the chilled clear sunlight that often teases Cape Codders in the early spring, he'd sit on that same weather-beaten bench at the foot of the dune and watch the gulls, the rolling surf.

Had it been July, the locals would have glanced at him, thought "tourist" and been on their way. But this was early April and they carried their speculations about him from one day to the next.

But he was oblivious to their speculation. Matthew Callahan knew who he was and why he was there and it never entered his mind that he might be a mystery to others.

In fact, he was doing some speculating of his own one late morning as the fog lay low on the dune. He was absent-mindedly rubbing it into his hands when he noticed an old man making his slow way along the edge of the surf, leaving wavering footprints and the mark of his crooked walking stick behind to be filled by the incoming tide.

As the figure got closer, Matthew saw the man was bent, wizened, and looked unfriendly. He'd focused on Matthew, headed right at him, and stopped short about six feet in front of him. He planted his walking stick firmly in the sand and stood there and stared for what seemed a long time.

"Got a powerful telescope up there," he said jerking his head to the side and looking up at a house nestled in sand and rock on a high promontory. "Been watching you for days. You walk and then sit on my bench doing nothing. Can't for the life of me figure out why you come here every day interrupting what I'm doing."

Curiosity got the best of Matthew. "What am I interrupting every day? What're you doing?"

"Looking," was the unflinching response.

"Sorry about that," Matthew said poker faced as he drew in his long legs and got up to leave. "Looks like it's time for me to mosey along and let you get back to your—looking."

When he was a few yards down the beach he turned and, as expected, the man was still planted firmly in the sand, bent over his walking stick, watching him. Matthew raised his hand in a jaunty wave and laughed quietly as he saw the man turn abruptly away.

A rainy spell hit the Cape and Matthew was the only one walking the beach for a few days but, when the sun came out again, the joggers and dog walkers returned. And so did the old man who, after a few days of curt nods and guarded hellos, stopped again almost nose to nose with Matthew who took a step back.

"Seems like now that you've totally interrupted my mornings, you might as well come up to the house and meet my daughter. She's been hounding me with questions about what I said to you. Told her I let you know I don't like you coming here and sitting on my bench every day. She claims it's not my bench, it's on the public beach, and I told her it's been my bench for forty years. Right down here in front of my house and I don't want anybody else sitting on it every damned day. Don't even know who you are. Least you can do is go up there and answer her questions before you _mosey along,_ he said with just a touch of sarcasm.

What the hell? Matthew thought. This should be an eye opener.

Without another word the old man turned and, rather than follow the surf as he'd done when he'd arrived, he headed straight for the dunes. Matthew followed him. Behind one of the dunes, unseen from the beach, was a stairway of sorts—huge, flat rocks bordered by beach roses and grasses—and a sturdy handrail that looked new.

"The wife and I had these rocks hauled in here when we bought the place forty years ago. Always served us just fine. Now the wife's gone and our Nell has decided I'm an old man and I need a handrail. Hate the goddamned thing. Don't use it and never will." He gave one of the posts a good whack with his walking stick.

3

"Only good thing about it was Bill Nickerson, the woodworker over in Truro? Know him do ya? He came and built it. Liked him. Took up with Katie, Nell's girl, for a spell but that didn't work out. Forty years old she is and she tells me she's not ready to settle down yet. Doesn't make a lick of sense. Always off to this place or that writing articles about where she's been. What she needs is a good man to share some of that stuff with but she won't listen to me. Always was thick headed. Stubborn. Can't tell kids anything these days."

With that, he stubbed his toe on the next step and instinctively grabbed the handrail for an instant, glared at it and let go. Regaining his footing, he kept on going. Matthew trudged along behind trying to figure the man's age. Pushing 100 had been his first thought, but now he was thinking 80 maybe. Or less?

"Name's Jonas Singer," the old man said when they got to the top. Matthew reached out to shake his hand but was promptly cut off by a scowl followed by "...don't know as that's necessary."

Turning to the side to conceal a grin, Matthew put his hand back in his pocket.

At the same moment, a plump woman with hair the color of the silvery cedar shakes on the house behind her appeared at the open gate at the top of the steps. Her blue eyes sparkled when she saw Matthew.

"This is Nell I told you about," Jonas said. "My daughter."

Unlike her father, Nell held out her hand in greeting. "Hi. My father doesn't usually bring people home with him. This is a real treat. Can you stay for lunch?"

"Just brought him up to meet you. Figured you'd have a bunch of questions," Jonas said. "Don't even know his name yet though. He's a quiet one."

"Matt Callahan," Matthew said, smiling as he took Nell's hand.

"Ignoring her father, Nell gave Matthew a warm smile. "Please stay. I've got clam chowder all made and corn muffins are just out of the oven."

"Nell makes chowder for some of the restaurants." Jonas was over-speaking his daughter without even noticing he was doing so.

"She works every day but Monday and gets fresh fish, clams, lobster, whatever she thinks she wants that day. She's got connections with the commercial fishermen and draggers."

Nell turned while her father was still talking and led them up a crushed oyster shell path to the front porch that went across the ocean-side front of the house and wrapped around both sides.

It was an unusually warm day for mid April on Cape Cod and Matthew took in the riot of sunlit color that surrounded the porches. There were tulips of every color, daffodils, some purple something-or-others, and forsythia bushes that were so big they must have been there when the Nauset Indians lived behind the dunes.

Jonas climbed the steps onto the porch and settled himself in what was obviously "his" chair at a small round wooden table that at one time someone had painted blue. There were three other chairs and Jonas gestured to the one he wanted Matthew to take.

"Guess you're staying for lunch. Sit there. You get a good view of Nauset Light from that one. I eat lunch out here anytime it's decent. You'd be surprised at all that goes on down there and this is a good place to watch the show."

ʿMatthew looked where Jonas was pointing. It was all dunes covered with brambles and grasses, then, way down below, empty beach leading to the crashing Atlantic. He agreed that it was awesome to behold—but a show? That one he couldn't figure out.

"You'll see. Just sit there and be quiet long enough and you'll start to see what I'm talking about," Jonas said. "The seabirds, the wind, the light. Bugs, clouds, sometimes jumping fish—you name it…"

But they didn't get a chance to sit quietly and observe because Nell reappeared with thick white crockery mugs of chowder, hot golden corn muffins, and a big green salad. She went back in the kitchen and came out with a pitcher of sun tea and three tall glasses filled with ice.

"Sit down Nell and stop fussing around," Jonas said, but not unkindly. "You worked hard enough making it, now enjoy it." He turned to Matthew. "She never lets up. Works all the time. No wonder her Katie is such a worka-holic. Came by it naturally."

"Come on, Dad. Matthew doesn't want to hear our family stuff. Tell us about you, Matthew. Is this your first visit to the Cape?"

"No, I…" Matthew began.

"…doesn't want us poking into his private life. If he wanted to tell us, he would have by now," Jonas interrupt-ed.

"It's okay. I don't mind telling it. It's just that it's not very interesting to anybody but me," Matthew said.

"Probably isn't," Jonas muttered. "But now that you got started, Nell won't give us any peace until you tell it."

"Maybe I just like to talk with somebody now and then about something other than quantum physics or the price of fish." Nell speared a lettuce leaf with more than a trace of impatience. It hadn't been easy for her raising Katie alone after her husband left her, then coming to care for her dad after her mother passed away. But she'd made a good-enough life for herself. She filled it with work she enjoyed doing, but the work left her little time for socializing. She rarely got to talk to anyone other than her father, the fishermen down at the harbor and the cooks she delivered her chowder to at the restaurants. She missed having good one-on-one conversations with people about their lives and about what was going on in the world and she was not going to let this real opportunity pass her by.

As added enticement, she set a yellow earthenware plate stacked with dark chocolate brownies near Matthew's elbow.

"You don't have to bribe me. I'll give you a rundown," he said as he picked one up and licked chocolate icing from his fingers.

"There's really not much to tell, though. I grew up in New Jersey thinking I was going to lead the simple life of an artist in a cottage by the sea, painting beautiful seascapes. My parents convinced me I needed to go to college just in case I needed a "real" job someday. Went for my degree, did a lot of drinking, met a rich girl and married her. Her family was loaded—Potter Department Stores, Boston to Baltimore?

Nell nodded. She had their label in a few of her "better" dresses and sweaters.

"I began to think of my little cottage by the sea and me being a great artist as a pipe dream."

"Typical," Jonas muttered.

"Typical of what, Dad?" Nell asked, annoyed at his interruption.

"Young people get all caught up in the high life. Forget the values their parents tried to teach them."

Nell bit her lip. "I'm sorry, Matthew. Go on."

"No need to apologize for me, girl. The truth is the truth. But go on young man. Get to the end of it."

"Not much more. My father-in-law introduced me to the right people and I got some impressive accounts. We built one of those McMansions down near Princeton, New Jersey, sent our two boys to a good prep school, traveled all over the world and hardly ever had anything of conse-quence to say to each other."

"Doesn't sound much different from a lot of marriages, except for all the money." Jonas was obviously getting im-patient with all the talk and Matthew got up to leave.

"Sorry to go on like that," he said.

"Sit down and finish it," Jonas said. "Might as well tell the whole thing and get it over with. Nell will never let me hear the end of it if you go now. There's got to be more to it than you didn't have anything to talk to your wife about."

"That's about it," Matthew said. There was no way he was going to tell these people he barely knew how he'd started drinking too much and Annaliese kept on spend-ing too much. He was ashamed to admit that his drink-ing started to show in his work and accounts began going elsewhere. It still hurt like hell to remember the day his partners called a meeting and laid it on the line: He needed to get a grip, to stop making excuses. He had to stop drinking.

Nell looked over at her father as if expecting him to break the silence, but all he did was glare at her and har-rumph once.

"Hey thanks for lunch," Matthew said to Nell as he folded his napkin and pushed in his chair. "I really should be going." He offered his hand to Jonas who just sat and stared over the porch railing watching gulls circle.

Matthew dropped his hand, shrugged, then turned to Nell. "Thank you again. I really enjoyed meeting you."

"Please come again," Nell said as she walked him to the top of the steps.

⁘

Matthew continued to walk the same stretch of beach every morning and whenever he stopped to rest on the bench he knew he was being watched from above.

This feels like I've pissed off God, he thought and turned to stare up at the house. I wonder what would happen if I gave the old guy the finger.

He no sooner sat on the bench a few days later when he saw Jonas making his way toward him along the edge of the water just as he'd done that first day. When he got close, he dug in the sand angrily with his walking stick, spewing some on Matthew's jeans and boat shoes.

"Nell's up there making chowder again. Want some?" he said. "She told me to ask you if I ever saw you down here again."

What the hell? Matthew thought. He'd liked Nell the day he'd met her and thought it can't be much of a life for her living with this old coot.

He followed Jonas up to the house again and when they got there he took the same chair he'd sat in the last time.

Nell had been hanging laundry and when she came around the side of the house and saw him, her face broke out in a wide smile.

"Wow, Matthew, it's so good to see you again," she said coming over and patting his arm. "Let me get you some iced tea."

"Sit down and stop fidgeting, girl," Jonas said and then turned to Matthew. "So you still trying to figure out your life?"

"Oh, I've got it figured out. I just don't know what to do about it."

"Maybe you ought to try getting a job. Doing something useful instead of just making tracks in the sand," Jonas said, then paused, took a deep breath and looked steadily at Matthew. "Would it help to tell the rest of it and get it off your chest?"

The kindly tone of Jonas's voice took Matthew by surprise. He looked questioningly at Nell whose eyes were wide with disbelief.

"Don't look at me that way," Jonas said. "Sometimes it helps a man to talk it through. Even I know that. Seems the least we can do is listen."

Matthew shrugged his shoulders and leaned forward, elbows on his knees. "Okay, so I'll bite the bullet," he said. "I started drinking and it got the best of me. Now I'm up here to get my life back together. End of story." He looked straight at Jonas waiting for the caustic remark he was sure would come.

Nell just sat smiling warmly at Matthew who, now that he'd finally spit out the truth to someone, was feeling less weighed down by it.

"Here I've been watching you every morning down there and I've been thinking, there's somebody trying to figure out something really important—a physics problem, a mathematical theorem," Jonas said. "Didn't know you were just another guy trying to figure out where he screwed up. A waste of your time, a waste of mine."

Suddenly Matthew regretted every word he'd let slip out of his mouth. He'd been a fool to be taken in by Jonas's momentary flash of kindness and was disgusted with himself for falling for it.

"Dad, you're being downright rude again," Nell said.

"Yea, so?" he answered without really seeming to care.

"You've got to realize, some people take stock and try to make changes," she said.

"What's that supposed to mean? Some people?"

"Just as I said, Dad. Some do, some don't."

"Meaning?'

"Well, meaning, maybe if you had..."

"Just what I thought you meant. If I had, maybe you'd have been one of those coddled Princeton brats at Miss Fine's School?"

"Matthew's jaw dropped. Princeton? What's he talking about?

"Maybe your brother would have recovered from his polio if I hadn't been holed up over there in Palmer Lab night after night? Is that it? Maybe if I'd been right there breathing for him, he would not have had to be put in that iron lung? Is that what you're saying, girl?"

Matthew could hardly believe what he was hearing. Princeton? No wonder there was that look between them when I mentioned it, he thought. They lived there too.

"No, papa," Nell said using the name she hadn't used for him since her childhood. "No, papa, I wasn't saying that at all."

"Maybe you should say it. Maybe it would clear the air," Jonas growled as he pushed back his chair, stood up and shuffled over to the door leading inside. "I've got work to do," he said, nodded curtly in Matthew's general direction and went inside letting the door slam behind him.

Both Matthew and Nell sat looking down at their plates, avoiding making eye contact. The silence lasted a minute or two and then, almost simultaneously, Nell stood up and started gathering bowls and plates and Matthew pushed his chair back and said he thought he'd better be going.

"I'm sorry..." Nell started to say just as Matthew said the same words. She held out her hand to him and he clasped it in one of his and covered it with the other. "It's okay," they both said at the same time and then started to laugh feebly.

Matthew turned and went down the steep steps that led to the beach—using the hand rail the whole way in case Jonas was watching.

— *Chapter 2* —

AFTER THAT, MATTHEW FOUND ANOTHER lonely beach for his morning walks. Hands in the pockets of his rolled-up khakis, he walked through the foamy edges of the cold waves as they turned his bare feet numb even though the day was warming up.

"The old guy was really right. I've been wasting a hell of a lot of time with all this self analyzing. I'm never going to be satisfied until I try out the cottage-by-the sea fantasy." He spoke into the gentle breeze coming in over the water and kept walking, the circling gulls landing about ten paces ahead of him and then taking off again.

"I'll do it," he told a speckled young gull that was perched warily on one of the jetty boulders and thought there had to be someplace with a decent view he could rent for a year. He began thinking finances. His severance package from the partnership would tide him over for a year if he didn't do any big spending.

"IF I don't do any big spending?" He laughed out loud. That was a joke. There was no way he could do any big spending with the phenomenal child support Annaleise claimed she needed for the boys. He was just about squeaking by as it was.

But the more he thought about it, the more determined he became. Picking up his pace, he went back and found his old Reeboks, slid his wet, sandy feet into them, and jogged back to his little silver Mazda parked in the Queen Anne's lace and cornflowers along the side of the beach road.

Driving back to the house he'd been renting a few blocks from the center of Harwich, he realized how much he'd come to love the place during the past months. The town wasn't much—Town Hall, a good library, a few small businesses. But he liked the look of the white clapboard, black-shuttered houses clustered around the pristine Congregational Church with its austere steeple. He liked joining the locals most mornings at The Stewed Tomato, ordering breakfast, blowing the steam off his mug of coffee while he read the morning news and grumbled about the price of gasoline and the careening stock market with the other patrons. He felt like he belonged someplace.

But he hadn't felt real secure with his no-lease rental arrangement and, sure enough, last week the owner called to tell him the rent was double now that the tourist season was about to begin. He'd gone right out and picked up a couple of local papers at the Stop & Shop and made sure to grab one of each of the freebie glossy ones that listed houses for sale.

❦

He scanned them for someplace small with an ocean view, but it didn't take long to find out the cost of living by the sea, whether as an owner or a renter, was astronomical. Deciding he didn't want to get involved with realtors, he got out a Cape Cod map, drew a wide circle around where he wanted to spend the next months and started driving in search of For Rent signs. Old Comers Road, Salt Meadow Way, Horsefoot Path, Mother Goose Lane. He turned the names over in his head and tasted them on his tongue.

To keep from getting too up tight about the whole thing, he tried to make his mind slow to the laconic pulse by which Cape Codders seemed to operate. He spent time talking with the fishermen at the harbor, with the guy in greasy overalls who serviced his car, with the white-haired ladies who ran the Thrift Shop he visited once a week to check the book and magazine shelves.

A week into the search he began his day as usual—at the counter in The Stewed Tomato with the classifieds and a hot cup of coffee he was waiting to cool. To kill time, he started reading the Help Wanteds. Buried in the middle of them, one caught his eye.

"Person Wanted to help edit and organize notes on experimental studies. Live-in situation. Some light housekeeping. E-mail or call if interested."

He circled the phone number and e-mail address, all the time thinking to himself, What am I, nuts?

⁂

He thought about it all day and finally, after cleaning up from his soup and sandwich supper, he sat down at his laptop and responded: "Interested. Please e-mail details." As soon as he hit the Send key, he started worrying that he should have written "MAY be interested" but then decided if he didn't like the sound of it, he just wouldn't write back. The person had no idea who he was. That's the beauty of e-mail.

But when he got up the next morning, he checked the computer before leaving for breakfast and he became even more interested in spite of himself.

The response said, "You didn't sign your name. How am I supposed to know if you're a man or a woman? Your e-mail address doesn't give me a clue. What are you?"

"Man. What about you? And why does it matter?" Matt wrote back and left for breakfast.

When he returned there was another response from JS82@seabrd.com: "Good. I am too. And it matters because that's what I decided I want. Now, if you're really interested, let's get to the point. I need someone as soon as possible."

Matthew thought about it long and hard, asking himself if he really wanted to hook up with someone who sounded as terse as he used to be. He decided to cut the crap with the few-word messages and get some real information.

"What kind of hours would you expect me to put in? I'm a painter and need blocks of uninterrupted time," he typed. "Is there room for me to set up my easel and spread out my paints? Is there a room where I could see the ocean and paint?"

He was on a roll and enjoying this. He grinned and went on typing. "What exactly is your house like? And what kind of 'light housekeeping' are you talking about? I'm not into dusting tabletops daily and starching doilies. And what about food? Would I be the cook and bottle washer? I could handle that as long as you know I didn't go to The Culinary Institute of America."

He hit Send and then walked out to the mailbox, stopping to talk to the lady next door who was checking on her roses that were just starting to bud and as he came back in his front door he heard, "You've Got Mail."

Sure enough, it was JS82. "How the hell did he have time to even read it, let alone type a response? This guy must be a keyboard whiz—wait'll he sees my hunt and peck system," he said out loud as he clicked on Read Mail.

It said, "Some days no work at all, some days full time, depending on how it's going for me. But full time for me means eight in the morning to noon. I'm getting up there and that's why I need some help. Don't want it, but need it. Yes you'd be cook and clean-up person. I guess I can handle ordinary meals for as long as you're here. I'll have to. And to me light housekeeping means taking out garbage, sweeping the floor and things like that. I hate starched doilies. Wouldn't have them. Not even when the wife was alive. But she didn't like them either.

"Yes, there's room for you to paint," he went on. "You can have the run of the house except for my study, my bedroom and my bathroom. There's a view of the sea from the front of the house and on the sun porch. The wife and I built a small house out back on the edge of the woods for our families to stay. Always had somebody visiting and we liked our quiet. It's small. Just two rooms and a bathroom. But you can see the ocean from both rooms and a big front porch. Don't know if you're a gardener, but maybe you could get the flower beds back in shape out there. Used to be pretty. There's a path over the dunes and down to the beach. You'd get solitude there. Maybe too much. There's a phone line connected from it to my house and I'd call you when I need you, don't worry about that. Let me know what you think. If you're still interested, you should come see instead of all this writing. I want to see what you look like anyway. By the way, house rules are no smoking, no drinking, no rock & roll music and nobody coming to visit without my say so."

Matthew wondered if he'd be sorry, if he'd end up bored, stuck with some old curmudgeon. The promise of an ocean view and a place of his own for four hours' work tempted him though and, in the end, he decided to bounce it off his mom.

He timed the call when his father was sure to be out because he knew what his father would say and he didn't want to hear it. "Get real, boy. Get a real job." He didn't feel like pointing out to his father again that he was 42 years old and not a boy.

He realized halfway through the conversation with his mom that he'd called her because he knew exactly what she'd say and it was just what he wanted to hear. "Give it a try, Matt. Sounds like it's a chance to do what's been eating at you for a long time. You can always leave if it doesn't turn out." Good old Mom. He could always count on her.

So instead of e-mailing, he picked up the phone and dialed the number from the ad. "JS82?" he asked when the man answered. "This is MatCal@bos.com. How about if we make a date for me to come and talk to you in person?"

After a short silence on the other end, a voice that sounded vaguely familiar said that would be good. He quickly rattled off directions and Matthew hurriedly wrote them down. They made arrangements for Matthew to be there in an hour.

He hung up the phone, picked up the paper with the directions on it and said, "Oh my God! It's him. That grouchy old physics guy. Holy shit!" He couldn't imagine working for that man, little house with an ocean view or not.

But as the clock ticked away, Matthew found himself getting more curious: What about the daughter, that blue-eyed woman, Nell? Where was she?

He knew it would take a half hour to drive out there and the time had come that he'd have to either leave or pick up the phone and say, "Forget it." Finally, he told himself what the hell, picked up the car keys and closed the door behind him. He was in the car when the phone in the house started ringing. He'd never know it had dawned on Jonas that MatCal was Matthew Callahan and was calling back to say, "Forget it."

— *Chapter 3* —

RATHER THAN PARK BY THE beach and walk up the dune steps, Matthew followed the directions Jonas had given on the phone. He turned off Rt. 6 onto a narrow dirt lane and immediately noticed a weathered sign, Singer Lane.

"Damn. I was right. It is the old bastard," Matt said aloud.

The lane climbed slowly through the woods and finally opened up to a clearing on a rock ledge that seemed suspended out over the crashing ocean below. Just to the left was the house he'd visited a couple of weeks ago. It looked different approaching it from the drive-in road rather than climbing up to it from the beach. And as he got out of the car and stood looking around to get his bearings, he turned to the right and there it was—the cottage overlooking the sea that he'd always pictured in his daydreams.

"Damn," he said again, only this time more strongly. "Damn," the third time but softer now, sadder. "I finally find this place and it comes with a price tag I don't want to pay."

Just then a door opened in the back of the main house and, sure enough, there stood Jonas, looking every bit as cranky as Matthew remembered him.

❧

"Don't get attached to it," Jonas said. "Don't need any-body. I'll get along just fine here by myself. Be good not to have somebody nagging at me all the time."

"That suits me fine," Matthew replied. "I just came ahead to tell you in person I'd changed my mind too." He turned his back on the cottage so he wouldn't be tempted to say, "Hey, c'mon, let's give it a try."

"Well, eh, guess you'd better be going then," Jonas said with a slight hesitation in his voice.

He expected me to grovel, Matthew thought. Damned if I will.

"See ya sometime," he called to the old man, got in the car and purposely not looking back either at Jonas or at the cottage, started back down the lane.

About halfway down, a small red VW convertible came bouncing around a bend not 100 feet in front of him. He slammed on his brakes and so did the other driver. It was a real "now what" situation. The road was so narrow one or the other would have to back a long way out. Immediately both doors of the VW swung open and a woman got out of each. The driver wore a baseball cap. He couldn't see her face, but he was sure impressed with her corkscrew curly red hair escaping from under the cap and the way she looked in her white shorts and bright green t-shirt. And the other woman—it was Nell! He was really glad to see her and greeted her with a big smile.

"Hey, Nell. Good to see you."

"Matthew! What're you doing here?" she responded right away, and then quickly added, "This is my Katie we talked about that day. Katie, Matthew Callahan."

He and Katie exchanged hellos and he immediately turned back to Nell. "I realize I barely know you and your dad, but I answered his Help Wanted ad in the <u>Cape Cod Times</u> for a live-in helper and can't help wondering about the sudden turn of events in your life."

"Help Wanted ad for a live-in?" Nell was shocked. "See Katie, I knew this would throw him for a loop."

"It's good for him, Ma. He depends too much on you and doesn't even appreciate all you do. And this will be good for you too."

Nell saw that Matthew looked puzzled and explained that Katie had landed a contract to write about all the riverships Bainbridge & Morven Cruiselines have plying the rivers of Europe. For three months she'd have first-class accommodations for two while they visited dozens of cities throughout Europe. She'd invited Nell to take three months off from her fish chowders to see some of the world with her.

Nell's life hadn't exactly been an easy one. When she was in college she'd had the misfortune of falling head over heels in love with Dan Vinnereli. Trouble was, he'd had his choice of women and he knew it. Maybe it was his sensuous ways. Or his thick black hair that almost concealed eyes the color of gunmetal. Whatever it was, the women gravitated to him. But not Nell. She'd learned as a child how to charm her father who, even back then, was often crusty and cranky. She'd known her dad was a softie and she quickly figured out how to get him to stop reading his dry old stuff and let her climb up on his lap with her own story book.

So when Dan Vinnereli crossed her path, arrogantly ignoring the girls who were always making up reasons to talk to him, Nell simply sat on the sidelines watching until he noticed her and sauntered over.

From that moment on it was Nell and Daniel and none of the other girls stood a chance. At least not until after Nell had become pregnant. Dan married her—her father had seen to that. But even before Katie was born, he was back to his old lifestyle.

One summer morning after he'd stayed out all night, Nell drove to the nearby 7-11 to get milk for breakfast and saw him lingering in the doorway of a neighbor. She saw Dan kiss the woman, brushing her tousled hair from her face and lifting the thin strap of her nightgown back onto her shoulder, kissing the place where it had rested. He was often like that with Nell and she had thought of those times as their own private tender moments.

She threw the car into Park and sat there frozen. The sudden movement woke Katie in her car seat and she'd begun to cry, her voice carrying out through the car's open windows. Dan turned and when he saw who it was, he stared right into Nell's eyes. Finally Nell put the car into gear and drove straight to her parents' house nestled in the dunes that hovered over the Atlantic—a safe haven. The last thing she'd wanted was to be home when Dan returned.

He never did. But Nell stayed in the house and raised their daughter there. She didn't remarry. Never wanted to.

When her mother took ill and Katie was off at college, Nell sold the house and moved back in with her parents. She'd reached a place of contentment. She worked hard, took care of her father after her mother died and looked forward to Katie's coming to stay with them when her schedule allowed.

Now this fabulous assignment landed in Kate's lap and she finally convinced her mom that Jonas could be left and they could have the time of their lives. Matthew could see both the bubbling excitement and the nagging guilt in Nell's eyes as Katie told him the plan.

"Go for it," he said and Katie gave him a big grin and a thumbs up.

"I want to, but, really, how can I? You see how worried he is already. I've only been over to Katie's in Boston for a few days, and he's got an ad in the paper for help."

"I took her shopping and she got all these great new outfits," Katie told Matthew then turned to her mother. "You going to wear that classy black pants suit down to the harbor when you pick up the fish, Ma?" she chided, then, for effect, exaggerated every syllable, "And the blue eye makeup and pearlescent nail polish? Come on, Ma. Don't back out on me. I'm so excited about this. Besides, I need an assistant—you—to go to one place while I go another on all the tours so I can give them full coverage."

Now Nell was clearly caught between duty to her father and duty to her daughter and Matthew could see that. "Nell," he said, "you owe it to yourself and to your father, and to Katie. If you keep passing up your own chances to enjoy life, you'll get as crotchety as he is and you won't be much good to either of them."

Katie started to laugh. "Here we are discussing a major crossroads in Ma's life with our car motors running and no room for either of us to pass. Somebody's going to have to back up. In more ways than one."

"I guess I'm closest. I will," Matt said. It took a lot of maneuvering to back up the winding narrow road for about a half mile to the clearing on the rock ledge. Every time he looked forward he saw Katie's tanned face shadowed by the visor of her Red Sox cap and her dazzling white grin.

When they got back to the house, Nell and Katie got right out of their car.

"Want to come in for awhile?" Nell asked.

"No thanks. I don't want another run-in with your dad."

"Run-in?"

"Yea. When he saw I was the one who answered his ad, he told me he's decided not to have anybody stay with him after all," Matt said. "I'd already decided not to take the job anyway when I realized it was him I'd be working for, so I told him that suited me fine and I left. I'd rather not run into him again now."

Katie was nodding her head in agreement when suddenly the door opened and Jonas came out on the porch.

"You're back," he said, and all three of them wondered if he was talking to Nell and Katie or to Matthew. "Yes, all three of you. Didn't expect to see any of you again any time soon."

"Well I'm leaving—again," Matthew said. He raised his hand in a friendly goodbye to the women. "Have a great trip," he said to Nell. "Call me when you get back and tell me all about it. Your father has my number and e-mail address."

He smiled directly at Katie, put the car in gear and left.

— *Chapter 4* —

MATTHEW WAS OUT ON HIS bike early the next morning. Cape Cod had pulled itself out of its long chilly spring. Lilacs were blooming all over the place and wildflowers were sprouting up along the Rail Trail that had been laid for bikers and walkers in the former train track beds. He got on in Harwich Center and rode north, stopping at the little red Pleasant Lake General Store that stood on the side of the path between Hinckley's Pond and Long Pond. He took his container of coffee and a donut out on the porch and when he saw the bench labeled "Democrats" was occupied, he shrugged his shoulders in a what-the-hell gesture and settled himself with a grin on the Republicans' bench.

Too bad Jonas is so hell-bent on being such an old coot, he whispered into his first sip of hot coffee. He'd been thinking about the whole situation all through the night and all morning. Actually, the reason for the bike ride was to stop thinking about it. He kept remembering the cottage and had spent the morning trying to convince himself if he'd just looked inside he probably would have found it so awful he wouldn't want to stay there anyway.

With an it's-too-late-now gesture, he crumbled his napkin, stuffed it in the Styrofoam cup and walked it over to the trash bin. Then, determined to think only about what he was seeing along the trail, he put his helmet back on and started pedaling.

⁂

The phone was ringing when he got home in late afternoon and when he answered it he was surprised to hear a woman's voice.

"Matthew? This is Kate Vinerreli. We met yesterday at my grandfather's house?"

Matthew closed his eyes and pictured that smile that had kept appearing all day in his mind.

"Yea, hi Kate. What's up?"

"My mom and I were wondering if you'd reconsider working for Jonas. He's really not so bad once you get under his crusty shell. He's kind of sweet actually," she said.

"Well even if I reconsidered—and I don't think I ever will—he's already told me he wouldn't want me."

Katie jumped right back in. "Mom and I talked with him until late last night and when I convinced him how good it would be for Mom to get away and how it would help me, he admitted maybe he'd been a little too hasty. When I asked if that meant he'd really have someone, he said, 'Not someone. Only that Matt guy. Only him if he'll do it.'"

"Well I'll be damned." Matt was surprised.

"Seems he took a liking to you, Matt," Katie said. "Said he liked the way you stood up for yourself. Won't you reconsider? Mom needs to finally start a life for herself. She's sixty-six years old. She's got to start soon and this riverboat trip with me would help her get her feet wet—no pun intended," she said with a laugh. "Won't you at least come back and talk to him about it? Come for supper tonight. Then if you still feel it wouldn't work, we won't bug you about it anymore."

Matthew paused. "Uh, I don't know…"

"C'mon, Matthew, I promise. It'll be whatever you say. No pressure—at least not after this strong-arm tactic," Katie said, laughing.

"All right, I give in." Matthew was laughing too.

"Great. Six o'clock. And it's just supper, nothing fancy, so keep your jeans on," she said.

Matthew reached under the sink and pulled out the bottle of Truro Vineyards Chardonnay he'd bought at Luke's Liquors the day before. After cautiously testing, he'd been glad to learn that he could enjoy a glass of wine with dinner occasionally without triggering that spiraling need for one more and one more. Never the hard stuff, but wine he could handle. Slipping the bottle back in the narrow brown bag it had come in, twisting its top and tucking it under his arm, he got in his car and drove to Singer Lane taking the back road in and parking on the rock promontory.

As he got out of the car, Nell came out to greet him. Matt thought he could see the change beginning to happen in her already. She looked younger, freer.

"So glad you agreed to come, Matthew," she said in greeting. "And don't worry, Katie told me the deal. Whatever you decide, we won't pressure you."

He handed her the bottle of wine and ventured a hello hug which was returned robustly.

Katie came out and offered her hand in greeting. Her hand and a big happy smile. "Thanks for coming, Matthew. He's in a pretty good frame of mind, so things should go well. He was surprised to hear you said you might reconsider and he even seemed happy about it."

They went inside and there was Jonas bent over his telescope looking at the far horizon.

"Dad, Matthew's here," Nell said.

"I heard him come in. Not deaf, you know."

The other three looked at each other and grimaced, but Jonas turned to them and offered his hand to Matt. "Glad you came back, boy. Maybe we can work things out," he said.

Dinner went well. Simple but good. Nell had grilled swordfish and they had early peas from the patch out back and a fresh garden salad. Katie had pickedup a loaf of crusty bread and an apple pie from Elizabeth in Truro who for years supported herself baking for her friends and neighbors.

They sat long over coffee and talked about Katie's assignment. Nell seemed transported already into a land of daydream possibilities.

Finally they got down to what Jonas would need and what Matthew might be willing to accept. Jonas was surprisingly docile and Matthew saw some of the sweetness Katie had mentioned. He could see Jonas setting aside his own pride so his daughter and granddaughter might have this special time together. Matthew liked what he saw.

They talked until the sun was beginning to set and still nothing definite was said.

"Katie, why don't you walk Matthew over to the cottage before it gets dark," Nell said. "Let him get a look at it before he leaves."

While Nell cleaned up and Jonas settled in to watch a biography of Theodore Roosevelt on the History Channel, Matthew and Katie crossed over to the cottage.

I'm probably sucked into this deal already, Matthew said to himself. But if this place is a disaster, I'm out of here anyway.

Katie turned the key in the lock and threw open the door. It smelled musty. But so did the house he was living in in Harwich.

The sun was low and cast a warm orange glow through the large west window and the white plaster walls were washed in it.

Katie repositioned with her toe one of several braided rugs that were scattered on the wide plank bare floors. A wooden table with two chairs stood by the east window where the sun would shine in at breakfast time. And a green and white porcelain-clad stove that reminded Matthew of the one in his grandmother's kitchen when he was a kid stood on its curved legs right up next to a Hoosier cabinet that he could see was well stocked with dishes, pots, and pans. It looked to him like the calico skirt that someone had wrapped around the wall-hung sink had been freshly washed and ironed.

"Isn't this fireplace great? Granddaddy says every stone was found right here on this property," Katie said. "Sometimes Ma and I would spend an overnight here when I was little. We'd get a big fire going and she'd sit in that chair and this one would be mine. These are the same slipcovers. Ma washed and ironed them not long ago when we decided to spruce up the place. I always loved the fact that each chair has its own ottoman. We'd stretch our legs out and fall asleep right here in front of the fire even though the bedroom and bathroom are right over there." When Katie pointed across the room, Matthew saw a screened-in porch that ran the length of the building on the ocean side. The whole thing was not large by any stretch of the imagination but, in Matthew's eyes, it was perfect.

He was sucked in. His decision was made. If Jonas could behave even half as well as he had tonight, he could handle him. And he'd have a lot of free time to spend here. In his mind he already had his easel set up on the porch, his tripod and camera set up by the west window to capture sunsets, his sketchpad on the "kitchen" table where he was sure to spend a good deal of time.

"What do you think?" Katie asked, looking deep into his eyes for an answer.

"I think I'd like to give it a try," he said.

With that, Katie let out a whoop and grabbed him in a bear hug. "Thanks, Matt. I know it will work out for the two of you."

Much aware of her slim but very female body pressed ever so briefly against his, Matthew gave her a return squeeze. "Don't worry. We'll make it work."

— Chapter 5 —

KATIE AND NELL TOOK OFF for Paris on a brilliantly lit May morning. Jonas wasn't up for the two-hour drive from the Cape to the airport in Boston, but wanted every detail when Matthew returned.

Before they left, Nell had given Matthew a Do and Don't list. Right at the top under "Do" was "Make sure his breakfast is ready by 8 a.m. or he'll be a bear all day." So Matthew, who liked to ease slowly into a day, made sure the coffee was perking and the juice poured before Jonas made his appearance each morning.

"How about if you don't show up until nine tomorrow," Jonas said one night. "I can pour my own cereal. And I like to watch the morning news and check the Weather Channel before I have to make small talk."

"Okay by me." Matthew smiled to himself and made a mental note to cross off #1 under the Do side of the list taped to his fridge door. Maybe he'd be making a list of his own to give Nell when she returned.

He'd moved into the cottage almost immediately. The day after they made the decision, he'd come back and started airing it out, washing windows and clearing out the cobwebs.

I'll bring over fresh linens and blankets," Nell said as she re-hung newly washed and ironed curtains.

Matthew was beating thirty years of dust out of the braided rugs he'd hung on the clothesline that tied together two massive red oaks when Katie arrived with bags of groceries, two bunches of red and white zinnias, and her own CD player with a stack of CDs.

"There's no cable hookup or tv antenna here. Sorry," she said. "But there's a good radio and tape player and you might as well use my CDs while I'm gone. Hope you like blues and classical because that's all I've got."

"That's perfect and I thank you," Matthew said. "I'm not a tv person except for an occasional Mets game. I like music while I'm working and NPR."

Katie put all she'd brought on the kitchen table and proceeded to stock the refrigerator and the cupboard shelves.

"This place is already feeling so much like home I think I'll go ahead and bring my clothes and stuff over right away," Matthew said. Within three days he was moved in.

Nell and Katie had made the transition not only smooth, but fun.

"Don't know what could be so funny over there," Jonas had said one day at lunch. "All I hear is this nonsensical laughing all day. Be glad when there's some peace and quiet around here again."

Matt, Nell and Katie glanced at each other in full understanding that Jonas wished he knew how to be part of the fun. They tried to include him, but he didn't know how to be playful.

⁖❀⁖

That became even more apparent as the two men started working together. Matt always saw the lighter side of things, and tended to turn a perplexing problem around by making a joke about it. Little by little he could see Jonas trying to loosen up.

They worked together from nine until noon each day organizing Jonas's notes and files. Matthew convinced him they needed a scanner and as soon as he brought it home from Staples in Orleans and got it set up, he started scanning documents into the computer and organizing a filing system for the hard copies.

Jonas liked to open his own mail, give each piece a quick read, then toss it across the table to Matthew with a "tell them no" or "put this in the Nell basket. She'll know what to do about it when she comes back—God knows when that will be."

E-mails were another story. He liked Matthew to open them, weed out the Spam then print the rest so he could read them on paper before telling Matthew to deep six them.

He was careful to keep all the correspondence from Princeton University, however, and Matthew was surprised to learn Princeton was setting up Singer archives in its library system. He began to think there might be more to the old guy than he'd imagined.

⁖❀⁖

They'd quit for lunch around noon and go their separate ways until Matthew came back to start supper around six.

As it turned out, Jonas rediscovered some cooking skills that had lain dormant for years.

"Used to cook when I was a bachelor. After that, always had a wife or daughter stirring something up in the kitchen," he told Matthew. They started grocery shopping together at the Stop'n Shop in Orleans and throwing some decent meals together. Evenings they went their separate ways.

It took several days for Matthew to settle himself in enough to get his paints out, to stretch a canvas and put it on his easel.

"Ahhh, this feels good," he said aloud as he squeezed globs of reds, yellows, and blue oils onto his palette. But when he tried to paint what he saw out his window it didn't happen. "Too soon," he told himself. He spent his free time biking and walking, but now he was describing what he saw on these solitary journeys in the notebooks he'd picked up at Staples. He walked every day, sometimes in the woods that encompassed acres of land on both sides of Singer Lane. And sometimes he walked along the beach where he'd walked when he first came to the Cape, where Jonas had spotted him. He even sat on that bench from time to time. One day when he was sure Jonas was watching him with his telescope, he stood up, turned and gave him a crisp military salute before leaving. It was a long time before Jonas ever mentioned it. By then the old man was learning how to laugh at himself sometimes.

⟨❦⟩

Weeks passed, a month. Notes and then a letter arrived from Nell and Katie cruising the Danube.

"I'm sitting on a bench in the marketplace here," Katie wrote on the back of a postcard from Melk, Austria showing a magnificent Abbey on a hill overlooking the town. "A Strauss waltz is coming from a window behind me and the local women are shopping with their baskets over their arms. Ma's off on a tour, having the time of her life."

Matthew was pleased that Nell was enjoying herself so much, and he just plain liked hearing from Katie. Besides, it put Jonas in a good mood.

The men found a comfort zone and made good progress in their work. One day, while Matthew was sitting at his kitchen table writing to his sons, he decided to ask Jonas's permission to invite them there for a weekend.

When they arrived it was in Annaleise's white Jaguar that came bursting out of the woods and stopped with a screeching halt dangerously near the edge of the promontory.

Matthew had to admit she still looked beautiful. Blonde hair windblown, a glowing tan, designer sunglasses. He thought his "Hey, good to see you. C'mon in for awhile" had just the right touch of warmth, but Annaleise refused to get out of the car. "I'm going to be late for my date in Boston. I had no idea it would take so long to get to this God-forsaken place. I'll be back Sunday at six," she told the boys. "Be out here waiting." Without a goodbye to their mother, Luke and Jason turned politely to their father. Each offered his hand as if meeting a distant relative. Later Matthew would tell Jonas, "And that was the highlight of the weekend."

"You really like living in this place?" Luke had said about an hour into the visit. He was looking around at the stove on legs, the skirt hiding the shelves under the kitchen sink, the worn slipcovers on the chairs. "It's funky, Dad. And small," Jason added.

"Yea, I know, but the light's great for painting and so are the views." Matthew had turned away to hide his disappointment. They tried to make it work. All three of them did. Matthew even felt sorry for them being dumped off there with a father who hadn't been much of a father to them in the past couple of years.

When he was in his bedroom with the door closed he heard Luke tell his brother, "I'm bored out of my skull, man."

"Yea," Jason had answered. "And only 26 hours to go."

"I feel kinda bad for him though, living in this crappy place and all. And with that old man over there and nobody else to talk to."

"Maybe we can get him to show us around or go down to the beach or something," Jason said. "Might as well. We're stuck here 'til tomorrow anyway."

He was relieved the weekend was over and he was sad to see the boys go. Annaleise had let him know in no uncertain terms what a burden it was for her to have them living with her full time. When he told her this gig would come to an end and he'd have to find a new, bigger, place to live and the boys could come spend summers with him, he caught the look of panic that passed from one brother to the other and his heart went out to them. What a mess I've made of our lives, he thought as he stood, hands in his jeans pockets, watching the taillights of Annaleise's Jaguar disappear into the woods.

~ *Chapter 6* ~

THE NEXT DAY HE STARTED his long walks in the woods again. Stepping over brambles and last year's leaves one day, he discovered a little brook running free. He followed it to a dense overgrowth of trees and wildflowers. Pushing his way through, he found a cabin—a small structure with trees and vines growing so close as to swallow it up.

He saw the windows were boarded up and so was the door. A wooden panel was nailed to the door, but the words written on it had long been obliterated. He pulled on the door but it wouldn't open. He circled around, tugged at the window boards, but knew he'd need pliers to loosen them. Finally he left for home.

He mentioned the cabin to Jonas that night at supper.

"You walk that far, do ya?" Jonas asked. "Must have good legs—and nothing very important to do with your time. How'd you even find it? Or find your way back?"

"It's probably less than an hour's walk from here and I like to keep in shape," Matthew said. "I found a stream, heard the water running over the rocks and went through the woods to the sound. Then I just walked along its banks.

Almost missed the cabin. Trees and vines and wild roses have it covered."

"People say it's haunted and there's a curse on it," Jonas said. "My Bridget wouldn't go within a mile of it. Story is somebody was murdered there back even before the Civil War. When Nell comes back ask her about it. She found something in the old newspapers at the library about a murder. Didn't say exactly where, except that the killer was put in leg irons right in the center of Wellfleet."

"Interesting," Matthew said as he cleared their dishes from the table, scraping chicken bones and cantaloupe rinds into the garbage. "Need anything else? If not, I'll go on back to the cottage. I want to get some of the weeds out from around the tomato plants. It's supposed to rain overnight."

"Go ahead," Jonas said. "I'll be glad for the quiet. Too much talking sometimes."

Matthew grinned as he hung up the dishtowel and let the screen door close softly behind him.

He didn't mention the cabin again to Jonas in the days to come. And he didn't talk about it to any of the guys he'd begun playing racquetball with at the gym he'd joined when he came to work with Jonas.

He didn't mention the cabin, but he thought about it from time to time. Then one day he put a pair of pliers and a small chisel in his back pocket and set off looking for the stream.

A stiff breeze was stirring the leaves and he strained to hear the bubbling water. Finally, the wind quieted for a few minutes and his ears picked up the water sounds. Following the stream, he came to the same flat rocks that had caught his attention the last time he was there. That time, before he'd discovered the cabin, he'd thought the fact that they were like steps leading down to the water was an interesting coincidence. Seeing them now, it was obvious someone had chosen them for their size and flat surfaces and carefully placed them where they were.

As he did the last time, he turned away from the stream and picked his way through the woods. Searching hard to find the cabin again, he tripped over something, fell, and then saw it was a rotting section of a picket fence. Using his penknife to cut away some of the vines underfoot, he discovered a piece of slate. About eight inches away he unearthed the edges of another, and another, a path that led right to the boarded-up door of the cabin that he could barely see.

It was even more concealed than he remembered and it felt like a whole forest of vines had grown just in the past week.

Fighting his way through the briars and wild rose thorns, he got to the door. Using his chisel, he pried the nailed-on boards loose and was able to get the rusty nails out with his pliers. He wondered about the piece of wood that was nailed to the door dead center, but assumed maybe Jonas or somebody had put up a No Trespassing sign there.

The lock was rusted fast and no amount of tugging got it to move. Determined, he got out his Swiss army knife again and started scraping back the rust. He was just about to give up when he felt a little give. Tapping his wedged knife with the end of the chisel, he was able to finally get it to slowly move upward. He pushed on the door and was surprised when it swung freely inward. He stepped inside and was immediately overcome by a feeling of having literally stepped back in time.

The room was damp and dark. It smelled like the root cellar in his grandparents' house in Vermont. There was only one small window in each of the outside walls and each was so thickly covered with cobwebs and grime on the inside and vines on the outside that no light could find its way in. He'd bring a flashlight if he came again.

There was an eerie stillness in the room and he began to shiver not only from the damp chill in the stagnant air, but from a fear he hadn't felt since he was a little boy.

He stood dead still waiting to feel acclimated, but every nerve in his body was alert.

"I'm getting out of here," he whispered to himself and went back out the door. He replaced the boards and even forced the rusty nails back into their holes. He tried to leave everything as concealed and untouched looking as he'd found it.

– Chapter 7 –

"YOU KNEW ALBERT EINSTEIN? You worked with him?"
Matthew stopped sorting through the papers he found in
a box he'd come across in the attic. He picked up some
of the top sheets to look at them more closely. The light
in the attic was poor even on a good day, but it had been
raining for three days and the leaves on the trees at the attic windows were sodden and let no light in. One 60-watt
bulb was all he had to go by, but it was enough for Matthew to see whose name was along with Jonas Singer's on
the notebooks.

"I guess it seems like a big deal now, but it wasn't then,"
Jonas said. "He was at the Institute For Advanced Study
when I was in Physics and we worked on a project together.
Got to be friends. Kind of. I was hoping we'd come across
this box."

When Jonas called the Princeton library archivist to
tell her what they'd found, she immediately made plans
to drive up to the Cape the next week to see for herself.
When they heard that, Matthew and Jonas dug in and
worked long hours to try to get some order to their find
before she arrived.

But now she'd come and gone, taking the box of note-books with her and Matt's work schedule was back to normal.

He'd been thinking of the cabin and decided the only reason he'd felt so weird there that day was because it was so dark and the air was so stagnant. He dug out his high-powered camping lantern and put new batteries in it. Armed again with his chisel and pliers and now the lantern and even a couple of candles and some matches, he headed back into the woods.

The stream, swollen from the recent rains, was noisy and easy to locate and he found the cabin in no time.

He again pried open the door and propped it wide open with a rock he'd found outside. Light and fresh air poured in. Also, having the lantern made a big difference. Even though there was still that feeling of stepping back in time, at least the place wasn't as spooky as it was before.

The room was sparsely furnished, but it was obvious that it had been someone's home. There were two uphol-stered chairs in front of a fireplace with a table between them that held an oil lamp. Years of nesting mouse families had taken their toll on the chairs. There was more stuffing on the floor around them than in the chairs themselves. Where the coverings had not been torn to shreds or rotted away, Matthew could see they had been patterned with flowers and must have been pretty.

A pair of glasses and a book rested on the table. Insects and mice had worked over the book pretty well too, but Matthew picked it up and read the title on the cover that was still intact. It was a guide for growing herbs "for flavorings and medicinal uses."

He set the book down and noticed the fireplace poker was laying on the floor where there was a huge black stain that was also on part of the raised hearth. That seemed strange because the rest of the room, though covered with dust, mildew and cobwebs, was orderly and it was clear that someone had once made every effort to make it homey and cheerful.

Something in a frame was centered over the mantle but the years had so totally left their film on the glass that protected it, he could barely tell what it was.

He took it down and carried it over to the open doorway, swiping at the glass with his shirtsleeve. Though it was faded and turning brown in places, he could read the alphabet and numerals 1 to 20. A sampler. It seemed appropriate that there was a garland of wildflower vines around the border very similar to those he'd just walked through to get there. And across the bottom, the legend read, "Nancy Titus, age 10. November 23, 1835."

With a sense of reverence, he hung it back on the nail over the mantle, wondering who Nancy Titus was and whether she'd grown up in the cabin. Did her mother proudly hang it here for visitors to see? Or, maybe, did Nancy come here as a young bride and hang it there herself?

He stood looking at the tiny stitches, marveling that a child of ten and younger would have the patience to stick with it. "It's a whole different world today," he said aloud, thinking of his sons.

Reaching up to adjust the sampler so it would exactly cover the lighter square on the wall that its hanging had created over the years, his arm brushed against a daguerreotype of a young couple. Stiff and self conscious, they sat before the camera. But undaunted was the merry twinkle in the young woman's eyes and the look of tenderness in the man's. He turned the frame over and read on the back, written in old script and dark black ink, "Mr. and Mrs. David Nadeau, Wedding Day: May 25, 1844." And in a less formal script in paler ink, he read, "Nancy Titus Nadeau and Davy Nadeau."

The pieces were falling into place. The girl who made the sampler married and came here to make a home with her husband, Davy. But why was their home abandoned and boarded up? And, it seemed, so suddenly?

It reminded Matthew of a book he'd read a few years back about the explosion of an atomic bomb and how the last people on earth to survive went into homes and found families had been interrupted by death from the radiation fallout right in the middle of a normal day. The cabin had that same feeling.

He set the daguerreotype back in precisely the same position in which he'd found it. He was now even more intent on keeping things as untouched as possible out of respect for the couple who had lived there.

There were other objects on the mantle. A baby's pewter cup and spoon with "DN" etched crudely on the spoon handle. And another daguerreotype of a family—parents and four children all sitting stiffly in their Sunday best. On the back was simply stated, "Titus Family, 1838." Matthew scanned the faded faces and was sure he found Nancy, then a shy girl looking wide-eyed at the camera.

Again, he put it back precisely where it had been, turned and took a few steps to the other side of the room.

There, under a small window, stood a wooden table that appeared to have been hand crafted. On one side it was set for a meal—a plate, cup, and saucer, flatware and the remains of what must have been a folded napkin and was now merely a powdery shape of one. A wooden chair was pulled up to the table. Hanging limply from its back-rest were shards of what may have been a colorful pad. On its seat were tatters of a matching cushion. A bowl in the middle of the table had hardened residue that Matthew thought might have been the remains of a supper dish that had just been set out more than 150 years ago.

It was the far side of the table that piqued his curiosity, however. Over there, the chair was pushed out and askew. The dish, cup, saucer, and flatware had been shoved aside and in their place was an open book. Walking around the table, Matt's foot rolled on the quill pen that had fallen or been thrown on the floor. He went to the other side and picked up the book. A journal. He closed it and then re-opened it to its first page. What he saw gripped him:

This Journal Belongs to Nancy Titus Nadeau. It was begun June 17, 1844 and ended~~ It was clear that it was just the latest in an ongoing series.

Matthew put his lantern on the table and pulled it close. He straightened the chair that seemed to have been pushed aside and began to read.

❧

There was entry after entry of the everyday life of the couple. The journal spoke of Davy going down into the town and building houses for the people there, doing repairs, general carpentry work.

It spoke of Nancy's love of gardening. Not only of bountiful beds of flowers, but of the herbs she grew and of how the townsfolk had begun coming to her for herbal remedies.

I don't know why these ladies think my herb potions are anything special, she wrote. They're just common sense. They're what Grammy Fuller taught me when she came to live with us after Grandpa died. Nothing mysterious or special about them.

Who wouldn't know that pine tar is good for skin ailments and a Tea made from chamomile will relax the nerves?

Matthew read every word and turned the pages slowly. Afternoon settled in on the old cabin and he realized he was actually feeling a sense of peace there. He read for a little longer then, with his stomach started sending messages, he looked at his watch, stretched and knew it was time to get back to start supper for Jonas. He was tempted to take the journal with him but, hesitant to take it out of the cabin into the modern world, he left it lying open on the table and prepared to leave.

As he picked up his lantern to turn it to the entry door, its light fell on the far wall and a door that was closed and secured with an antiquated version of a padlock. He thought "storeroom" and left.

– *Chapter 8* –

THE CABIN BECAME MATTHEW'S SECRET. He didn't want to discuss it with Jonas or anyone else, for that matter. He went back when he could and read more of the journal each time. He was annoyed the day Jonas asked for a ride to Cambridge so he could meet with one of his former colleagues. Grudgingly Matthew gave up his plan to get back there that day and they left early to beat the morning rush.

While Jonas met with his friends, Matthew, rather sheepishly, succumbed to something he'd wanted to do for a long time but never allowed himself to do because it was so touristy. He bought a ticket and boarded a harbor cruise ship in Boston. Seeing the city from the water and hearing its history recited on the canned narrative tape, gave him the much-needed break from his job with Jonas and his afternoons at the cabin. He became totally immersed in the city's history and, when they returned to the dock, he found a bookstore and bought two of the books the clerk touted as the best on the subject. He was beginning to get a picture of what the world might have been like when

Nancy and Davy Nadeau lived in it and he wanted to learn more.

He took Windex and paper towels with him to the cabin the next day and washed the windows so more light could come in. He also took pruning shears and cut vines away from the two windows. Since the cabin was on Singer private land, he had little fear that trespassers would venture upon it. Clearing the windows made a huge difference and now that he didn't need the lantern, he had some sense of the way it had looked when Nancy and Davy had lived there.

Now he was able to notice little things like what must have been a broom propped against the wall in a corner. The bristles were mostly gone but there were a few left and, surprisingly, it still stood upright—probably held in place by the thick cobwebs that connected it to the wall.

He went over and opened the doors on a cupboard and found neatly stacked cast iron pots and a skillet on one side and earthenware dishes on the other—two of each. Two plates, two bowls, two mugs, a platter and a bowl. They were plain and oatmeal colored, but each had a flower centered on it.

Another cupboard held tins and in one that had been sealed tight he found dried tea leaves. He sniffed and caught a hint of faint aroma. Another, marked Flour, held only the shell remains of the worms that must have feasted there before dying. There was salt in one that had turned to stone and the other marked sugar held only black crusted grime.

He found a shelf that held a few books: A Bible, a <u>Goodwin's Home Remedies</u>, an <u>Atlas of the World</u> dated 1825 and an account book in which someone had faithfully recorded every penny earned and spent. Matthew took that one to the table to read when he finished the journal.

Next to a chair by the hearth he found what must have been Nancy's sewing basket. Carefully sorting through, he saw some of the threads still wound on their wooden spools—black, tan, white and one that must have been pink at one time. There was a small assortment of needles and a delicate pair of scissors shaped like a bird with a long bill that was, in reality, the blades.

A pair of men's heavy cotton twill trousers in surprisingly good condition was folded neatly in a second basket which also held square patches waiting to be sewn on.

And also in the basket were the tattered remains of three tiny nightgowns cut out and waiting to be sewn. Could it be Nancy and Davy were expecting a child? Or were they being made for a friend's growing family?

Matthew was tempted to fiddle with the lock on the storeroom door but decided instead to read more of Nancy's journal.

In the next entry he realized she must have gotten a letter from her mother. Nancy wrote:

> _These letters from home always do two things to me. I'm so excited to hear all the news, and I miss them all so much and am sad to be so far away. Davy says we can go visit come September. He's chopping wood after his long work days and putting the money away he earns when he sells the wood to go toward the fare. I don't earn much with my herbs and flowers, but every penny also goes in the pickle jar._
>
> _When I wrote back to Mama I wanted so much to tell her our good news, but I'd rather tell her in person about the baby so when she hears it she can put_

her hand on my swelling belly and maybe even feel it move. Davy worries the trip will be too hard on me, but I should be far enough along by then, 4 months, that this morning sickness will be gone. I do so want to see everybody back home. Grammy Fuller is slowing down now, Ma says. She spends a lot of time in the rocker by the window. And Ma says Prissy has a beau—tall skinny Ethan who she met that time the church group went over to the Stout farm in Concord to help with the harvesting. It's hard to believe Prissy is old enough to have a beau, but I just counted up and it's been three years since I left, so she must be sixteen by now. And the twins—that's hard to picture too. Ma says they're starting to be some help on the farm. She says Will feeds the geese and the chickens and Peter manages to gather eggs every day without breaking too many. Hard to picture them almost six years old. They weren't much more than babies when I left.

Matthew sat back and closed his eyes picturing the young woman in the daguerreotype as she must have been on the farm before she left home. How did she and Davy meet, he wondered? What brought them to this place? Where was Davy's family?

Warm sunshine filtering through the newly cleared window warmed Matthew's cheek. He stretched and yawned contentedly, the gripping fear he'd felt in the darkness that first day was gone.

Looking around the little room, he was tempted to clean the decades of dirt and decay away, but decided Not Yet. Maybe someday, but not yet. There was something sacred and untouched there and he was unwilling to disturb that.

He only visited the cabin once or twice a week and that was because he wanted it that way. He clearly saw that he could become immersed in the past life of the place.

He was doing less painting and more just plain thinking—about what he'd discovered there. He, like Nancy, had always liked to journal and he found his entries were getting longer. One day, reaching for a yellow legal pad he'd picked up at Staples, he started putting to paper his imaginings of what Nancy and Davy's life might have been. He became engrossed in filling in details as he saw them, drawn from what he'd read in Nancy's journal that day.

He spoke of what he'd found to no one, but he began writing some of it to Katie. They'd fallen into writing letters back and forth during her first weeks away and now they were e-mailing every couple of days. Katie wrote of the towns and cities they were seeing, of the river crafts where she and Nell were living, passing through the locks, visiting cathedrals and abbeys, enjoying all the local food and wines.

Matt told her how Jonas was thriving and enjoying cataloging his life's work.

"He's actually even laughing now and then," he added in a short p.s.

When he was finally able to get back to the cabin a week later, he saw the rugosa roses had burst into bloom and were all entangled with the honeysuckle that had climbed even across the roof. The air smelled sweet from it all and he brought the journal outside, cleared off a large boulder that rested down near the stream and read on.

It's a pretty June day, Nancy had written, *and I won't let Rev. Heady spoil it for me I won't let his anger scare me. I was washing our undergarments down at the stream this morning when I heard thrashing in the bushes and saw his black suit and that strange hat he always wears. I was scared, but held my ground. He is so angry because the ladies in town are coming to me to buy herbs when they have their monthlies or when their babies are colicky. They used to turn to him with their troubles and he'd tell them it was all caused by their evil doings. He'd pray over them and expel their devils. In time they'd feel better because that's nature's way and they'd thank him and put extra coins in the offering. But we started friendships, some of the women and I, when we'd meet at the market in town and when they came to visit I took to sending them home with a bunch of roses or zinnias or some herbs and I'd tell them things like the way chamomile could help them sleep or how it would ease a baby's tummy. They got relief and told other women who started talking to me in town and coming here.*

So many of us are good friends now and I like exchanging my recipes and sharing stories of our men and their sometimes perplexing ways. It's good for women to have other women to talk to.

But Reverend Heady doesn't like it at all. He's threatened me with ex-communication from "the society of the community" (I don't attend church services) and promises hellfire will rain down on me for my evil ways. I don't feel evil. I pray as much as he does I'm sure and I know God knows I'm not an evil woman. Still Reverend Heady frightens me. As for evil, I see

*it in his eyes. I see jealousy and mean spiritedness. I
don't tell Davy about Reverend Heady's visits (which
are becoming too frequent) because he would worry
about me and our child and he might go after the evil
man and I'm afraid my Davy might be harmed. You
never know how an evil person will strike.*

Matthew shuddered and closed the book. Suddenly
that tranquil place amid the wild roses felt threatening.
He took the journal back to the cabin, boarded the door
and left.

— *Chapter 9* —

Jonas was sitting on the back porch of the main house when Matthew came walking out of the woods. As soon as he saw Matthew he got up and stood, rigidly tapping his fingers on the railing.

"'bout time you decided to wander back. What's the big attraction in those woods that you go there every week?"

"I just like the solitude. I can think things through in there with no one to interrupt me," Matthew said. "I'm thinking of writing a book—things are just starting to fall into place and I need to be alone and quiet for my mind to tell me what's coming next."

"For your mind to tell you? What kind of gibberish is that? Either you know what you're going to say or you don't is my way of thinking. Anyway, got something to tell you."

"I can tell," Matthew said with a smile.

"Got a letter from Princeton today. Seems like they've cooked up this thing where they want to have some kind of reception for me to thank me for the gift of all those notebooks we sent them. August 30th. The faculty starts the Fall semester that week. What do you think? Should

I tell them I'll go? With Nell gone, I'll need you to drive me. Those two aren't supposed to be back from their gallivanting until the middle of September, right?"

"Right. But I'll be glad to drive you down. It'll be fun for me to see the old stomping grounds again too. Tell them you'll be there with bells on. And see what kind of specifics you can get about exactly what's going to be going on, how long we'll be there, whatever. That's less than a month away so we've got to start making plans."

Before Matthew even finished what he was saying, Jonas was out of his chair and going to the computer. With lightning speed, he typed out a letter of acceptance saying he'd be honored to attend.

Matthew tried not to let Jonas see his surprise. *That sly old fox has been pretending he could hardly type so I'd do all the grunt work*, he thought and suddenly remembered those swift-as-lightning e-mails Jonas had fired back at him the day he'd answered the ad. *Look at him go. Mr. Nimble Fingers himself when he wants to be.*

Jonas printed the letter on his best stationery, signed it and had it ready for mailing even before supper was ready.

"…he's been much happier lately," Matthew wrote in an e-mail to Katie later. "He even seems younger. Maybe it's getting his life's work organized and ready for the archives. And probably having another man around, someone he can needle and not feel guilty."

Lost in his own thoughts, he was surprised when an Instant Message from her popped up on his screen. He didn't know she'd put him on her Buddy List. He'd added her name to his about a week before but when he saw that she was online he held back from sending her a message.

He told himself he didn't want her to get the wrong idea, didn't want her to think he was more interested in her than he really was. But his heart raced when he saw who was Im-ing him.

"I see you—how come you're online and not at the easel, pal?" she wrote.

He grinned and wrote back, "Because I was writing to you. Got some fun news about Jonas to tell you."

"What?" she asked and he responded with the details about the upcoming trip to New Jersey. Then he added his observations about how animated and cheerful Jonas was these days and how he had actually become fond of the old guy.

"Thanks for telling me. It'll make Mom happy. She misses him. Feels guilty having a good time here. She's been talking about flying out a couple of weeks early."

"Tell her not to do that. He's having himself a good old time," Matt replied.

"But what about this event? How big a deal? Should we plan to come home early?" Katie typed in reply. "We end the cruise on the Seine 8/25 and the final cruises through Italy depart 9/1 and 10/1. Should we leave from France and return in a month for Italy?"

"When he raced through his acceptance tonight, he asked them for details. When we get them, I'll let you know. Right now, I'd say stick to your planned itinerary with your Mom. It would be a shame for her to have to miss Italy. And I'd bet you wouldn't be able to talk her into going back with you to do it a month later."

"You're right," Katie answered. "I'll talk with her in the morning. Right now I need to get back to sleep. It's two a.m. here. The ship went through the locks and we must have bumped sides. Something woke me up and I saw the computer was still on and you were on line. I'll e-mail you tomorrow, okay?"

"Okay. G'night, Katie. Sleep well." He clicked off and shut down the computer then sat there thinking of Katie and that dazzling smile of hers. Yes, he'd be glad to see her when she returned.

It was still early evening for Matthew and though Katie was sleepy, he was wide awake—even more wide awake than he was before he'd talked with her.

Hands in his back pockets he walked over to the west windows and watched the light of the full moon playing on the whitecaps as they rolled in and then spread out on the sand. He reached for his sketchpad and some pastels, began making color notes, then decided to take his French easel down to the beach to see what he could do with a painting of moonlight on incoming surf.

The handrail that Jonas hated on the dune steps saved him a couple of times as he lugged the easel and camping lantern down to the beach. But when he got there he knew he'd made the right decision. The light was perfect on the whitecaps. And it was still light enough that when the waves broke and spilled thinly onto the sand he could still see their translucency. This would be no brilliant setting sun painting—it would be the pale moonlight, the deepening ultramarine sky, the almost silhouetted dunes. While his eye traced outlines and his hand took his brush to the right hues, his mind was remembering Katie and wondering how much their talk had to do with his wanting to capture every moment of beauty the world was offering.

He completed two small studies of the colors, the movement, the atmosphere he was seeing. He would use them later in the studio as reference for larger, more formal paintings. But these, too, he would frame because he knew they were fresh, spontaneous and well done.

He was starting to think about going back up to the cottage and when he turned to look in that direction he saw it nestled against the woods behind it, all perched comfortably on the rock ledge above the dunes. The moonlight fell silvery on its roof and on the roses and flowers that were, under his encouraging hand, growing abundantly around it. There was no color to record because it was night, but there was light and there was a myriad of shapes and there was the cottage itself.

He quickly put another small canvas up on the easel and started laying out a palette of rich but grayed-down colors. He worked for about an hour using his camping lantern to illuminate his palette so he could mix colors, but relying on the light of the moon to illuminate not only his subject, but his canvas as well.

When he felt he could go no farther, he packed up his gear and wrapped his brushes in plastic wrap to keep them until he could clean them in turps. He fastened the canvases to the outside of the easel and made his way back up and over the dunes.

When he got there he saw the light on his answering machine blinking. It was then almost midnight and he wondered what might be wrong and with whom.

"You have one new message," the machine told him. He waited apprehensively, then heard, "Hi, this is Katie" and he smiled. "I still can't sleep," she said. "I've been thinking about that journal entry you said in your e-mail that you read at the cabin today. I can't get it out of my mind. Matthew, I think something bad happened to Nancy. I know it was a century ago and I can't do anything about it, but I still can't get it out of my mind. No need to call me back though. I'm going to try to get back to sleep. I just called Room Service and asked someone to bring me a blackberry brandy. That usually helps. Just felt like talking to you some more about the journal and the cabin. Will you take me there when I get back home?"

He looked at his watch, looked at the phone, and then back at his watch again.

"I just picked up your phone message," he wrote in an e-mail. "Was going to call you back, but I don't want to wake you up if you've gone back to sleep. The answer is yes. I'll take you to the cabin when you get home."

He shut down the computer, got in bed, and tried not to think about her so he could get to sleep.

– Chapter 10 –

THE EVENT IN PRINCETON WAS still a few weeks away but Matthew started prodding Jonas to get out any clothes he wanted to take so he could get them dry cleaned or laundered. He dug around in the attic of the old house and found a vintage Samsonite hard-sides suitcase that Jonas declared was good enough.

Whistling some nameless tune that had been bouncing around in his head all morning, he got the one suit he'd brought to the Cape out of his closet and pulled out a couple of dress shirts to be laundered and ironed.

Jonas poked his head in the door. "What's going on in there? You that happy to be going back to the scene of all your crimes?"

Matthew grimaced, but then laughed. "Yea, I'm going to get to see my boys play soccer. That way I'll get to see them and I won't have to see their mother. Soccer fields are too dirty for her."

He began making a list of people he'd like to visit while he was back in his home area, but then quickly realized there weren't that many he was interested in seeing anymore. His parents had decided to stay on in Florida after their annual winter sojourn this year to get a feel for the summers in case they wanted to retire there. And his lifestyle had become so different from his former friends' in these few short months they wouldn't have enough in common to even sustain a lunch conversation. The list was short: Nick, his AA sponsor, and maybe his kid brother Joe who was probably back from his trip to Ireland by this time. He'd have to check with Mom.

But never during all the planning for the trip did Matthew stop thinking about the cabin and that last disturbing journal entry he'd read. He'd been filling his journal with wondering what had happened and continued the story he'd started writing about Nancy and Davy and the life he imagined they might have led. But what he needed now were Nancy's words, not his own. He knew he had to get back there.

His break came one evening as he and Jonas were cleaning up after supper.

"Don't need you over here tomorrow. Got things to do," Jonas said.

Matthew looked at him, one eyebrow raised.

"What's that look all about?" Jonas glared at him. "Can't I have some privacy in my own house when I want it? I've got a speech to write and I can't think with you hanging around here humming and whistling. I'm gonna need the whole day, so you go paint or write or do whatever it is you do over there."

"Sounds good to me," Matthew said. "Call me in the afternoon if you want me to come make supper."

"Just come. I'll need a break by then."

Matthew got a slow start the next morning. He'd been on the computer until late instant messaging with Katie and it took a while for him to pull himself up out of sleep. But once he was up, he was motivated. He went right to the cabin and right from the pried-open door to the book on the table.

But when he turned to the next entry, he was surprised to see nothing written about Rev. Heady. Instead, Nancy had launched into long reminiscences about her girlhood on her family's farm, and the fun times in the youth group of the church in Concord.

He decided Rev. Heady must have settled down and stopped bothering Nancy and when he saw her next entry was all about when she and Davy met, all thought about the reverend left his mind.

I was just sitting here at the table looking at our wedding picture and remembering the first time I ever saw my Davy, Nancy had written. It was that night Prissy and I went to Youth Group for pumpkin carving. We were helping the young ones so they wouldn't cut themselves and I looked up and there he was. He came with Jonathan Evans and when I saw Davy my heart started beating so hard and fast and I knew, I just knew... I remember how nervous I was when he came over and introduced himself. And when he stayed and carved his pumpkin right by me I could hardly do mine, my hand was shaking so much. I'll never forget what happened when we took them out to the Green and Davy helped me light the candle for mine and I looked into his eyes. Yes, I knew. We both knew.

Matthew read that passage over and over. He'd never had that kind of experience and he liked thinking about what it might be like to meet someone and to know. For both of you to know.

Ever since then, candlelight has a special mean-
ing for us. We both remember how it was that first
night—and still is, she wrote.

Nancy had left a little space after that on the page and had drawn a little sketch of two candles with one flame. When Matthew saw that, a lump rose in his throat. Would he ever find a love like that?

Further down on the page Nancy wrote how she'd felt sad when Davy told her about leaving his father and two older brothers who were whalers and lived down in New Bedford:

They didn't understand him. He loved to write
stories and to write down things he was thinking. His
words were beautiful, but they told him that was for
womenfolk to do.

They expected him to be a whaler too, and when
he told them he wanted to build houses, they didn't
understand. He misses them a lot, but he wants to
build really good, strong houses for farmers who have
to be out in the fields and for fishermen who have to be
out to sea. He says they can't spare the time to build
a house and they're not skilled at it, so he wants to do
it for them. It's a simple ambition, but one that isn't
lofty or foolhardy and I admire that so. He took me
to see two of the houses he built. They're really special
and he has plans all laid out for a two-story house he's
going to build for us as soon as he can.

Right now though we're so very happy in this cabin. I've prettied it up with curtains and pads for the wooden chairs. We have mama and papa's soft fireplace chairs and Davy built us this nice big fireplace to keep us warm—and the raised hearth to make cooking easier. I remember mama and both grandmas always having back trouble from bending low to stir the soup and turn the griddle cakes. Davy's made sure that won't happen to me.

He showed me the plans for the house that he had made up even before we got married. When he told me he already started making this table and chairs, I pictured them right beneath a window like this where the morning light would come in just like it is right now. He showed me on his plans where he was going to build a separate room for sleeping and for keeping our clothing so we wouldn't have to sleep in the main room like so many other couples starting out have to do. And he did build it, right off this main room. I can see the sun coming in there too while I'm writing this. And it even has a real closet with a door on it. We don't have to hang our clothes on hooks on the wall where they'd get all dusty and damp from the moisture that hangs too heavy in these woods by the sea.

Matthew smiled as he read what Nancy wrote about the four-poster bed Davy had made for them with the high spindle head and footboards that he had carefully turned and lovingly buffed and made smooth until they shone:

The bed is wide and instead of just ropes and a straw mattress, Davy sent all the way to Philadelphia for our one luxury—metal springs and a real fiber mattress! He told me, "I'm not going to make love to

my beautiful wife on a bed of straw. We're going to
curl up together in real comfort on a real mattress."
Can you imagine? We weren't even married yet when
he told me that. I couldn't stop blushing. I still do
when I remember him saying it.

Matthew closed the book and sat back musing about
how sweet and tender Nancy's love for Davy had been, and
compared it to what he'd had with Annaliese. A heavy sadness came over him. A longing for what he'd never had.

He was glad what he'd read had none of the foreboding
of the previous entry, but now he wanted to get back to his
cottage to sort out the feelings that were milling around
inside him.

When he came out of the woods, he glanced up at the
sky to make sure the sun was still high enough that he
wouldn't have to start making dinner. Then he checked his
watch and confirmed it.

He'd started it on the computer but when he found he
was more comfortable writing it in long hand, he picked up
one of those thick spiral notebooks his boys had brought
up with them the last time they came. There was something about the story that felt alien to a computer and as
soon as he closed his door he went right over, picked up the
notebook and settled in.

He chewed on the top of his pen, doodled in the mar-
gins of the pad resting on his knees, and finally started
writing, giving his imagination free rein, editing little as he
went along. Editing and tightening would come later. For
now he'd come to believe Nancy and Davy wanted their
story told and trusted him with the telling.

— *Chapter 11* —

DEALING WITH JONAS'S MOOD SWINGS that went from happy anticipation to "Call them and tell them I'm not coming" was wearing on Matthew. Organizing papers and files for the trip, and then re-organizing the same things after Jonas went through them and changed everything was driving him nuts. Besides, he was itching to get back to the cabin. It had been almost two weeks.

But finally everything seemed to fall into place and the pace slowed down and Matthew seized the opportunity.

He knew now he'd been wrong to think of the little room behind the old-fashioned padlock as a storage room. It was the bedroom Nancy had described with such love in her journal.

He rooted through Jonas's meager cache of tools and took an old hacksaw along with the camping lantern and the tools he always carried there and started along the path by the brook.

When he entered the cabin, which now felt familiar and comfortable to him and almost homey, he walked right over to the locked door and started working on the padlock. He tried prying at it with his Swiss army knife but that didn't work, so he began sawing at it with the hacksaw. It took a long time and from time to time he stopped and wiped his brow wondering why in hell someone would padlock a bedroom door. He was tempted to take the crowbar to the old wood but, remembering Nancy's description of the work Davy had done for his bride, he just kept on sawing. It seemed to take forever and his shirt was damp with sweat when he finally broke through and the lock came apart. He pushed the door and it opened freely.

He was right. It was the bedroom. Though the room was dim, he could make out a bed, it's four posts rising toward the ceiling, its surface rumpled with old linens and a wooden chair that still seemed to bear the remnants of the last clothes someone had draped on it.

Vines covered the two windows inside and out and Matthew went back out into the main room, got the camping lantern and entered the room again. He shined the light on the far wall and there was the closet. The door was ajar and he could see the shredded remains of some of the clothes on hooks inside. The mice had been here too. The shambles of Nancy and Davy's few garments would probably have distressed Nancy, whom he had come to envision as a caring housekeeper.

His light finally fell on the four-poster bed. It was just as Nancy had described it in her journal with high posts turned delicately. When his light fell on the surface of the bed itself, he could see remnants of what must have been a handmade quilt that was covering something that lay beneath it. He couldn't make out what it was, so he moved closer to the bed with his lantern and then stopped short and gasped.

On a pillow whose ticking had turned brittle and brown was the skull of a human. Feathers had been torn free from the rotting pillow and were strewn about. A few even lay on the cheekbones of the skull. The shredded quilt was carefully tucked up under what must have been the chin of the person and spread down over the bones that lay beneath. Next to the carefully tucked-in skeleton, however, the quilt was crumpled and turned back as if someone had risen and not gone back to straighten it.

Matthew could not take his eyes off what he was seeing. Nor could he stare. He was caught between horror and macabre fascination. His hands shook as he rubbed his arms trying to stop the chill that was creeping from his feet to his scalp that was crinkling with goose bumps. His teeth began to chatter, and his knees were trembling.

He wanted to run, but couldn't get his feet to leave the floorboards. He wanted to scream, but no sound came from his throat. He could scarcely breathe. Still trembling, he stepped backward toward the door he had just entered, went through it and closed it quietly. He replaced the padlock but now it could no longer lock. He had broken into a terrible secret, one that could no longer be locked away. Even if he told no one else about what he'd found, he would carry the secret of this cabin with him the rest of his life.

Still stepping backward, he felt his muscles clench and contract as if to protect him from absorbing the awful truth. He collapsed in the chair that he had found askew when he first arrived in the cabin all those weeks ago.

For a long time he just sat there trembling, his mind not able to comprehend what he'd found. Then, slowly, he began to think more clearly. He wondered if there might be a clue in Nancy's journal. Words that might answer at least some of the questions racing around in his brain.

He reached for the book that he'd always left on the table where he'd first found it. He turned through the cracking, worm-eaten pages to the ones he'd read with Nancy's sweet reminiscences. What he saw next sent another chill through him:

Reverend Heady is back again, she wrote and Matthew noticed her hand was unsteady. Yesterday and today I saw him hiding in the bushes watching me.

Matthew's hand shook as he turned the page to see what she'd written next. Nothing. That had been Nancy's last entry.

He thumbed through the next pages which were yellowed, but blank also, his mind desperately searching for answers. Finally, he came upon pages written in a totally different hand—more hastily written, more bold and clearly written by someone distraught.

Matthew read and quickly realized. Davy.

July 2nd. If anyone should read this, I want you to know what happened to my Nancy this day. Davy had begun in a shaky hand, some of the words roughly scratched on the page, some gouged deeply into the paper.

I came home from hunting, heard a man yelling. Evil. Ugly. Screaming at my Nancy. I ran fast. Our door was open and there was a man all dressed in black. My Nancy was crying, begging, No Please No. I was running so fast my knees gave way. I screamed for him to stop but before I got there he raised his hand and struck her across her chest with our fireplace

poker. It was that evil Rev. Heady who had the devil
in him. I've seen the way he looked at my Nancy.
Hated her. I should have protected her more. Should
have told him stay away or I'll kill you. I should have
killed him.

My Nancy cried out and bent over when he hit
her and put her hands on her belly to protect our baby.
Rev. Heady (Rev. was crossed out, slashed heavily
several times.) I can no longer call him reverend.
He is not a man of God. He called my Nancy a blas-
phemer, a child of the devil. He pushed her. It happened fast. My God, I couldn't get to her. I couldn't.
My Nancy fell back, hit her head on our fireplace then
lay still with blood coming from her head. She was
silent. I screamed. Loaded my shotgun and he turned
on me, snarling. I shot him and he fell to the floor.
I wished him dead. So help me God, I wished him
dead. But he was not so I hog tied him fast with rope
tied to my belt for a deer if I got one. I made sure he
could do us no more harm and I went to my Nancy.
Her eyes were open in horror, but I knew she could no
longer see me. I put my hand to her soft breast that
I have loved to caress but I felt no warm heartbeat. I
held her wrist between my fingers and there was no
beat there either. My Nancy was gone from me.

I hate Heady. It's near choking me. I threw his
vile self in my wagon bed and drove him to Wellfleet
and told the Constable what happened. He put him
in leg irons and chained him to that big red oak tree
by the inn in the middle of town to wait for the coach
to take him to Plimouth to stand trial there before

he's sure to be hung for murder. If he isn't, I'll go do it myself.

People came to spit on him. What he deserved. I hope he rots in hell forever for what he did to my Nancy and our child.

Matthew's hands were shaking as he read the journal entry and he could barely turn the pages. He stopped reading, although there was more written, and he put his head down on his folded arms and let his tears soak his shirt sleeves. His heart was breaking for this good young man who had lost the love of his life. Knowing that he'd sat here so many days reading Nancy's journal while her remains lay just a few feet away behind that closed door felt overwhelming to him. He looked over at the fireplace poker laying on the hearth and the black stain on the floor and it all became real.

Finally, he knew he had to read on and he did:

I wanted my Nancy standing at the door smiling when I got home. But she was still lying where I left her, Davy had written. She was dead. There was nothing I could do but love her. The rest of my life.

I lifted her and laid her in our bed. Got water in our bucket from the stream. Warmed it over the fire still burning in the fireplace, careful not to step in her blood. Tried to not look at our poker that was still where Heady dropped it when I shot him.

I washed my Nancy's face, her hands, arms. Took her dress off her. It was covered with blood across her chest where he had hit her so hard. Her camisole was bloodied too. I took it from her precious body. Threw them in the fireplace and watched them burn away. Went back to my lovely Nancy and washed her with

*the warm water, passing the cloth gently down over
her little breasts that were just starting to swell for our
little one inside. Pulled a clean flannel nightgown over
her head and put her arms in the long sleeves. Lifted
her sweet body and smoothed the nightgown under
her and over her beautiful long legs. Brushed her hair
100 times like she did every night. Her lovely golden
hair. Smoothed it back from her lovely face and kissed
her brow.*

*Slipped in beside her under the quilt she made
for us. The quilt that had covered us as we fell asleep
and then woke up all wrapped around each other. The
quilt that covered us the morning we made love and
knew we had conceived a child.*

*Pulled her close to me and wept. Whispered to
her all night long. Told her how much I love her, how
sweet she is and how happy I was when she told me we
were right and would be having a child come spring.
Told her I will never love another and I will, God
willing, be with her and our child again someday in
Heaven.*

Again, Matthew had to stop reading. His own tears
were blinding him. His shoulders shook with quiet sobs
as he again rested his head on his folded arms on the table
top and gave way to grief. He never questioned how Davy
could have spent the night holding his beloved Nancy.
Matthew knew he too was capable of that kind of love and
that made his reading Davy's words even more difficult for
him. Matthew had never known a love like that, but he
knew he would have loved that way if he'd had a Nancy in
his life.

Compelled to stay with Davy through his agony, Matthew read on:

Didn't sleep. Davy's words went on, _sometimes hard to decipher_ because of the emotion that propelled his hand. _Didn't want to give up one minute holding my Nancy and talking to her. She grew cold in my arms and I kept the quilt around us and tried to warm her with my body._

When the sun came in our east window, I knew what I had to do. Kissed my Nancy's cold lips one last time and whispered my words of love to her. Left our bed, tucked the quilt in around her, and pulled it up under her sweet chin to keep her warm. Put some clothes in a sack and whatever food we had that won't spoil and will last my journey.

I can't bury my Nancy in the ground. I can't cover her with dirt. I have to leave her sleeping in our bed.

I found a board out back and wrote this cabin is now sacred ground and any who enter it will be answerable to God. I wrote my beloved wife and child lie dead inside and no one is to enter and desecrate their peaceful sleep.

Now I'm writing this in my Nancy's book. I leave it on our table and if her spirit is allowed to live in this place we loved, then maybe it will comfort her.

I leave now. I will board up this place where my love and our child lie and I leave it to our Lord to protect and preserve it, for it is sacred.

I go first to Concord to tell my Nancy's family what has happened. Then to New Bedford to go on

*the whaling ships with my father and brothers until I
can be with My Nancy again.*

I go now.

The journal still had many blank pages to follow, but
this was the last entry. Matthew sat with it a very long time.
He didn't cry anymore. There were no tears left. Eventually he stood up, left the journal open to Davy's last words
and left the cabin. He was now even more careful to board
it up and leave it as he had found it that first day.

— *Chapter 12* —

HE STAGGERED BACK THROUGH THE woods in a stupor. Stumbling down to the stream, he followed it home hardly noticing where he was walking. His foot slipped once in the mud and he went down on one knee in the water which brought him back to reality, but only until he got back up on his feet and tried unsuccessfully to get the mud off his jeans. Hardly aware of the now-wet and chilly denim clinging to his left leg, he just kept moving forward while his mind remained back in the cabin with what he had seen, read, experienced.

When he reached the edge of the woods, he saw Jonas pulling weeds out of Nell's bed of blue delphinium. Not wanting to talk to anyone and most especially not to Jonas, Matt stopped short, backtracked, and took the narrow winding path down over the dunes to the beach below.

There were a few groups of people scattered on the broad expanse of sand and he took a wide path around them. He took off his sneakers, tucked his socks in them and, carrying them, walked along the edge of the surf letting it splash and curl over his feet and around his ankles as it lazily found its way onto the shore and then washed back out again.

He walked for an hour or more, going long past the public bathing area to the rocky shoals where he found a secluded spot in among the boulders and he sat there to rest.

He wondered if he needed to call police or tell some other authority what he'd found. What does a person do if he's stumbled on the skeleton of somebody who was murdered 150 years ago?

He didn't know the answers to the questions he was asking himself, but he did know he wasn't ready to reveal any of it yet. He couldn't bear to think of exposing Nancy and her journal and Davy's entry in it to the curious world. There was no doubt that it would make big news and he shuddered at the image of tv cameramen and broadcasters descending on the cabin and having it all appear on the evening news. It had been a secret, sacred place for 150 years and Matthew was certain he didn't want to violate it.

There was no sign of Jonas by the time Matt got back to the house and he slipped into his cottage unnoticed. He peeled off his jeans that were by that time not only wet from his fall into the stream, but were sandy wet for about five inches up from the bottom where the surf had caught him by surprise a few times. The sun was pouring in the west window as he collapsed in one of the overstuffed chairs wearing just his boxers and a t-shirt. He put his feet up on the ottoman and promptly fell into an agitated sleep.

The phone woke him and he was surprised to see the room was turning dark. He grabbed the phone and heard Jonas shouting as he always did on the phone as if he had to yell to be heard on the other end of the line.

"Is something wrong over there or have you just decided to get into a snit about something today?" Jonas shouted.
"Supper's over. I scrambled myself some eggs and burned
a couple of pieces of toast but I managed just fine on my
own." He paused, waiting for an apology, but Matthew
wasn't up to giving one. "Saw you sneaking out of the
woods and high-tailing it down the dune path. Figured
something was eating at you and I decided I'd just as soon
not have to get mixed up in it. Thought I'd better check on
you before the news comes on so I don't have to be interrupted. You okay?"

Matt rubbed his eyes and ran his hand through his hair
trying to orient himself. "Yea," he said. I'm okay. I just fell
asleep. Maybe I'm coming down with something. Sorry
about supper, Jonas. Didn't mean to leave you in the lurch,"
he finally said.

"Well you did, but so be it. You hungry now? You can
come get something if you want. But I don't want any big
talk time, the news is coming on."

"No, I have a couple of apples here if I get hungry.
No big deal. I think I'll just go to bed early. See you after
breakfast."

Jonas muttered something that might have been "good
night" and they hung up.

Matthew went in the bathroom and while he was there
he got a look at himself in the medicine cabinet mirror—
messed up hair, a day's worth of beard stubble and eyes that
looked bewildered.

"God, I look awful," he said aloud. "Maybe I really am
coming down with something."

But he knew better and, as he fixed himself a few peanut butter crackers and bit into the tart green apple, his

mind wandered back over all that he had seen and experienced that day and the sadness came back over him.
He knew he needed to talk about it with someone and he
knew exactly who the right person was. He booted up his
computer and started typing.

"Katie," he wrote, "I found something today that is so awful and so sad. I need to talk with someone about it and I
suspect you'll understand how I'm feeling. But please keep it
a secret at least for now. Don't even tell your mom."

He wrote on telling her about sawing through the padlock on the "storeroom" and finding that it was a bedroom.
He described the room to her and he told her about finding
Nancy's skeleton under the rotting quilt in the bed Davy
had made. And he told her about finding Davy's entry in
the journal and all of what Davy had written. Then he told
her about the horror he felt and the overwhelming sadness.
He asked her the questions he'd asked himself down on the
beach and told her he'd decided, at least for now, he would
not tell anyone except her about it.

He typed on and on pouring out his thoughts and
feelings and finally got online and sent it. He sat back in
the chair, exhausted but more at peace with it all now that
he had shared it with someone—with Katie. He stood,
stretched and yawned, put the lid back on the peanut butter jar, closed the cracker box and put it on the shelf. He
tossed the apple core out the door for the raccoons to find,
turned out the lights and went to bed.

Again he was awakened by the phone ringing, but this
time the cottage was totally dark. Grappling for the phone,
he noticed the illuminated dial of his alarm clock: Just after
midnight. He got hold of the phone just before his answering machine would click on.

"Matthew, it's Katie," he heard.

"Katie. Where are you? Is everything okay? Why are you calling? It's after midnight."

"Matthew, everything's okay and it's not after midnight here. I'm in France and it's a bright new morning, but I just got up and picked up your e-mail from last night. Oh God, Matthew, how horrible. And how awful for you. I just had to call you and talk about it. How're you doing?"

"I don't really know, Kate," he answered. I just know I felt a lot better after I wrote to you and was able to come in here and fall asleep.

"And now I woke you up. I guess I shouldn't have done that. I did think about that before I called but, Matthew, I just had to call and make sure you're all right. Please don't be mad at me."

"Are you kidding, Katie? How could I be upset with you for doing something so sweet? I'm glad you called. Why don't I call you back sometime tomorrow? What's a good time for you?"

She gave him a time and a number where she could be reached. They talked just a minute or so more and then Katie said, "Matthew, I'm thinking about you and wish I could be there with you."

"Thanks, Katie. This phone call means a lot to me and I do feel like you're right here with me. I'll call you later. G'night—I mean good morning. Or whatever... Talk to you later."

They both hung up chuckling. She at his muddled sleepiness and he with the sweet contentment that she'd called.

— *Chapter 13* —

Jonas was his usual morning self at breakfast, a mix of gruff and sometimes almost pleasant.

"You feeling okay today?"

"Yea, just tired still," Matthew answered. "I think I'll spend the morning printing up and collating all your notes from Fall Semester '64. I'll get them in binders and then I'll start on Spring '65 when you were working out your theories on the Matterhorn Project. That okay with you? If I can get them all organized, that will be a big job done.

"Suits me fine," Jonas said. "And maybe I'll get into the next filing cabinet and see what's in that one."

They worked straight through to lunch time, made sandwiches from the barbecued chicken they'd gotten two nights before at the Shop & Stop and ate almost in silence as they listened to Jonas's new Mozart CD that had come in the mail earlier. The music was beautiful and restful and Matthew lingered longer than he'd meant to.

He barely made it back to his cottage for the appointed time to call Katie and was nervous as a schoolboy. When he heard her voice, he almost started stuttering.

He asked her about her day and she told him she'd spent it transcribing notes and writing about the marketplace she and Nell had visited where the local craftspeople were selling their work. She said Nell had met some women her age aboard ship and they were out on the town, going to have dinner and then hit some of the night spots. Matt made a funny comment about Nell and her sixty-something friends bellying up to the bar in some strobe-lit club packed with bumping and grinding college kids. They laughed and then grew silent.

"How are you, Matt?" Katie asked softly.

"Doing a little better today," he answered. "Jonas and I got a lot done on his files this morning and that keeps the mind occupied. We plan to stick with it all afternoon too. I decided I had to set all that other aside for a day or two in order to get a better perspective on it. What do you think I should do about it eventually, Katie?"

"I don't know," she said, "but I do agree it's best to do nothing for the time being. Do you plan to go back there?"

"No. At least not any time soon," Matthew said quickly, then added quietly, "It's too strange. I felt like I'd burst into something very private, very intimate between those two people. They were so much in love, Katie. Imagine him bathing and dressing her in her nightgown, brushing her hair and then holding her all night to try to keep her warm. I kept thinking of that when I left there and went walking on the beach. What a beautiful and rare thing a love like that is and how horrible it was for it to be taken from them so violently. And her being pregnant and all. I don't know how Davy could have survived that. I'm wondering if he did."

Katie was silent as Matt spoke and afterward for a moment or two. Then she said, "You know what, Matthew? I think you're capable of a love like that."

And he answered right away. "Yes, Kate, I know I am. I felt that as I was reading Davy's words and I felt so sad for him and what he lost and I guess for myself too for what I've never had."

They were both silent and then Katie whispered, "Maybe you'll find that someday."

Hearing the tenderness in her voice, Matthew felt tears welling up. He swallowed hard and said, "I hope so, Katie. I hope so."

They talked a few minutes more about ordinary things. She asked him what he planned to do with the rest of his day and he told her he'd just keep working at the house with Jonas. She said she was going to turn in and, after promising to e-mail, he wished her good night.

He sat for awhile staring out the window picturing Katie's bright smile and then got up and went back across to the main house. He and Jonas spent the entire afternoon quietly working, Jonas at the big rolltop desk and Matthew at the computer and printer across the room. It was just the kind of day Matthew needed to get himself absorbed in something other than the cabin and what he'd found there.

They decided on an early supper and Matthew put a couple of steaks on the gas grill on the back porch along with couple of ears of corn, still in their husks, which he'd wrapped in foil. Jonas sliced cucumbers and tomatoes from the garden and set plates and flatware on the old blue table on the porch.

They were a little more talkative over supper than they had been at lunch.

"Heard anything from Nell or Katie lately?" Jonas asked, startling Matthew with the question.

No way was he going to admit the phone talks with Katie. Without meeting the old man's eyes, he said yes, there'd been some e-mails and a few phone calls. "Nell's able to relax when she knows everything's all right at home."

"Seems like you could have told me without my asking," Jonas said. "Been more than a week since I heard from Nell. Guess she's pretty relaxed these days."

Trying to smooth things over, Matthew told Jonas about Nell's having met some women her age but he didn't mention their going out on the town. No sense giving him ammunition to badger her with when she got home.

"Won't be long and they'll be back, Nell trying to boss me around, Katie talking non-stop like she always does when she gets home from a trip," Jonas said.

"Well, we've got our trip to Princeton to think about before then," Matthew said, still trying to divert him and get him in a better mood.

They talked about all the work they'd done that day as they started clearing the dishes. Jonas tossed the corn cobs over the rail for the raccoons and filled the dish on the porch step with dry food for CalleyCat, the feral cat who dropped by for all her meals. When all was cleaned up, the two men said goodnight. Jonas retiring to the evening news and Matthew to his thoughts of Katie.

❦

Day after day they worked almost non-stop, pulling files together, dating, cataloging. Jonas kept getting caught up in remembering the stumbling blocks on some of the projects, the struggles to work out his theory. But then he'd also remember the satisfaction he'd felt when his theory proved true.

Being privy to the evolution of Jonas's ideas and theories and also to the man himself intrigued Matthew especially because he sensed Jonas was unaware of the way his own growth was so evident in what they were transcribing.

Matthew thought about his own development from the callow young artist who just wanted to live the fairytale life of an artist painting glorious seascapes, to the guy who got caught up in the high life of young advertising execs with all the money to be spent. Standing by the printer, collating, stapling, he wished again he could influence Luke and Jason to seek a more rewarding, if more difficult, way. But he knew the best way to help them is to be there for them whenever possible. Like Matthew, like Jonas, like Davy, they'd make the decisions that determined the course of their lives.

As the date of their departure came closer, Matthew e-mailed the boys and Nick, telling them he was planning to be in Princeton and giving them the dates. He said he wanted to spend time with each of them and hoped they'd be free.

It was hard not to think about the cabin and his sad and grisly find there. It worked around the edges of his mind and kept rising to the surface. To deal with it, he tried submerging all those energetic thoughts into painting. He spent hours on his sun porch painting seascapes. Other times he set up his easel on the rock promontory and tried to catch the play of light on the boulders that found their way there during the ice age.

After several days of this kind of painting, he lined the studies up around the main room of the cottage, standing them on the floor with their backs against the walls. When he stood back to get a feel for what he'd done, he was uncomfortable. He'd always enjoyed the many moods of the ocean, but what he saw in these recent paintings was not the energy, the peacefulness, or the turbulence of the sea, but his own agitation. His strokes were not fluid. Where they should have been strong and dynamic, they were disjointed and unresolved. What could have been a painting of the ocean in any one of its many moods was, instead, a confused interpretation of an undecided sea. He knew something deep inside of him was unsettled.

Searching for some feeling of contentment, he did sketches of his cottage and the flowers surrounding it. He bought a macro lens for his camera and spent hours getting deep inside the blooming yellow daylilies and the furls of grasses that grew on the dunes. The rugosa roses were blooming profusely and he let his macro lens pretend it was a honeybee getting down inside the rose to the sweet nectar and the convoluting shapes inside. He scanned the images in his computer to use for future paintings and printed one from which he did a large canvas that he filled with just the heart of what he intended to be a deep pink rose. Instead, as he painted, the colors grew stronger, more intense. His beach rose ended up blood red and looked threatening.

Finally he stopped trying to force himself to not think of the cabin and Nancy and Davy and when he returned to his cottage after working all morning with Jonas, he filled the pages of his spiral-bound journal with his thoughts and feelings about it. Slowly he realized he could suppress the story no longer. It needed to be told, but he was still reluctant to open it to the world. Not yet.

He dug out the notes he'd written weeks back when he was going to the cabin regularly. He'd started writing his vision of what their lives might have been. But when he read those notes now, knowing the final outcome of their story, they seemed trite and fanciful.

He told Katie all this in his e-mails and her response was, "Start again, Matthew. Delete all the other stuff and start fresh. Some of it will find its way back, but now your story will have more substance. Just start writing and see what happens."

He gave in to it one afternoon. It was one of those dreary Cape Cod days when the rain pelted continuously, the kind of day when all Matthew wanted to do was stay indoors with a low fire burning in the fireplace to keep the damp chill away. The work with Jonas was just about completed and now they were tying up loose ends for their trip. They'd finished long before noon that day and Jonas, reverting to his old taciturn manner, told Matthew, "Why don't you go back to the cottage and do whatever it is you used to do there. You've been hanging around over here planning this, organizing that, getting as bad as Nell was. I've got reading I want to do and I can't do it with you inter-rupting me all the time."

Matthew knew Jonas well enough by now to realize he was just getting nervous as their time to leave drew near and he agreed that it was best they spend some time apart.

"Yea, well I've got stuff I've been wanting to get to too but I've put it aside so I could be planning this and organizing that and interrupting you all the time," Matt said, giving it right back.

"Well, go do it then," Jonas snapped.

Matthew grinned and said if Jonas could be trusted to put the roast in the oven by three, he'd just do his thing and would let him be. He'd be back in time to start the vegetables for supper.

"I think I can manage that," Jonas said. "Not feeble-minded yet."

Matthew grabbed his windbreaker, threw it over his head and made a dash through the downpour to his cottage.

It took him a while to settle. He spent the best part of an hour getting a fire going, making a pot of coffee, sorting through and piling up old newspapers. Busy stuff. Avoidance they call it in AA, he thought. He knew it was time to stop procrastinating and take Katie's advice. Start fresh and see what happens.

He let the story flow with no direction. Because he had no intention of ever formalizing it, he was letting it course through him and come out on paper. Two hours passed, then three, and he was still writing. Once again, he started with Nancy as a little girl growing up on the farm near Concord. This time, however, his words weren't just a recitation of how she looked, some of the things she must have said and done. This time it was emerging as a full-bodied story of a girl who was learning about growing up female. It was the story of a girl who was being taught how to take care of a home, how to cook, to sew and be the anchor of a family. He wrote about her learning gardening, the planting of vegetables, flowers, and herbs and how she was being taught by her grandmother Fuller about the medicinal uses of the herbs she was growing, how to preserve them and use them to make poultices and tonics.

He got up to put another log on the fire and stretched, trying to get the kinks out of his back and neck. Sitting hunched over the keyboard for that long a spell without a break wasn't good. He stretched out flat on his back on the floor, arms out to the sides, legs spread eagle and stretched as far as his muscles would allow.

He felt like calling Katie to tell her what he'd done, but the timing was wrong. She'd probably just gotten to sleep. He'd be glad when they were both in the same time zone again. It was only a matter of a few weeks now and she and Nell would be returning. Of course, she'd probably go right to her apartment in Boston, but still that was only two hours away and, if it worked out, he could drive in now and then and take her to a show or out to dinner. Maybe she'd come visit her mom and he'd get to see her then too.

They'd been writing to each other every day. Some days more than once. They found they were getting to know each other on the computer screen far better than they had ever come to know other significant people in their previous lives.

They wrote about their growing up years, their career hopes and plans, their disappointments in the field of romance. She told him she'd been seeing someone pretty regularly until about a month before she and Nell left on this trip.

"His name is Ian. He's a great dancer and can be fun to be with, but that's all there is to him," she'd written. "I need someone I can get into good talks with, not just gossipy stuff about who's making it with whom."

Matthew told her about his marriage and why it failed. He told her about his alcoholism and how AA had helped him get sober and stay that way.

The printer had long since stopped and its silence finally penetrated his daydreams.

"Okay, Jonas, hold your pants on, I'm on my way," he said to the wind as he threw his windbreaker over his head again and ran back to the main house through the pelting rain.

Hours later, when he returned, he picked up the printed pages and settled in the easy chair to read what he'd written.

"This is good stuff," he said out loud when he was finished.

He'd done a fair amount of journalism in his time and, of course, had written advertising copy in his job, but this kind of writing was different, more from the gut.

Reading the pages made him think he ought to take the writing more seriously. The story had been eating at him ever since he'd started going to the cabin. Since he went into the bedroom there he'd become as taciturn as old Jonas and his agitation was showing up in his paintings and in just about everything he did. Maybe the story needed to be told.

If he was going to share their story, he knew he had to give it some structure. He returned to the computer and began writing a loose story line, envisioning how it would develop and finally conclude. Not wanting to confine the flow that so far was working well for him, he wrote an outline, read it through a couple of times and then put it away. He could refer to it now and then if need be, but he trusted that now he had some direction and he'd see how it went from there.

The weather cleared by the next day and the sun shone brightly the rest of the week. The day before they were scheduled to leave for Princeton, both men packed their suitcases, shined their shoes, made sure everything they'd need was in their briefcases. Jonas had gotten through his tenseness of the week before and was now almost like a young man going off on a fun vacation with a buddy. He was even trying to make jokes.

When he was crossing over from his cottage to the main house to start dinner, Matthew stopped dead in his tracks. "What the hell is that?" he said out loud. He stood listening, thinking maybe it was a CD or a radio playing. But it was too awful for that. Then he realized Jonas was doing something in the kitchen—and singing! "Holy Mother of God," Matthew said, aghast.

Matthew started up the porch steps, the singing stopped abruptly and Jonas looked up blankly from the potato he was peeling when Matthew walked in. "Guess we've got everything ready to go," he said. "You're sure you told Nell and Kate where we'll be staying?"

"Yup—phone number and address as ordered."

"Good. The wife and I always made sure we left a phone number and whatever when we went places. Kind of silly maybe, but you never know."

"Well, I'm sure they'll want to call to find out how it all went and to get details on who was there and who said and did what," Matthew said.

"You're right. Women can be pains in the ass about that kind of thing. I always say when a thing's over it's over, but they have to rehash and rehash. Can drive you crazy."

"Not if it was a real special time and you enjoy remembering all about it," Matthew said.

"Humph" was Jonas's only answer to that.

After they ate, they watched the evening news together and then Jonas said he wanted to go over what he was going to say at the dinner. Matthew offered to stay and be his audience, but Jonas said he wanted to be alone. "Why should I make an ass of myself twice, being all that gracious and nice once for you and once for them? Once is enough. Then I can get it over with and come home."

That man will never admit when he's happy about something, Matthew thought as he stood up, stretched, and went to the door. He's happy as a lark about this whole thing but God forbid he let anyone know. I hope I never get like that.

— *Chapter 14* —

THE MORNING FOG HADN'T HAD a chance to burn off yet when they started off the next morning. They bumped down Singer Lane, turned out onto Route 6, and drove only a mile or so when Jonas said, "Got to go back. Forgot my briefcase with my speech in it."

"Goddamn it," Matt said under his breath. He turned the car around, bumped back up Singer Lane again and sat in the car waiting while Jonas went inside and got the briefcase.

Nothing had gone smoothly since he walked into the kitchen all ready to go at six that morning. Jonas was a bundle of nerves and Matt had learned when Jonas is a bundle of nerves it takes the patience of a saint to be around him. And now there he was frying up a batch of bacon.

"Need a hearty breakfast to hold us on the road," he said.

"Whatever that means," Matthew said. He would have been content to stop for an Egg McMuffin at a McDonald's when they got off Cape. Trouble was, Jonas forgot to turn the heat down and the bacon burned to a crisp, the smoke alarm went off and they had to open all the windows and doors to air the place out.

They ate the remains of breakfast in silence and when they were done Matthew cleaned up the mess while Jonas disappeared into the other end of the house—for an exceptionally long time. The kitchen was in order, all the windows and doors closed again and securely locked. CalleyCat had come for breakfast and was gone and still no Jonas. Finally, after Matthew had read the entire front section of the <u>Cape Cod Times</u>, Jonas came into the kitchen and walked strait to the door to leave.

"Diarrhea," he said. "Big trip ahead." And he walked out and got into the car.

Just what I need, Matthew thought. He closed and locked the door, trying the handle again to make sure it was locked and then he, too, got in the car and started it up.

Now on this second go-round when Jonas got back in the car with the briefcase, Matthew just sat there and said, "Maybe you'd better check inside to make sure the speech is there."

"It's there."

"Check anyway for my sake, okay?" Matthew knew he was being testy and it felt good to let some of his annoyance seep out.

Now it was Jonas's turn to mutter an epithet but, because he knew they wouldn't be going anywhere until he did it, he opened the briefcase and, with an "I-told-you-so" attitude showed Matthew the speech that was lying right on top.

By the time they got back down to Route 6, the fog had burned off and the sun was coming through the rising mist. It was going to be a wonderful Cape Cod morning.

Matthew put Ocean 103.9 on the car radio because he knew Jonas liked listening to the Oldies they played. He kind of liked them too.

He didn't know if it was the music or the sunshine or the fact that they were setting off on an adventure, but he felt his own spirit rise and knew Jonas was feeling lighter too. It wasn't long before they both relaxed and by the time they reached the Sagamore Bridge they were talking about everyday things.

The stopped for lunch in Guilford, Connecticut, in a nice little place Matthew remembered taking a date once when he was a student.

"Food's still good here," he told Jonas as he leaned back and relaxed, glad to have a respite from driving. The second half of the journey would not be as easy as the first. Traffic through Connecticut was always horrendous and it didn't matter whether you took the Merritt Parkway or stayed on I-95.

They got to the Hyatt in Princeton by late afternoon and as soon as Matthew closed the door of his room, he kicked his shoes off, gave in to the yawns that were coming one after another, and lay down across the bed exhausted from the long drive in heavy traffic. Almost immediately his phone rang and, stifling another yawn, he answered it.

"Want to take a ride and see if anything's changed?" Jonas shouted into the phone.

I've just fought traffic for the past six hours while you dozed, Matthew thought. All I want is a good dinner, then back to this room with my feet up watching something mindless on tv—alone. I sure as hell don't want to go for a ride to see if anything has changed in the last frigin' forty years. Jesus, Mary and Joseph.

His mother's old Catholic mutterings always surfaced when he was tired and exasperated but he forced himself to push past his annoyance. "When do you want to leave?"

"Now's a good time," Jonas said, sounding like a young boy anxious to get out to the soccer field.

As they stepped out of the elevator, Matthew heard the desk clerk saying, "Oh, there they are now. Dr. Singer, Mr. Callahan, these ladies were just asking for you."

Matthew stopped dead in his tracks, He turned a questioning look at Jonas and saw the old man was as astonished as he was.

At that moment, Nell and Katie came rushing across the lobby toward them. Nell swept her father up in a big bear hug and Katie stopped herself just short of doing the same with Matthew. Seeing her hesitation, he saved the awkward moment giving her a quick cordial hug.

"Wow! It's great to see you," he said. "This is some surprise!"

Nell released Jonas and gave Matthew another of her whopping, jovial hugs as Katie put her arm around Jonas's waist, kissed him on the cheek and then rested her head on his chest.

"What are you two doing back early?" Jonas asked. "You didn't come just for this little thing Friday night did you? I told Matthew to tell you not to bother. Guess you didn't do what I told you to do," he said turning on Matthew.

"Yes, Granddaddy, he told us," Katie said. "But we came anyway because we wanted to."

"Shouldn't have," Jonas said. "Might as well stay if you want to though. Can't send you back now."

"We want to stay, Dad," Nell put in, "and we're already booked in here. We were just going to our rooms to take a little nap. It was a long flight from Paris and then a long drive down from JFK airport."

"Well, we were just going out for a ride to see if anything's changed since I lived here," Jonas said. "As long as you're going to sleep anyway, we'll just go ahead. Right, Matthew?"

Matt had been standing back a little letting Jonas be fussed over—and trying the whole time to keep from looking at Kate. She might see how good she looked to him. As Jonas spoke Matthew's name, Katie turned and caught him watching her and it was his turn to feel awkward.

She reached over and took his hand. "You two go ahead and we'll all meet for dinner. Let's meet right here at six, okay?"

⁂

Matthew found an upbeat music station on the car radio and didn't yawn once as he drove back over Route 1 and went into Princeton.

"A lot more traffic," Jonas said as they slowed for the light at Nassau and VanDeventer. But his eyes lit up when he saw the old Garden Theater was still there. And the Nassau Tavern was still operating on Palmer Square even though the Square itself had changed. A big new parking garage was there now and stores like The Gap and Crabtree & Evelyn were where privately owned little shops had been.

Jonas wanted to check out Dillon Gym where he'd spent his young years working out and when they stopped at the security guard's kiosk at the main entrance to the campus and gave the guard Jonas's name, they were waved right through with an "Oh yes, we've been expecting you, Dr. Singer." Matthew concealed a grin when, out of the corner of his eye, he noticed Jonas sat up a little straighter when he heard that.

The gym was still as Jonas remembered it. It still smelled of sweat in the locker rooms and disinfectant everyplace else. They walked past the art museum and the chapel. Jonas grumbled about the abstract sculptures that were now sited in different locations and he stared in wonderment at the massive expansion of Firestone Library. Back in their car, they drove past the tennis courts where Jonas said he'd walloped (probably exaggerated, Matthew thought) a number of opponents, over to the new Math/Physics building on Washington Road.

As they walked the halls, Matthew could see Jonas tensing up. "Doesn't have the feel of my old classroom and lab at Palmer Lab," he said. "Too sterile. Too much glass. How can you think about what you need to think about with all that outside coming in at you?"

He grumbled up one hall and down another. Although the Fall semester hadn't started yet, some lecture courses for grad students were going on. When he poked his head testily into one of the classrooms, a young professor stepped away from a blackboard and, recognizing Jonas, asked, "Aren't you Dr. Singer?"

A bit surprised, Jonas answered that he was.

"We've been looking forward to your coming. I teach your theories and my students are excited that you're going to be here. I have to warn you though, they have a whole roster of questions for you."

Jonas seemed taken aback by what he was hearing, but only momentarily.

"Well, I've got answers for any questions they have, he said with a grin and a cockiness Matthew hadn't seen in him before.

"I'm sure you have, sir, and we'll be glad to hear them," the professor said smiling as he turned back to his students who, Matthew noticed, were looking impressed with the whole exchange.

"They've got questions, have they?" Jonas said as he slammed the car door briskly. "I can talk circles around those kids. They'll end up with more answers than they bargained for."

— *Chapter 15* —

MATTHEW SHOWERED, CURSED WHEN HE nicked himself trying to shave too close, and swore again when he realized he hadn't brought much of a variety of shirts and ties to pick from. Finally he decided to go with the Princeton look and chose a blue button-down collar shirt and striped tie to wear with his khaki pants and navy blazer. He called Jonas when it was time and they met Katie and Nell in the lobby.

"Mom and I don't feel like anything too upscale, do you care?" Katie asked when Matthew started to mention places they might go. "We thought maybe the Nassau would be a place we could just relax and talk. What do you think?"

They agreed and were there in a matter of minutes. They made their way downstairs to the pub where generations of Princeton students had carved their initials and "Class of…" into the thick wooden tables.

Matthew held back uncertainly as the foursome chose seats in the high-backed wooden booths, but Nell slipped in beside her father and left the way open for Katie and Matthew to sit side by side.

Matthew started intently looking over the menu to hide what was going through his head—is it better to feel her sitting next to me or across the table so I can just enjoy looking at her in that classy black knit kind of thing she's wearing?

Her only jewelry was a silver pendant and a bunch of silver bangle bracelets that jingled as she played nervously with the flatware, the menu, her water glass.

This is one sexy woman, Matthew thought, remembering how she'd looked as she walked across the hotel lobby toward them earlier. The first thing he'd noticed was her open-backed, high-heeled shoes and a pair of long shapely legs. That and the fact that she'd pulled her curly red hair up and it was already spilling out of the silver combs she'd used to try to contain its energy.

To cover his own nervousness, he leaned back in the booth and said, "Now, Nell, Kate, tell us about it."

And they did. Hesitantly, as drinks were served and then their salads. "It's hard to come back and tell it all in one fell swoop," Katie said. "It'll all come out over time. But, Ma, what were some of the highlights for you?"

Nell mentioned a few of the sights they'd seen and then paused, trying to think of what else might interest the others when Katie prompted her with the names of some of the friends Nell had made aboard ship. Then she opened up and it was non-stop.

Katie sat there and grinned as she sipped her wine and buttered chunks of warm bread from the basket the waiter had brought.

Jonas was quiet, obviously giving Nell and Katie center stage intentionally and that impressed Matthew even more about the man behind the curmudgeon.

While Katie was full of descriptions of quaint villages they'd visited and scenic wonders, Nell kept talking about the friends she'd met—and especially Tom who, to her obvious delight, was a fisherman from Gloucester, Massachusetts whose wife had died when they were young. He'd raised three boys and a girl who, for his 65th birthday, had sent him off with his widowed sister, Margaret, to cruise the rivers of Europe.

Nell told them she'd met Margaret one morning at breakfast on the Po River Cruise when they'd each arrived before anyone else, even the servers. They'd gotten coffees from the urn set up for early risers and took them up to the open deck to watch the little villages they were passing wake up to the new day. They'd become immediate friends and spent a lot of time together for the rest of the cruise. Margaret's brother, Tom, joined them occasionally and Nell said she liked being with him too.

"I was really glad when they told me they were going to be on the Danube cruise too," Nell said. "We already felt like old friends and we signed up for the same land tours and had drinks together in the lounge every night. Katie and some of our other friends came and sat with us too and it was fun."

What she didn't choose to share with her father and Matthew was about the night Margaret decided to have dinner with other people aboard ship and Tom asked her to dinner with him in Regensburg where they were docked. She pretended to be studying the menu, but she was seeing herself walking the winding streets with Tom and sipping wine in that small café where they'd told each other their life stories.

Tom was a far cry from Dan Vinerelli whom she'd carried in her heart memory all these years, but he was a good guy and it was fun talking to him over there in Europe about the Massachusetts seacoast, the place they both called home.

When they returned from dinner that night he'd drawn her aside before they boarded the ship and kissed her sweetly on the lips. It was the first time in years someone had done that and Nell's color rose now as she remembered how much she'd liked it—and knew Tom did too.

For the rest of the cruise they always managed to sign up for the same land tours, and they stretched out side by side on the chaise lounges on the upper deck as the ship passed through riverfront villages. Margaret, noticing their attraction to each other had started giving them more and more time alone. It made her happy to see her brother laughing and even flirting again.

"So what happened with this Tom fellow?" Jonas asked after the waiter refilled their water glasses.

"Nothing," Nell said a bit too casually. "He was scheduled to go home and Katie and I had to finish what we'd started. We exchanged phone numbers and I said I'd call him when I got back. That's all."

Their food came and Nell was glad for the distraction. She had no intention of telling them about their last night aboard ship.

They'd slipped away from the others who were gathered around the bar in the ship's lounge and had gone up on the deserted upper deck where they stood leaning on the rail watching the lights on shore pass by.

"I think this is more than a shipboard romance," Tom said as he leaned down and kissed her lightly. "We're past all that fly-by-night stuff at our age, don't you think?"

"I'd like to think so," Nell answered.

"It's hard to tell in a romantic setting like this if it's real or not, but what do you say about us seeing each other back home and finding out for sure?"

"I'd like that, Tom," Nell had said quietly as he took her in his arms and kissed her again. As the kiss lingered, Nell felt responses she'd long forgotten and soon Tom was kissing her with all the passion of a much younger man. And she was responding as she had to the kisses of Dan Vinerelli.

Without even discussing it, Nell took Tom's hand and led him down to her stateroom. It happened as the most natural thing in the world. They made love with all the passion of young lovers and all the tenderness of a man and a woman who have survived some tough stuff and have reached the place where they could embrace life's tender moments.

Tom disembarked in the morning to fly home to the U.S. They embraced a little shyly as he and Margaret gathered their luggage and headed out to the waiting minibus that would take them to the airport, but they renewed their promises to see each other back home.

Now as Nell talked about their trip, it was Tom who kept coming up, surpassing any stories about cathedrals, castles, and river vistas. It was Katie who gave the travelogue describing some of the things Nell hadn't even seemed to notice once Tom had come into the picture.

And the whole time, Matthew found himself becoming more and more mesmerized not only by Katie's dazzling smile, but by her fun way of telling a story and her obvious tenderness toward both her mother and her grandfather.

They decided to walk once around Palmer Square after dinner, then went back to the hotel. When they got there, Jonas announced he was going to bed and Nell agreed it had been a long day, but even though it was already nearing midnight, neither Katie nor Matthew was ready to let the day go.

"None of those desserts at the Nassau grabbed me, but I could sure go for some hot apple pie with vanilla ice cream," Matthew said licking his lips. "What about you, Kate?"

"Ummm, I shouldn't but…yeah, so what if I can't zip my dress for tomorrow night's affair. Let's go for it."

"I know just the place," Matthew said as she linked her arm in his. "A little hole-in-the-wall on Alexander Road. It's nothing fancy, but they used to have the best pie ala mode and I stopped there all the time when I lived here. Let's go."

They played catch up while they savored their desserts, then Katie steered the conversation to the cabin in the woods.

"It haunts me, Kate," he said. "I haven't gone back since the day I found Nancy's skeleton in the bed and Davy's writing about what happened, but I can't get them out of my mind. And I don't know if I should be doing something about it.

"On one hand, I understand Davy's wanting to leave her there in their bed instead of burying her in the ground. But on the other hand, it's been all these years now and maybe she should finally be laid to rest. I feel like I want to protect her. Is that silly? I keep thinking if I could find her, maybe someone else would and I hate the thought of that."

"No, Matthew, it's not silly at all for you to feel that way. Will you take me there when we get back?"

"Yes. Only you."

"I want to go. Not out of morbid curiosity, although I have to be honest and admit there's some of that, but I've just gotten caught up in their story too and it's a feeling of wanting to get to know them better. I know that sounds creepy, but…"

"Not creepy at all. I have those same feelings," Matthew said. "We'll go together one day next week when we get back."

They talked until they noticed the staff turning lights out and putting chairs up on tables waiting for the morning's floor cleaners. When they finally left, the night had turned foggy and a thick mist hung low over the narrow iron bridge spanning the canal that ran along the edge of town. Matt drove across at a creeping pace.

"They built this bridge right next to the old one over there just a few years ago and I never could understand why they didn't build it wider," he said.

Driving carefully over it and into the sharp curve ahead, Matthew kept his attention on the road, but once they pulled into the Hyatt parking lot, it was Katie who filled his mind and senses once again.

He took her hand as they walked to the entrance and across the lobby to the elevators. As the elevator door closed, he drew her close and they simply looked deep into each other's eyes until the door opened on her floor. Matthew walked her to her door, aware of his rising desire for her. He helped her unlock the door and she invited him in.

It was only a bedroom, not a suite, and there was the bed, covers turned down and inviting. And here was Katie resting against him in the crook of his arm. He began kissing her with a longing she quickly shared. It was hard to cut it off, but Matthew knew it wasn't the right time for them—yet.

It's late, Katie. We've both had a long day," he said.

Looking a little surprised, but then in total agreement, Katie stepped back and said, "You're right Matt. We both need to get to bed—separately."

They both grinned, agreed, and kissed once again but more lightly and said goodnight.

– Chapter 16 –

"Well Granddaddy, are you ready for your big day?" Katie stifled a yawn and smiled at the waiter who was pouring her first coffee of the day.

"Cut out the big day nonsense will you?" Jonas snapped. "We'll let them have their little celebration, then we'll go home and get back to normal. Can't be soon enough to suit me."

"Dammit, Dad, lighten up, will you?" Nell's voice was louder than she'd intended.

"You watch your language, girl," Jonas shot back at her. "You might be too big for me to paddle now, but I can give you a good tongue lashing that'll tone you down for awhile."

"I'm sure of that," Nell said under her breath.

"Come on, Granddaddy," Katie said. "Even if you're uptight today, don't spoil it for the rest of us."

"Not uptight."

"Okay, you're not uptight, but maybe the rest of us are and you can help us through it. You're special to us and we want it all to work out really nice for you. Come on, just relax and enjoy it."

The waiter returned to take Matthew and Jonas's orders and that gave them all a chance to regroup a little.

"What do you want to do between now and two o'clock when you're scheduled to meet the physics students, Jonas?" Matthew asked.

"Don't care." Jonas was obviously still hanging on to his grouchy mood.

Ignoring his response, Katie said she wanted to check out the art museum. She'd seen in the hotel copy of the <u>Princeton Packet</u> newspaper they were running an exhibit drawn from Princeton alums.

"There should be some pretty good stuff in an exhibit like that," Nell said. "Let's check it out. Maybe there are a couple of seascapes, Matthew."

"Yea, I'd like to check it out too. There are a lot of good museums in this area, but that one has always been my favorite. What about you, Jonas? You up for it?"

"Whatever."

This guy's his own worst enemy, Matthew thought. I don't know why he can't relax and let himself enjoy things.

Katie looked over at Matthew, locked eyes with him, shrugged her shoulders and began gathering her things to get up and leave.

At the museum, Katie went directly to VanGogh's "Tarascon Diligence," which she said she'd seen there years before and had been hoping to see again. Matthew had always visited it on his previous visits and was glad to see it again too. That and Monet's "The Houses of Parliament, Seagulls" which intrigued him because of the way Monet was able to portray the buildings and a boat shrouded in a dense pink-gray fog. But his favorite was a small Boudin,

"The Beach at Trouville," and he took Katie's hand and led her to it.

When they stopped in front of the painting, Matthew glanced across the gallery just in time to see Nell nudge Jonas and say something to him. "Don't look now," he told Katie, "But your mother looks mighty pleased that we're holding hands."

"Yea, I know. I heard her telling Granddaddy that we've been emailing every day. She called you 'a really decent sort' and said you're kind of handsome too."

"Your Ma's got a good eye," Matthew grinned and whispered back. Katie gave him a playful punch and they both laughed. Then Matthew asked, "What did Jonas have to say about all that?"

"'Humph.' That's what he said, 'Humph,'"

"That's all?"

"Well that and he added that maybe I'm finally getting some sense. I heard him tell Ma he's gotten to know you pretty well while we were 'off gallivanting'. He called you 'solid'—pretty high praise from Granddaddy."

After they left the museum, Jonas and Nell were walking up Witherspoon Street behind Matthew and Katie who were still holding hands and looking for all the world like young lovers.

"…he hasn't done as much painting as I thought he would, but he sure has done a lot of writing," they heard Jonas say in a voice that was louder than he realized. "Especially since he found that old cabin back there in the woods. Seemed spooked by it."

They had to slow down a little to hear Nell's reply. "I know," she was saying. "He wrote a lot about it to Katie and she was full of questions to me. I told her I knew nothing about it because Mom told me it was haunted and scared the be-Jesus out of me so bad I wouldn't go anywhere near it."

Katie started giggling. "That's right," she whispered to Matthew. "She didn't want to talk about it. I could tell it made her nervous to even think about the place."

"I had a feeling he found something that upset him there," they heard Jonas say. "Came back looking pretty shook up one day and hasn't been back since. He's been a big help to me though. Easy to work with too. Got so I like him. That was a good idea of mine to have him. Glad I didn't let you women talk me out of it."

Katie had all she could do to restrain herself from turning around and looking aghast at her mother. She just grimaced at Matthew and let the remark pass.

By that time they'd gotten to the car and Matthew dropped Katie and her mom off back at the hotel and drove Jonas back to the Math-Physics building on campus.

"What shall I do? Come back for you?" Matt asked.

"How about if you just stay? Maybe learn something in spite of yourself. Then we'll go back and get ourselves all gussied up for this big shindig tonight."

When they got inside, Matthew was glad to see the lecture hall was filled and not only with students, but older people too. He'd been worried that with Jonas being a recluse for so long not many would remember him and come to hear what he had to say. He quickly saw how wrong he was. They were actually setting up folding chairs in the aisles.

Matthew hung back and watched as Jonas was taken forward, being introduced to people all along the way. Many of the people seemed awed by his presence and Matthew couldn't help but be impressed. And he also couldn't help thinking about what a cranky old coot Jonas could be sometimes—times when he was unsure of himself, Matthew had finally learned. Far different from the affable man he was in these circumstances.

When Jonas was finally introduced, the applause was vigorous and lasted long, but when he cleared his throat to speak, a silence fell over the room. Matthew watched with fascination as Jonas the scholar, the teacher, emerged from Jonas the curmudgeon, the man who had been so apprehensive just the day before at the start of the trip that he'd had an acute attack of diarrhea. There was no hesitation in his delivery. He knew his material, he loved it, and he wanted to give it to his listeners.

At the end, he received a standing ovation and was greeted by warm handclasps and pats on the back as he stepped away from the lectern. It was another good hour or more before they could gracefully break away from the well wishers to return to the hotel.

"Well did you learn anything?" Jonas asked as soon as they got in the car.

"Sure did," Matthew said.

"Yea? What?"

Oh shit, Matthew thought. What could he say? The whole lecture had been way over his head, though everyone else in the room hung on Jonas's every word and seemed to be understanding it all. But all his years in advertising taught Matthew to think on his feet and quickly.

"I learned how important you are in your field. And how respected you are," he said.

"Good save, boy," Jonas said with a grin. "In other words, you didn't understand a word of it."

"Well…" Matthew said sheepishly.

"Don't worry about it. It took me years of study to begin to get a handle on it," Jonas said.

"I'm not sure even years of study would open up this brain," Matthew admitted. "I'm a right-brain artist type, you know."

"An artist who hasn't done much painting lately," Jonas said.

"You're right. I haven't. But now this is behind us, I plan to. And, by the way, how much longer can I stay in the cottage? I'll pay you a good rent now that our work is about done."

"Who says our work is about done?" Jonas asked. "We have to tie up loose ends on this and then I want to get back to the book I started last year. Thought maybe you could stick around and help me with that—not much everyday work, but like driving me in to Boston or over to Harvard now and then when I need to do research. How's that sound? You'd have a lot more time to paint or do that infernal writing you've been doing lately. No great salary to speak of, but free rent and meals—Nell's meals—and you'd get to see Katie whenever she comes. We might even see more of her with you there, looks like," he added with a stone face but clearly hoping for some comment from Matthew.

"Hmmm sounds like a deal I can't refuse. Thanks, Jonas. How about if we try it for another few months and maybe talk about it again after Christmas? I'd like to paint the ocean under some steely gray winter skies."

"That the only reason?"

"Well Nell's meals sound good too."

"And seeing Katie?"

"Yes, Jonas, seeing Katie. I've been thinking of talking to you about her, but since, so far, we're just getting to know each other, I decided to wait to see if anything develops. But, yes, Jonas. I'm really enjoying her company a lot."

"That all?"

"Actually, no. That's not all. I was thinking last night I could probably fall in love with her."

"So go ahead and do it," Jonas said looking straight ahead out the car windshield as they crossed Route 1 and pulled into the hotel parking lot.

"Maybe I will. Now that I have your blessing." Grinning sardonically, Matthew pulled into a parking space and turned off the engine.

"None of this, 'maybe I will' stuff. Do it," Jonas said. "And it's not my blessing. It's my trying to talk some sense into you for God's sake."

"Okay then, since it's now escalated to being for God's sake, I guess I'd better do it."

"Smart ass," he heard Jonas grumble as he opened the car door, but when he looked over the hood at him, Jonas was smiling.

— *Chapter 17* —

THE RECEPTION WAS GOING TO be held at Prospect, the former home of Princeton University presidents which was now used for faculty dining and special functions. Set under the towering trees in the middle of campus and surrounded by lush beds of flowers, it was an elegant setting.

"Whoa, I'm impressed," Katie whispered to her mother as soon as they got to the ladies' room to check themselves out in the full-length mirrors.

"And are you also impressed at how elegant our 'dates' look?"

"Two handsomest guys I've seen so far tonight," Katie said with a wink.

Jonas was wearing a navy blue pinstripe suit (maybe a decade or so out of fashion, Nell conceded, but somehow it was who he was). The collar of his white shirt was starched, Nell noticed, and he had on his years-old Princeton necktie, the one with the shield and motto on it.

Matthew was wearing a soft grey suit, white shirt and blue tie that made his eyes look even bluer—a fact that made Katie's heart skip a beat.

The cocktail hour turned out to be a welcome-back-Jonas party. He'd shed his nervousness and ill humor of the morning and was, finally, enjoying himself immensely.

Dinner started out to be a formal affair with Jonas seated at the head table between the university president and the chair of the physics department. The appetizers were served after only a few words of introduction and a promise of hearing from Jonas after they'd all eaten.

Nell, Katie, and Matthew, seated as honored guests in a spot where they could be seen and could see all that was happening, were enjoying the good-old-days-at-Palmer-Lab stories being told by two of Jonas's former colleagues and their wives who were also at their table. Nell hung onto every word about her dad in his younger days and the glimpses of him through the eyes of his friends. For far too long it had been just the two of them living together on the Cape and, she was realizing, she'd lost the sense of him as a man who had a place in this world of academia and congenial colleagues.

The affair was turning out to be more than Matthew or Jonas had expected. Everyone—and Matthew guessed there were more than a hundred there—was having a good time. He leaned over and mentioned that to Katie who was seated next to him.

"I agree. And it's all just because Granddaddy's here. Just look at him, Matt, he's having the time of his life."

And he was. Right at that moment, he was leaning around the president and telling some kind of story to the provost and the three of them were laughing.

"It's so good to see him like this," Nell, who was sitting on the other side of Matthew, said in a whisper. "Don't you wish we could bottle it and take it back to the Cape with us?"

Just then the president stood up to speak and the room got quiet. He spoke of Jonas's long affiliation with the university and of the many contributions he'd made to the body of knowledge of physics in general. He spoke respectfully of Jonas's research projects and of how he'd reached his goals. He spoke warmly about Jonas's exceptional skills as a teacher and as a one-on-one mentor to many aspiring physicists.

Then the president paused and said, "We know all these things about Dr. Jonas Singer, and we are here to celebrate them. But how about some of the things that are not known by everyone? Several of his colleagues got together and decided a formal dinner steeped with accolades is nice, but what our austere professor really needs is a good roasting. So let 'im have it, gentlemen."

There was a burst of applause and cheering as the two former colleagues who had been sitting at the table with Nell, Kate, and Matt, rose and went to the microphone.

Jonas looked surprised, but not at all upset at the prospect of what was about to be said—even eager to hear what was coming next.

"I'll be damned," Matt whispered to Katie, "he likes being the center of attention. After all the fuss he made this morning, just look at him now. He's eating this up."

Katie laughed. "Yea, isn't it great?"

"Jonas, do you remember the time you…" his old friend began and from then on it was story after story, all of which poked lighthearted fun at something Jonas had said or done, or had forgotten to say or do all those years ago. They teased him about his veneer of gruffness and how every

September the incoming students were scared to death of him—fear that lasted until they finally found out what a softie he was.

There were Dillon Gym jokes, some locker-room humor, and even a story about the time Jonas and his friend, Albert Einstein, got to arguing about something as they walked across campus one snowy afternoon. Jonas, so intent on his argument, didn't watch where he was going, tripped over a curb hidden in a small drift, fell flat on his back in the snow and lay there continuing his argument while Albert laughed so hard he could barely stand up.

By that time, everyone in the dining room, including the wait staff, was laughing. And Jonas most of all. After the roasting, Jonas got up to the mike and threw some good-natured barbs and told some stories of his own. But then he got serious and told those assembled how much the evening meant to him.

"The best years of my life were spent here in Princeton with my sweet wife, Bridget, and our dear Nell. It's been a good life. I've done the work I set out to do and now I leave it as a gift to all of you. And when you decide to honor these two old codgers," he said gesturing toward his two old friends who had just roasted him, "let me know. I'll be back with some tales about them that will set your ears on fire."

"But before I leave here tonight, I want to introduce you all to my Nell who has brought joy to her late mother and me from the moment she was born. And this is Nell's daughter, my lovely granddaughter, Kathryn Rose, our Katie. And between them is my assistant, Matthew Callahan, without whom the collection of my notes that are now in

119

the archives here would still be in boxes in my storage room on the Cape."

There was warm applause until Jonas said, with a slight crack in his voice giving away the emotion he was feeling, "And now I want to thank you for this wonderful evening, my friends. Thank you. Thank you. From the bottom of my heart."

He stepped away from the microphone and was immediately swept into conversations with the many people who wanted to wish him well before they said goodnight.

⁂

By the time they stepped out into the garden to make their way to their cars, the line of thunderstorms that had earlier been predicted was starting to move in. Lightning lit up the sky followed by a very quick clap of thunder.

"Kate, let's you and I run for our cars. Nell, you stay with your Dad and watch for us. We'll pull up as close as we can," Matthew said.

He grabbed Katie's hand and they made a dash for it. The rain hadn't started yet, but it was about to. They managed to get back to Nell and Jonas just as the big drops started pelting them. They'd driven over in separate cars and now Matthew wished they hadn't.

Glad it was such a short ride back to the hotel, he thought maybe they could even make it before the worst of it hit.

Jonas got in with Matthew and Nell ran to Katie's car just behind them and got in. They started down the campus drive that would take them to Faculty Road and then to Alexander Road. From there it would be a quick shot to the Hyatt. Trouble was, everyone else was leaving at the same time and traffic was backed up bumper to bumper and just creeping along as the full force of the storm hit with blinding rain.

"I'm glad we don't have to do any highway driving with all that kick-back spray from tractor trailers," Matthew said, squinting to see as he edged his way slowly into the left turn onto Alexander Road. He'd been first at the traffic light, so when he finally made the turn there was no one ahead of him, no red tail lights to guide him. He was glad the tail lights of his car would guide Katie.

The rain seemed to ease up a little as they passed the coffee shop where he and Katie had been the night before. He saw the iron work of the narrow bridge ahead and was feeling good that visibility was a little better. He just started to cross the bridge when suddenly a white box truck came too fast around the sharp curve ahead. The driver lost control on the wet road and the truck came swerving at them. It hit the side of the bridge, ricocheted off, hit the other side, and then came at them head on.

Matthew hit the brakes, but it was too late. There was nothing he could do to stop the tragedy. The next thing he knew, the airbags were deploying, glass and pieces of metal were flying, and there was the windshield of the truck just feet from his face, its wipers still flopping back and forth, back and forth. He could see the truck driver's head slumped over the wheel.

"You okay, Jonas?" he asked.

"Jonas! Jonas, answer me," he screamed.

Silence.

He tried to unlatch his seatbelt and realized he was pinned under the steering wheel. Blood was running fast down over his face and his head began to pound. Lightning was flashing incessantly outside and the thunder rolled one clap after the other.

He tried again to yell for Jonas, but realized he was too weak. No sound would come. "Katie," he whispered. "Oh my God, Katie…"

The last thing he heard as darkness overcame him was Katie's voice screaming, "No, No, No-o-o-o."

– *Chapter 18* –

MATTHEW CAME TO CONSCIOUSNESS IN the glaring lights of the Emergency Room at Princeton Medical Center. He was lying on a gurney in a curtained-off alcove and Katie was standing next to him, tears flowing freely down her cheeks.

He wanted to ask her how he'd gotten there but he didn't have the strength. He wanted to tell her how glad he was to see that she had not been injured, but then he saw the bruises on the other side of her face, her swollen lips, one arm bound across her chest.

He fastened his eyes on Katie's and once again tried to speak but was unable to. My God, how can this be happening?

It's okay, Matthew, just rest now," she said. "We'll talk later." And with that she bent down and kissed him tenderly on his brow.

He wanted to stay awake and ask her a dozen questions, but he couldn't seem to fight sleep. It crept in around the edges and soon engulfed him.

When he woke again he was someplace else, and he didn't understand what was happening. Someone was calling his name over and over again and he was trying to answer.

"Matthew. Matthew. Can you hear me, Matthew?"

He opened his eyes and a pleasant-looking nurse was hovering over him.

Everything's okay, Matthew, you're in Recovery, she said as he began to drift away again.

He felt a strong need to tell the nurse he'd been in recovery for a long time and had been sober for almost two years, but he slipped away again.

"Matthew, stay with me, Matthew," the nurse said. "You can do it. Here, hold my hand, hold on to me. I'll help you hang on."

He grasped her fingers and felt her warmth flow into him. He wanted badly to be able to speak, to be able to understand what was happening.

The nurse stayed with him urging him back to consciousness, back to being alive, and finally she noted that his vital signs were stabilizing, and she knew he would pull through.

The surgery had been extensive. He'd had almost-fatal injuries to his liver and spleen, one lung had collapsed, and there had been internal abdominal bleeding. A team of doctors had worked for several hours to save his life. He'd probably have permanent facial scars from the lacerations, but it looked as if the internal injuries had been repaired.

Jonas had not been as fortunate. When the paramedics reached the accident scene, they found he was already dead. His injuries did not appear to be as extensive as Matthew's, at least not visibly so, but it was thought that perhaps the trauma had been too much for his eighty-four year old heart. An autopsy was required and would give the answer.

Katie and Nell had survived with broken bones, cuts and bruises—and broken hearts. Katie had been told at the scene that Jonas was gone and she had also been told that Matthew might not make it. Her mother had been knocked unconscious when their car rammed into the rear of Matthew's. Nell, obstinate as ever, had refused to buckle her seatbelt and the impact had thrown her forward against the dash and then to the side where she hit her head on the doorframe. In the silence that followed the crash, she'd lain there with her jaw agape and her right leg twisted and jammed over onto Katie's side of the vehicle. They learned later that the leg was broken in two places. She was taken in a separate ambulance to the Medical Center and into another operating room to have the leg reset and then casted. Like Matthew, she didn't yet know of Jonas's death.

Only Katie knew. She had been firmly buckled into her seat and rear-ending Matthew's car didn't throw her around as it did her mother. Her left knee was swollen twice its size from being rammed up under the dashboard and she'd broken three ribs—that's why she was trussed up as she was. Despite the injuries and the assault on her heart and her mind, she was faring the best of the four of them.

But it was left to her to tell the others about Jonas's death and she didn't know how she would be able to do that.

Her mother, heavily sedated, slept through the rest of the night and when she woke in the morning and saw Katie sleeping in the other bed it took her a few minutes to realize where they were and why they were there. A nurse came in to take vital signs and, while Katie still slept, Nell tried to question her but she was evasive.

Slowly, the events of the night before seeped back in on Nell and when the vivid memory of what happened came crashing in on her, she gasped aloud and began weeping.

Katie heard her and awakened. Sitting up suddenly in her bed, she was swept with a wave of vertigo, but she fought through it and slipped into the other bed with her mother. Ignoring the pain in her own chest, Katie took her mother in her arms and simply held her while she cried and Katie cried with her.

"Granddaddy?" her mother asked her. "Is your Granddaddy okay?"

Katie couldn't bring herself to answer. To say it would make it so. She just continued to hold her mother to her, trying to comfort her with her love.

"Katie, he's gone, isn't he?" Nell asked. "Katie? Is he? Please, you have to answer me. I have to know."

Katie continued to hold her mother close, now not only to offer comfort but to ease her own grief. Finally, sobbing, she nodded her head up and down on her mother's shoulder and they cried together.

"And Matthew, honey? What about Matthew?"

"Critical," was all Katie could say. And they were silent, holding on to each other trying to make sense of it all.

"Oh, God, Katie. If I hadn't been off gallivanting all over Europe having myself a good old time, I could have had more time with Granddaddy. I should have been the one to go through all those Princeton boxes with him. Maybe he found things that brought back memories and we could've talked about it all."

"I know, Ma. I'm feeling the same way. What kind of a granddaughter have I been lately, all wrapped up in my own life?"

They cried and tried to comfort each other with memories of good times they'd spent with him, letting him know how loved he was.

After awhile Nell began smoothing Katie's unruly hair. She took the edge of the sheet and tenderly dried the tears on her daughter's face and kissed the place where they had been.

"It's okay, girl," she said. "He said last night he'd finished the work he'd set out to do. He was happy last night, Katie dear. We have to remember him that way. We'll just have to learn to go on without him."

Katie sniffled, nodded and then raised her head and looked into her mother's eyes. "I'm so glad you're okay, Ma," she said. "I don't know what I'd do if I didn't have you."

"Nor I you, my sweet girl," Nell replied tenderly. "Now tell me, honey, what do you know about Matthew?"

Katie told her all she knew so far was that Matthew was critically injured, had had extensive surgery and he was in the Intensive Care Unit. "As soon as they let me, I'm going to go up there and see if they'll let me see him," she said.

⁕

When the doctors made their morning rounds, Katie was told she was free to go home as soon as the floor nurse came to check her out.

"Home" sounded good to Katie except for the fact that, for now, "home" would be her room at the Hyatt. Nell was told she'd probably have to stay another day or two so they could monitor the results of the concussion she'd had and to make sure the leg was not going to give her major problems. She'd be in a full cast for six to eight weeks and then there would be a long period of physical therapy after that.

As soon as the residents left their room Katie got out of bed and went into the bathroom. She was shocked when she saw herself in the mirror. Her lip was grotesquely swollen as was her jaw on the left. The entire left side of her face was beginning to turn a ripe red purple. In a few days she'd look like an eggplant ready for market.

Her chest ached and if she moved even a little bit the wrong way a sharp pain would shoot across her broken ribs. She was quickly learning what she could and could not do.

The nurse's aide had brought her a toothbrush, comb and all the things she'd need for a basic cleanup and getting herself somewhat presentable. She couldn't shower with her chest all bound up as it was, but an aide came in to help her wash and get into the clothes she'd been wearing the night before. When she glanced back into the mirror she caught an amused look on the aide's face as the woman took in the long sleek black dress with the slit up one side and the aqua hospital slipper sox with their gripper soles. But there was no way she was going to put on high heeled pumps until the last possible minute when she'd have to go out in public. She was too shaky and tottery this morning to even think about looking proper.

"Come on over here and let me brush your hair and fix it for you," Nell told her when she saw Katie struggling to do it one handed. "You'll never untangle that mop of yours with one hand."

Katie sat on the edge of Nell's bed smiling contentedly while her mother brushed and brushed as she'd done when Katie was a child.

"Wish I could go up to ICU with you honey," Nell said. "Hate to have you have to do that by yourself."

"I'll be okay, ma," Katie said. "Just say lots of prayers that he's going to make it."

Katie had called earlier to inquire about Matthew's condition and was told it had been upgraded from Critical to Serious.

Not wanting to wait until the floor nurse came to sign her out, Katie slowly made her way down the hall to the elevator and up to the ICU unit. She was told at the nurse's station that Matthew had been showing signs of improvement and if that continued he might be moved to the Step-Down Unit later that morning.

Katie's spirits rose and when she was told she could go in to see him for five minutes, she entered the room smiling. But the smile froze on her lips. He was hooked up to beeping monitors, tubes, and wires affixed to seemingly every part of him. His usual ruddy color had faded and he was ashen. He, too, had cuts, angry looking bruises and swelling. His head was wrapped in gauze and his right eye was swollen shut. If she hadn't been told by the nurse that this was Matthew Callahan, she would have not known him.

He seemed to be sleeping but when she approached the bed he opened his one good eye and looked at her.

"Matthew..." she said softly. "How're you doing?"

He heard her and he wanted to answer but he was too weak. Instead, he just kept looking at her and after awhile a tear slipped from his eye and puddled above the swelling on his cheek. Very gently, Katie wiped it away with her fingertip.

"I know, Matthew, this is just terrible. And you must be in so much pain," she said.

And still he just looked at her.

She smiled tenderly at him and told him not to worry about anything, to rest and when he was stronger, they could talk. It seemed as if she'd only arrived when the nurse came in and gestured that her five minutes were up.

Katie leaned down to kiss him goodbye but, finding no place on his face to kiss that she wasn't afraid would be painful to him, she rested her hand lightly on his, told him she'd be back a little later and she left.

He wanted to beg her to stay, to stand there by his bed so he could keep looking at her. He saw how injured she was too and he wanted to tell her how sorry he was it had happened to her, but he couldn't summon the energy to speak. Just knowing she was there, being able to see her looking so beautiful despite her bruises had felt life giving to him. He closed his eye again and slept remembering her words, "I'll be back a little later."

The nurse was waiting for Katie when she got back to her room. She was given instructions about what she needed to do, who she needed to see about her broken ribs and other bruises. Then she signed the papers and was told she could leave whenever she wanted to.

But she stayed. She didn't want to leave Nell. She didn't want to be too far from Matthew, just in case… And she really didn't want to be alone. Not yet. Housekeeping came and got what had been her bed ready for the next patient who might need it and Katie stayed by Nell as a visitor now rather than a patient. Every bone in her body seemed to ache, every muscle felt on fire. She was so tired that looking at the empty bed across the room, she longed to get in it and sleep for hours.

Nell saw that and stepped into her mother role. "Katie, you must go back to the hotel and get some rest," she said. "It will do you a world of good and it will help me. I can't sleep with you sitting there looking at me like that. I'm well taken care of, Matthew needs to sleep and so do you. After you get a good nap, then come back and we'll talk about things we have to take care of. Now go, girl. I'll call you later on.

Katie knew her mother was right and, reluctant as she was, reached for the phone and called for a taxi to pick her up at the main entrance. Then she put on her shoes, steadied herself for a few moments and bent and kissed her mother goodbye.

"I'll call you before I come back later to see what you want me to bring back with me," she said as she lingered at the door a moment, blew her mother another kiss and left.

The elevator door opened and as she was just about to step in, John Bellows and Langdon Hall, Jonas's two friends who had roasted him at the dinner the night before stepped out.

When she saw them, all of a sudden she was in tears again. Each man put an arm around her and led her to a group of chairs in the nearby solarium which, at that hour, was fortunately empty.

She'd felt so frightened and so vulnerable and had had no one to tell that to. She'd felt she had to be the strong one, the one to take care of her mother and Matthew. But now, seeing these two kind men whom her Granddaddy had liked so much, she felt comforted.

They told her everybody in the university community was terribly shaken by what had happened and she was not alone.

"There are so many people who want to do something to help," Langdon Hall said. "And we both want you to think of us and our wives as family. Come stay at our homes. You can stay as long as you want to."

Katie found she didn't have words enough to thank them for their kindness and she just sat there holding their hands, trying to stop the sobs that were still coming like hiccups and jarring her damaged ribs.

"We've got to get you back to the hotel for now so you can rest," John Bellows said. "Lang, why don't you go ahead and see Jonas's daughter, Room 322, and I'll drive this gal back to the hotel and get her settled in. Then I'll come back for you."

Katie was grateful that she didn't have to do that on her own and thanked him. They went down to the lobby and John told her to wait there and he'd get the car and come around for her. The taxi was waiting at the curb and when she told him she'd called for it, he told her he'd take care of it.

Katie sank down shakily on the chair he'd led her to and tried to relax. She absent-mindedly picked up a newspaper that was lying nearby. When she saw the front page she gasped. It was the Trenton Times and there on the front page was the bold-type headline: World-known Physicist, Dr. Jonas Singer, Killed in Princeton Car Crash. Driver Of Truck Also Killed. Three Others Seriously Hurt. And there was a big picture of the scene of the crash. She was horrified and could not take her eyes off what she was seeing. A white box truck with some kind of Seafood logo on the side was mounted atop the front of Matthew's crumpled car and they were both smashed against the side of the bridge. Rescue workers were crowded around the vehicles and she could see part of a stretcher with someone on it on the ground nearby. And almost out of the picture, there was the front of her rental car smashed up against the rear bumper of Matthew's. It was horrible. Seeing the picture, she wondered how anyone had escaped alive.

She looked up and saw John Bellows coming in the revolving door for her. Tucking the newspaper under her arm, she shakily made her way over to him. He took her by the arm and guided her to the car. Helped her in and closed the door. A group of reporters who had been told they could not congregate in the lobby had been standing outside waiting for any sign of the survivors. One of them spotted Katie and they all rushed over to the car, but John just slowly pulled away and left them there.

"Oh my God," Katie said. "I didn't think about that aspect of it. I always forget Granddaddy is so well known. I guess I'm going to have to deal with them sooner or later. I hope they leave me alone for awhile though. I can't talk about it yet."

They were silent as they drove through the town and out to the highway. John had a classical music CD playing softly and that, as well as his quiet presence, soothed Katie as she couldn't help but see the places she had walked just a day ago with Matthew, her mother and Jonas. It seemed as if that had been years ago. She cried softly thinking of how her grandfather would never get to see again this lovely college town he'd loved so much.

The hotel desk clerk saw them walking across the parking lot as they approached the hotel and he called Henry Gruber, the manager, as he'd been told to do. As they entered, Mr. Gruber, fending off the reporters who had been hovering since early morning, came to them immediately and led them to his private office.

"I'd like you to meet my grandfather's dear friend, John Bellows," Katie told him. "He and another close friend, Langdon Hall, and their wives have offered to help me while I'm here in Princeton."

Henry Gruber asked how she was feeling and how her mother and Matthew were. And he spoke about how sad he was to learn of Jonas's death. He said his staff would be at her disposal and she was to let them know whatever they could do for her. He also told her he'd taken the liberty of moving her and her mother into the executive suite and it would be theirs for as long as they would need it. "And when Mr. Callahan is released we will make a similar arrangement for him," he said.

Katie tried to say thank you, but all she could do was look at him and nod as her tears welled up and weakness and extreme grief threatened to overwhelm her.

The men helped her to the manager's private elevator and took her to the suite. They stayed just long enough to see she was settled in and to tell her they were only a phone call away.

As soon as they left, Katie kicked off her shoes, took off her dress, slipped under the covers of the king-size bed and was almost immediately asleep.

– Chapter 19 –

ALL THE LOCAL NEWSPAPERS CARRIED graphic accounts and photographs of the accident. The New York Times and other national newspapers picked it up off the wire and television shows gave it mention. Jonas Singer was not exactly a household name, but he was well known in academia and even much of the general public knew at least that they'd heard of him and that he'd made some kind of significant contribution to the world even if they didn't understand quite what it was.

The morning after it happened, Matthew's son, Jason, was having breakfast and checking out the sports page of the paper. His mother reached over for the front section to have something to scan while she drank her first cup of coffee of the day and smoked her first cigarette.

"Oh my God," she said. "Oh my God."

"What?" Jason was alarmed. His mother rarely ever spoke before she had at least a couple of cups of coffee in the morning.

"Your father. He was in a bad accident last night. Oh my God. Oh my…"

"No way." Matthew's older son, Luke had just come into the dining room and heard what his mother said.

"No way," Jason echoed his brother. "Let's see." He got up and walked around the table to read over her shoulder.

They saw the same headlines and photograph that Katie had seen earlier.

"Yea, he was coming down here with the old guy, Singer. We met him when we went to stay with Dad on the Cape," Jason said. "What does it say about Dad?"

Annaliese motioned for her sons to be quiet and go sit down but they ignored her. Luke began reading aloud over her shoulder.

"Look, it says Dad's alive. He's in critical condition though," he whispered.

Annaliese sat there staring into space, tapping the ash from her cigarette into a porcelain ashtray, sipping coffee from a delicate china cup. Things hadn't been going well for her lately. Not only had her financial advisor steered her in the wrong direction more than once in the past months, but her father, who was supporting her in this style that she so loved, had been losing a great deal in the long bear market slide. Just the week before he'd told her the boys would not be able to attend Lawrenceville again the next year, that they'd have to apply to a more affordable private school. And he'd told her she'd have to hold onto her year old Mazarati for another year. He couldn't afford to get her the new model she'd been talking up to him.

"This says Matthew was the old guy's assistant and that he lived with him. Singer's famous—well almost," she said to herself. "I'll bet he had a lot of money. I'll bet he's been paying Matthew a bundle and now Matthew is going to be sitting pretty. Plus he'll get a pretty good insurance payoff from this."

She folded the newspaper and sat up straight. "We should go see your father this morning, boys."

"You too?" asked Luke. "I thought you never wanted to see his face or speak to him again."

"Go get yourselves dressed," she said ignoring the barb. "We should get over there as soon as we can. Says here he's in bad shape."

Picking up her cigarette and ashtray, Annaliese started up the white carpeted stairway. "Let's go boys. Get a move on. We'll leave in a half hour."

When they arrived at the nurse's station in the ICU unit, Annaliese informed the nurse she was Matthew Callahan's wife, these were their sons, and they were to see him right away. She neglected to say she was divorced from Matthew and was now the soon-to-be-divorced again, Mrs. Rightmier. "Mr. Callahan is no longer here," the nurse said. "He's been moved to the Step-Down Unit. You'll have to check in there."

Luke and Jason followed along behind her as her high heels clicked an agitated pace on the marble floors. "What's with her?" Jason grumbled. "All of a sudden Dad matters to her again? I don't get it."

"Neither do I," said Luke. "A couple of weeks ago when I tried to talk to her about us going up there to visit him over Christmas she told me, 'Forget it. That man doesn't exist for us anymore, so get used to it.' Now she's in a frenzy to go to his bedside? I don't get it either."

They were told at the Step-Down Unit they could only go in to see him one at a time and only for a couple of minutes each. Being transferred had tired him and he needed to rest to be able to make the adjustment.

Annaliese didn't even offer to let the boys go in first. She almost ran to Matthew's bedside—then stopped dead in her tracks when she saw how bruised and battered he was. Not appealing at all, she thought as she steeled herself for the contact she felt she had to make.

"Matt, honey, it's me. Annaliese," she cooed as if they were once again twenty-one and still in love. "Wake up, sweetie. As soon as I found out what happened I rushed right over here."

Matthew heard her and thought it must be the drugs. He must be hallucinating. He opened his one good eye and, sure enough, there was Annaliese hovering over him looking all concerned. He closed his eye again and thought, O God, now what?

"We're going to get you better real fast, honey, and I'm going to take you home with me and take care of you. We'll get you the best doctors and before you know it you'll be up and around," she said. "Of course we won't let the insurance company know you're up and around, but I'll keep you real happy and you won't mind hiding out for a few months until our lawyers get this whole mess settled. Then we can go have ourselves a long vacation someplace nice.

What? Matthew was thinking. What the hell is she talking about?

Fortunately, the nurse came in and told Annaliese her time was up and she had to leave.

"Maybe you don't know who I am," Annaliese said. "I'm his wife and I'll leave when I'm ready to leave."

"I'm afraid that has to be now," the nurse insisted as she took Annaliese by the arm and propelled her toward the door.

Shrugging herself free with a look of distaste, Annaliese went back to the bed, leaned over, kissed Matthew on the lips and told him she'd return as soon as "this creature" allowed her to.

Luke and Jason, standing by the open door, watched their mother's display and looked at each other quizzically.

"Okay, boys," the nurse said pleasantly to them. "Why don't you both go in together, but make it a very short visit, okay?"

Although Matthew looked like he was in a deep sleep, he was fully aware of all that was going on. He opened his eye and gave the boys the widest smile his damaged face would allow.

"Hi guys," he whispered.

"Hi, Dad," they said. "How's it going?"

"Not real well at the moment, but I'm on my way back." It was the longest sentence Matthew had spoken since the accident.

The boys saw the nurse approaching again and Luke said, "We'll come back as much as we can, Dad. Hang in there."

"Love you, Dad," Jason said, barely getting it past the lump in his throat.

"Me too," Matthew whispered. He smiled again and watched them as the nurse ushered them out.

They're good kids underneath all that crap their mother has dumped all over them, he thought. If I could only

get them away from her influence…   Then, the encounter drained him of all energy, he fell back into a deep sleep.

– Chapter 20 –

It was late afternoon by the time hunger woke Katie up. Except for some orange juice and a half of a muffin that had come on her breakfast tray at the hospital, she hadn't eaten anything since the dinner the night before. She struggled to get out of the king-size bed. Not an easy thing to do when you wake up in the middle and you have one arm strapped across your chest.

Padding across the room to the desk, she found the room service menu and called down to order scrambled eggs, toast, a fruit cup, and a pot of herb tea. She thought her request might be a problem for this time of day, but was told it would be there in fifteen minutes.

In the meantime, she went to the closet where someone had hung the clothes she'd brought and picked out a pair of gray moleskin slacks and the jacket that matched them. From a drawer she got her soft white short sleeve sweater. I need soft clothes today, soft and loose, she thought. She'd been told she could unstrap her arm when she needed to bathe and dress but then she had to strap it up again. It would just be a few days she was told. To support the weight of that arm and give the ribs a chance to heal.

Every bone in her body ached and much more now, after her nap. After she ate her late-afternoon breakfast, she got in the shower and luxuriated in the hot water and steam. She dressed, called for a taxi and was back at Nell's bedside just as Nell's dinner tray was arriving.

"They think I'll be able to leave tomorrow," Nell told her happily. "As long as I stay nearby and come back in two days to be checked over."

Katie told her about their having been moved to the hotel's executive suite. Nell laughed. "Me in an executive suite? The guys at Rock Harbor will never believe that one!

"I called Tom, by the way. He wanted to come right down but I told him to hold off. Maybe he would be the one to drive us home. What do you think?"

"Yes, maybe," Katie answered. "And I guess we have to make some decisions now about Granddaddy, don't we?"

Nell had already thought it all through and Katie quickly acquiesced to her plan. According to his wishes, he would be cremated the next day and they would try to arrange a memorial service at the University chapel for early the next week. Langdon Hall and John Bellows were looking into that for them. They'd also made arrangements with the funeral home and contacted the Unitarian minister from the church he and Bridget had attended when they'd lived in Princeton. Half of Jonas's ashes would be buried next to his beloved Bridget in the old cemetery off Witherspoon Street. The other half would be taken back to Cape Cod where they would be, at his request, scattered in the wind so they would go where the wind carried them and land where it set them down—on the rolling, tossing sea, amidst the grains of sand on the beach, on the petals of Nell's flowers. Part of him would be in that place he'd come to love. And part of him would be here in Princeton in the place he'd loved first.

"Strange isn't it that he died here?" Nell mused. "Kind of like he came full circle."

"It's going to be so hard to be without him," Katie said. Especially for you, Ma. The two of you were so close."

"Yea, we were. Although most of the time nobody would have ever guessed it. He was always growling at me for something or other. But, funny, I never once doubted he loved me very much. And he knew I loved him. It didn't look that way to outsiders, but we were really peaceful. We each had our work, our routines and we were comfortable with each other. You're right, this is going to take a lot of getting used to. But we'll do it, Katie. We have to.

"And did you know Matthew is in the Step-Down now?" she said, changing the subject.

"Wow, that's great. I'm going to go see him now, okay?" Katie got up and headed for the door. "I'll be back in a little while."

The nurse on duty recited the rule on visiting to her and then added, "I'm sorry we have to be so strict," she said, "but it's like I told Mrs. Callahan when she was here earlier, it's for Mr. Callahan's own good. He needs a peaceful environment. Another upset like what happened a little while ago would set him back. He seems to have rested a lot since that happened, so maybe it didn't do too much harm, but we do have to protect him."

What's she talking about? Katie wondered. Mrs. Callahan? She was puzzled, but when she entered the room and saw that he was looking better than when she'd left this morning, she was so happy she stood there grinning from ear to ear.

"Ahhhh, the Katie smile," Matt said. Even his voice was already getting stronger.

"Well you're giving me something to smile about," Katie said. "Matthew, you're looking better. Your color is coming back."

"It's all this good stuff they're pumping into me." He lifted his arm with all the i.v.s hooked into it.

"So what did you do all day, lie around here like a lazy man being fussed over and waited on?" Katie teased.

Matthew's face clouded over. "I was fussed over all right." His voice grew weaker but he continued. "Annaliese, my ex-wife? came. I don't know why. I certainly haven't been one of her favorite people for the last few years, but it seems like I am now. But she brought Luke and Jason and it was good to see them."

"Well that was nice of her, Matt. And she probably is very concerned about you. After all, you were her husband. She's remarried now isn't she?"

"Remarried and divorcing," he answered. "I heard husband #2 ran out of money." By now he was almost whispering.

"Time's just about up for now," the nurse said quietly, poking her head in the open door.

Immediately, Katie bent over Matthew and kissed him on his forehead, smoothed his hair back and smiled tenderly at him. "Take a little nap now, Matt. I'll be back before I leave for the night."

"Ah, if all visitors could be as cooperative," the nurse said as they left the room together. "That episode this morning was uncalled for."

"What happened?" Katie asked.

"When I told Mrs. Callahan it was time to leave, she put up a big fuss. Said she'd leave when she was good and ready. He was embarrassed. I could tell. He doesn't need that kind of carrying on. And with the kids there to see it too."

Katie agreed and left, not wanting to get caught up on the whole thing. But she was curious about what was going on—and it did seem like something was going on.

She spent the evening visiting with Nell and even took her for a ride all around the third floor in her wheel chair. "Better get used to this, Ma. You're going to be riding for awhile now."

"Not for long," Nell said. "They want me up on crutches in a day or two and I'll be coming every day for physical therapy. I'll be running races around you before we know it."

"I don't doubt it," Katie said with a chuckle.

Nell was discharged the next day and after Katie got her settled into their suite, they told Henry Gruber he could let the press people come up and they'd talk with them.

And when the reporters left, Nell sighed deeply. "Well that's one less thing we have to deal with. Wasn't as bad as I thought it was going to be."

Katie agreed. "Next we have to meet with the lawyer. Mr. Voorhees said he'd stop by around eleven tomorrow. Wanted to give us a good chance to sleep in."

"And John Bellows said the memorial service is all set up for next Thursday," Nell said. "Then what, Kate? I should be able to get therapy on the Cape and my doctor up there can take care of me. And you're doing okay now, right? But what about Matthew? He won't be strong enough to make the trip for awhile yet."

"I don't know, Ma. I've been thinking about the logistics of this too."

"Well the nurses said his wife has been there and is planning on taking him back home with her, so maybe that's how it will be," Nell said, looking at Katie to measure her reaction.

There was none. At least none that showed.

The next days passed in a blur. The doctors told Katie she could remove the binding. She was able to use her right arm again and she was surprised her chest didn't hurt much at all. The arm was a little weak and still but they told her that was okay and with normal use the stiffness would disappear. She rented a car and was now carefully driving the short distance from the hotel to the hospital and back for Nell's therapy sessions and their visits to Matthew who seemed to be improving every time they stopped by to chat with him. The doctors removed some of the tubes and wires and, on the third day after the accident, he was taken down to a private room on the same floor where Nell and Katie had been. The swelling in his eye went down and he was looking more like himself.

On Monday, Katie did a little shopping on Palmer Square before she went to the hospital. She bought Matthew a big bag of fresh cashews, a box of assorted dark chocolates and, just for fun, a cuddly teddy bear who carried a balloon that said, "You're Just Too Cute For Words." She thought now that his bruises had ripened (as had hers) to flagrant purple, he might get a laugh out of the irony of that.

All this is coming down on him now, she thought. His own infirmity, not to mention his discomfort and his grieving Jonas who had become a good friend.

She stepped eagerly off the hospital elevator when it got to the third floor and walked quickly to his room looking forward to seeing him and to giving him her fun gifts.

"Hi there," she said as she stepped into the room smiling happily—then stopped abruptly. A chic and attractive blonde woman was buttoning the front of a fresh pajama top that Matthew had obviously just put on. He said something to the woman that made her laugh. She straightened his collar and kissed him on the tip of his nose. When she turned to sit on the edge of the bed she saw Katie.

"Oh Matthew honey, you have company," she said with a sneer on her face and in her voice.

Matthew looked over and saw Katie standing there holding the colorful wrapped packages and the teddy bear. She looked so confused and sad that he was at a loss for words. He didn't understand what was going on himself, so how could he expect anyone else to, especially someone who had just come into this absurd scene of domesticity.

"Katie, this is my former wife, Annaliese. Annaliese, Kate Vinerelli," he said.

"It looks like your little friend has brought you some toys and goodies, Matthew honey," Annaliese said. And then to Katie, "Aren't you the girl who was in the other car? Dr. Singer's granddaughter? It's sad the accident had to happen, but then he was old anyway, right? Probably wouldn't have lasted much longer. And look at the wonderful thing that has come out of all of it. It brought Matthew back to his family."

Katie looked at Matthew to see how he was reacting to the woman's callousness, but he was lying there with his eyes closed. She knew, of course, that he wasn't sleeping and was hurt that he didn't tell that awful person how cruel she was being. Refusing to give either one of them the satisfaction of seeing how hurt she was, she said, "Matthew, Ma and I thought you might like some treats. I have to go meet her in therapy now. Hope you're feeling better."

She put the gifts on the foot of his bed and, as she started to leave, she saw Annaliese pick up the bear and heard her read the sign, "'You're Just Too Cute For Words.' Unbelievably tacky, Matt, but, ah, cutsey, I guess."

Katie rushed to the stairway exit, her cheeks flaming, tears welling up in her eyes. What she didn't hear in her haste to leave was Matthew saying coldly, "Just go, Annaliese. Get out of here and please don't keep coming back. It's no use. I know you for what you are and what little love I had for you all those years ago has been dead a long time."

"Now honey, you're tired and overwrought. That girl bothers you too much anyway. She probably won't be back and you're well rid of her," Annaliese said. I'll go on home now, but I'll be back tomorrow. We have to start making plans for your release and when you'll be coming back home."

"You don't get it do you?" Matthew said wearily. "Just go."

– Chapter 21 –

KATIE WAS UNUSUALLY QUIET AS she drove Nell back from her therapy session and Nell watched her closely.

"I'm going to bed now. Just let me sleep, Ma, okay?" she'd said as she kicked off her shoes and went straight to the bedroom. She closed the door and that had been the last Nell saw of her. She didn't come out for dinner, so Nell ordered room service for herself. She picked at the Chicken Divan the steward brought and tried to figure out what was going on. She suspected it wasn't just that Katie was tired. This was unlike her and, besides, she'd been so exuberant earlier in the day, what with the fun presents for Matthew and all. No, something was going on.

When the phone rang at about ten that night, Nell was the only one up to answer it.

"Ian Swayze here," a male voice said. "Kate Vinerelli please."

He didn't have to identify himself. Nell would know Katie's old boyfriend's pompous tone of voice anywhere. Nell told him Katie was sleeping.

"I'm in the airport getting ready to board for Germany," he said as if that were a good reason to summon Katie after months of his silence. "Saw in the papers what happened. I want to talk to her."

Always was an arrogant bastard, Nell thought. "I'll give her the message you called," she told him and hung up.

Katie stood in her open bedroom doorway. "Was that Matthew?" she asked.

"No, Kate. It wasn't. It was Ian."

"Ian?"

"Yes, about to board a plane for Germany. Wanted me to wake you up but I said no. Figured you needed your sleep."

"I wasn't sleeping, Ma. Just thinking."

"Oh yeah? About what?"

"Just things," Katie said. "Well, things like maybe we should take Tom up on his offer to drive us back to the Cape after Granddaddy's memorial service on Thursday. You were right. You can get therapy there and the doctors can treat you just as well there as they can here now that you're all casted."

"What's bringing this on today, Kate?" her mother asked.

"I don't know. I guess I just feel it'll be the right time to go."

"And what about Matthew? Just take off and leave him here to fend for himself?"

"He won't be fending for himself, Ma. He's got his wife and sons here."

"Ex-wife," Nell reminded her.

As Katie opened her mouth to respond, the phone rang again and she picked it up. It was Ian calling back.

"Listen, Kate," he said as soon as he heard her voice. "I'm getting ready to take off for Germany to pick up a client who's being extradited on a murder charge. Heard about the accident. You okay?"

Katie opened her mouth to say she was fine but he didn't wait to hear her answer.

"Look, I'm really glad you're okay. Just wanted to let you know I'm thinking about you. I've been missing you. I'll call you when I get back. What say we patch things up and start all over again?"

"Ian, I…" Katie started to say.

"Gotta go, Kate. They're boarding first class," he said and hung up.

"Just like that? Patch things up? Start over again? After all these fucking months? Men!" Katie glared at the phone. She slammed it down, stalked across the floor and slammed her bedroom door for good measure.

"Whew," Nell said to herself. "So it does have to do with Matthew. Thought so."

The next day at breakfast, Katie was subdued and apologized to her mother for her outburst the night before. They went through the motions of getting through that day and the next. When they talked it was about who John Bellows and Langdon Hall invited to give eulogies at the memorial service, who would be doing the chosen readings.

Matthew called several times but Katie never picked up the phone when it rang. She hadn't been to see him since Monday and he was calling to try to tell her he missed her visits. Nell spoke to him a few times when she happened to be there to answer when he called. He told her Katie hadn't been to see him and asked if she was okay. One of those times Nell said, "She's right here. You can ask her yourself" and handed the phone to Katie.

"I'm all right. I've just been busy," she heard Katie tell him. Then she heard her say, "Ma and I are going to leave for the Cape after the memorial service tomorrow. We're driving back with Tom. Yes, sure, we'll both come to see you later today. That would be best because we'll want to get on the road right from the cemetery tomorrow."

I'd like to wring her little neck, Nell thought to herself. Why the hell is she doing this to him and to herself?

Katie hung up and Nell asked her just that: "Why the hell are you doing this, Kate Vinerelli?"

"Because I want to, Ma. Just leave it alone, okay?"

"Okay, I will," Nell said, "but not until I tell you that you're making one big foolish mistake. Something's hurt your feelings and you're scared of being hurt some more so you put up this big thick wall around yourself just like you've always done since you were little kid. But you know what, Katie my girl? It gets dark and lonesome behind those walls and you're the one who's alone back there and doing the hurting—you're hurting yourself."

Having said that, Nell hobbled on her crutches into the bathroom and closed the door.

❀

Later that afternoon they drove to the hospital to see Matthew one last time. He looked gaunt and listless and all the conversations they started fell flat. It was as if the three of them no longer had anything to say to each other. After awhile Nell told them she'd called ahead and made a date to have coffee downstairs in the cafeteria with a couple of her favorite nurses when they went off duty at three.

"I'll be back in a short while," she told them and, quickly, before Katie could protest, she turned on her crutches and left. Left Katie and Matt alone and avoiding looking at each other.

Finally Matthew said, "Katie, I'm sorry Annaleise was so rude to you on Monday. She really didn't mean to hurt you, she's just that way."

"She did mean it, Matthew," Katie said. "And maybe you can make excuses for her meanness, but I can't. But I'm leaving tomorrow and won't have to deal with her again, thank God."

"Katie, do you have to leave tomorrow? Can't you stay on for at least another week? You can do your writing here on your laptop and Nell can continue with the therapists who've been working with her from the start. Please say you'll stay, Kate. I'm going to miss the two of you."

"No, Matthew. It's time for us to go. We'll keep in touch by phone and by e-mail when you get out of here. And when you're ready, we can ship all your stuff down to you."

"Katie, no. Please don't say that," Matthew pleaded. "Jonas and I talked the afternoon of the accident and he told me I could stay in the cottage as long as I wanted and we agreed I'd stay at least until Christmas and then talk about it after that. I still want to do that. As soon as I can get strong enough to get out of here and get up there. The doctors told me I'm going to have a long convalescence and I want to spend it painting and writing the story I started about Nancy and Davy and the cabin."

"Maybe when you're well enough you can come up and stay there awhile—if your *family* will let you. I'm sure Nell would enjoy having the company. I'm going right back to my place in Boston by next week probably."

"What's happened, Kate?" Matthew asked. "This can't all be because someone said some mean things to you. What about the things we planned to do when we returned to the Cape? You said you wanted to go to the cabin with me, that you felt like you wanted to get to know more about Nancy and Davy and the life they led there together. We were going to do some research on them together, you were going to help me write their story. What happened to all that, Katie?"

"That was just being caught up in some fantasy, Matthew. I do that sometimes." Avoiding his eyes, Katie was smoothing non-existent wrinkles out of the sheet at the foot of his bed. "This is reality and the reality is that we're leaving tomorrow and I'm getting back to my real life."

"I can't change your mind, Kate?" Matthew asked.

"No, you can't change my mind." Katie finally looked at him directly. "And now I'd better go hurry Ma up. We have to get our clothes ready for the service tomorrow and get busy packing. Tom's due to arrive in about an hour and we want to get his car packed tonight so we can leave right from the cemetery."

"If I could get out of this goddamn bed, Katie, you wouldn't be leaving because I'd bar the door and not let you go."

Matthew no sooner got the words out of his mouth when the door to his room swung open and Annaleise came bursting in with the boys in tow.

"Hi honey," she said, ignoring Katie and going right to Matthew and kissing him on the mouth. "Guess what? We have permission to get you up in a wheel chair and take you to the director's private dining room for a nice candlelight dinner tonight. Just you, me and the boys. Daddy arranged it when he was playing golf with the director this afternoon. And look, I brought you this gorgeous new monogrammed bathrobe to wear for the occasion."

"Goodbye, Matthew," Katie said. She turned, walked past Luke and Jason and left.

— *Chapter 22* —

THE UNIVERSITY CHAPEL WAS FILLED the next morning for the memorial service. It was a real cross section of students, faculty, friends, and administration people. Brilliant sunlight flooded the vast space with shafts of crimson, sapphire, emerald, and gold as it filtered through the exquisite stained glass windows.

Those gathered sat in a shared sadness as they listened to one speaker after another tell how Jonas had touched their lives. There was soft laughter now and then as many of them remembered some of his foibles. There was interested silence as his achievements were mentioned and the list went on. And, for those who knew him best and had shared their lives with him, there were tears of deep sadness as they thought about their lives to be lived now without him.

Matthew should be here, Katie kept thinking. If that stupid woman could have arranged for him to be wheeled to the fancy dining room for dinner, why couldn't she have had him brought here for this service? Of course, Katie knew he was nowhere near well enough to do either one of those things, but she missed him so much it helped to change that missing to unreasonable anger.

Nell had a pretty good idea of what was going on inside her daughter. They were holding hands and, for a moment, Nell withdrew her other hand from Tom's who was sitting on her other side and she covered Katie's hand with hers, rubbing it softly as she did so. Katie turned to her and smiled through the tears that were freely flowing.

At the cemetery as the container with half of Jonas's ashes was placed in the ground, Nell had a real sense of his being with her—both Jonas and her mother, Bridget. She sighed deeply and Katie understood that it was a sigh of real peace.

"It's like something is complete now," she whispered to Katie. "It's real sad, but it feels right too."

Because it was announced that the interment would be private, only a handful of people whom they'd invited had accompanied them to the cemetery. After the minister said his last words and handfuls of dirt and flower petals were thrown into the open earth, the small group moved away toward their cars.

There were hugs and tears, promises to keep in touch and before long only Katie, Nell and Tom were left. Tom stayed back by the car while the women walked back and said one last farewell to Jonas, then they all got in the car, drove out of town to Route One and headed north.

Matthew lay in his hospital bed listening to the audio tape John Bellows had had made of the funeral service. He still found it hard to believe Jonas was really gone. He'd been such a strong presence that it hardly seemed possible that the two of them wouldn't be cooking supper together one day next week or digging into more boxes in the attic pulling out more files to be organized.

The day of the funeral had been tough. When Liz, his morning nurse, came in to check his temp, pulse, and blood pressure, she saw how down he was.

"I should be with them now. I feel like we're family and I should be there," he told her. "I want to be there." He was gazing out the window looking toward the chapel just a few blocks away.

He'd talked to his doctors about the possibility of going in a wheelchair then being brought right back to the hospital afterward, but they'd said absolutely no. He was too weak, too vulnerable.

He knew they were right. Just getting out of bed to sit in that chair by the window took all the strength and energy he could summon up.

"That fiasco dinner my ex-wife arranged in the director's dining room last night wiped me out." He shifted to try to be more comfortable. "I hated having the kids see my hands shaking so bad when I tried to get the food to my mouth. And then when I looked at her to see if she noticed, she was all annoyed. It was like I was spoiling her evening."

Liz kept her fingers on his wrist and her eyes on her watch, letting him grouse, glancing up at him now and then.

"I'm sorry, Liz," he finally said. "Just pissed off."

"No problem. You're weak and everything's coming down on you. I'd be pissed off too." She picked up a vase of wilting roses Annaleise had sent and carried them out to the dumpster.

Matthew was silent the rest of the day, barely answering when spoken to and not caring if he was being rude or not. As every hour passed, he felt the growing distance between himself and Katie.

When Nell called that night to let him know they'd arrived back on the Cape, he asked to speak to Katie but Nell followed her daughter's instructions and told him she was in the shower and had said she was going to go right to bed.

❦

Matthew's recovering was continuing in a steady but slow pace. After the dinner in the director's dining room, Annaleise claimed that her life had gotten "unbelievably busy" and her visits became shorter, changing from the one midday visit to a breezy hello when she dropped the boys off or picked them up. They came daily, sometimes as a pair and sometimes separately, depending on who had what after-school sport that day.

A week after the accident, Annaleise paid a call on her attorney to get his views on Matthew's chances to collect damages from the truck driver's insurance company. She also wanted to find out what he thought the chances were of winning a lawsuit against the truck driver's company. She was told it was "iffy" but certainly worth giving it a try.

After that, she paid a call on her financial advisor who told her her situation had gotten much worse than they'd expected. Because of his own drop in income, her father had stopped making the hefty monthly deposits in her account and she was now having to draw down principal in order to pay the monstrous bills she continued to pile up.

"You're going to have to take some drastic steps or you're going to be in very serious trouble, Mrs. Rightmier," she was told.

Adding to these worries was the fact that she could see Matthew wasn't going to be the pushover she'd at first thought he would be.

The boys are the key here, she thought. He'll get all fatherly with them and won't want to leave them. It's happening already. Her bright orange painted lips parted in a smile that never reached her cold blue eyes as she laid out her action plan. In the first few weeks after he's strong enough I'll probably have to have sex with him, but I remember what he likes and I'll give him as much of it as he wants. It'll be a bore, but I need to do it. With that and the boys, he'll stay. Then we can get moving on collecting big on this. After the money comes in, probably no more than a year or so, I don't give a damn what the hell he does with himself. He can even go make an ass of himself with the brillo-head redhead for all I care.

By the time she got away from the meeting with her financial advisor, it was time to pick the boys up from the hospital and get them home for dinner so Mrs. Mercer, the new cook, wouldn't be angry at them all again for being late.

She could hear the laughter coming from Matthew's room as soon as she got off the elevator. She quickened her step and grinned to herself thinking about how right she was, that he was already hooked on the kids and it was all going to work out as planned. She pulled a chair up next to Matthew's, completely oblivious to the fact that when she arrived all the laughter stopped. She kissed him sweetly on the cheek, took his hand and held it.

"It feels so good for us to be family again, Matthew," she said. "It's great, isn't it guys? Guys? Isn't it?"

"Yea, I guess so," Luke said. He turned off the hand-held electronic hoops game the three of them had been playing trying to beat each other's score and began putting his things in his backpack. Jason just got quiet and stared out the window and Matthew distantly smiled and said hello.

"We'll be down in the lobby, Mom." Jason gathered up his things and went over and gave his father a high-five. "See ya tomorrow, Dad."

The boys left looking sullen and annoyed but Annaleise either didn't notice or didn't care.

"They're so much happier now that you're back in our lives. Have you noticed? Luke's test grades are better and Jason isn't nearly as surly as he was getting to be. You're a good influence on them. It'll be good for them to have their dad back home again," she said, not noticing that Matthew seemed dismayed. "We should never have split. I was selfish and caused us all a lot of pain. But I know better now and I'm going to make it up to you and to the boys."

"You always could put on a good act. What's up, Annaleise?"

"I know it's going to take a while for you to trust me again, honey, but you'll see," she said. "It's going to all work out."

Matthew looked at her and just shook his head. "You'd better go. I'm tired. And the boys are waiting downstairs."

When she leaned over to kiss him on the lips, he turned away and said, "No. Just go."

The hospital had notified Matthew's parents about the accident and they called daily to check on his recovery. They didn't have a whole lot of money and Matthew talked them out of flying up to be with him, convincing them he was really better than he sounded.

Other than the boys and Annaleise he didn't have visitors and the days seemed to drag on endlessly. He called the Cape house several times, always got Nell and was always told Katie was not available for one reason or another.

Then one time he called, Nell told him Katie had moved back to her apartment in Boston. She was finishing up her European river cruises project and about to embark on a new one—river cruises here in America. Nell also mentioned that Katie was back to dating her old boyfriend, Ian, the lawyer. Nell didn't sound pleased about that, but Matthew refrained from asking questions.

He remembered some of the things Katie had told him in her early e-mails from Europe about her relationship with Ian. The guy had a mean streak and when Katie had finally gotten the courage to end it with him she'd said unequivocally that she would never see him again. And now she was. Matthew wondered what had changed her mind.

"Please be kind to her, Ian," he whispered to himself, then added through clenched teeth, "and you can bet your ass if I could get out of this fucking hospital and get up there, you wouldn't stand a chance."

— Chapter 23 —

"I never know where to find you anymore. I come to check your temp and blood pressure first thing in the morning and you're already chatting up old Mrs. Riley next door or sitting by Mr. Sanchez's bed reading his morning paper with him. You're supposed to stay in bed until I make my rounds."

"C'mon, Liz, don't scold me," Matthew said. "The morning nurse is supposed to be all sunshine and smiles."

"Come over here and roll up your sleeve," Liz said as she wrapped the blood pressure cuff around his arm. "You can be Mr. Personality of the Recovery Unit when I'm done with you."

Matthew sat on the edge of his bed and did as he was told. "I'm just trying to pass the days as pleasantly as possible until I get my walking papers," he said.

He'd become a favorite of all the nurses on the floor. His room was right across from the nurse's station and each day when his sons came after school the bantering and laughter lightened everybody's mood.

But in addition to the fun of those visits, Matthew and the boys had been having good talks too and it was clear that their home life left a lot to be desired. Apparently Annaleise was rarely there and they were left to the reserved politeness of Mrs. Mercer and the ever-changing housekeeping help that seemed to last only a few days before leaving in a huff. Matthew was beginning to understand why they had been turning to material things for a sense of security and pleasure. They sure weren't getting it from their mother.

One day while he was sitting in the lounge chair next to his bed, there was a tap at his door and when he looked up there stood Nick his old AA buddy. Nick had been his AA sponsor and they'd become closer than brothers.

Matthew had called Nick a couple of days before he and Jonas were to leave for Princeton trying to set something up but Nick's secretary said he was in South America where he'd taken a group of teens on a Habitat for Humanity project.

"Hey, buddy! You're back!" Matt was across the room in a matter of seconds giving Nick a big bear hug. "It's great to see you. How'd the project go? Did you get the house built?"

"House? Singular? Houses. Two of them. We had more kids sign up than we expected and there was a good team down there—carpenters, electricians, plumbers, you name it. So we got two done. But how the hell are you, buddy? Sorry I've been away when you needed me. I couldn't believe it when I picked up the Princeton Packet on line and read what happened. How're you doing? When're you getting out of here?"

"I'm feeling stronger every day and, actually, the doctors are hinting about maybe setting me free next week if all keeps going so well."

"Where're you going when you get out? Got a place to stay?" Nick asked.

"Well---- Annaliese has a campaign going to get me to move back in..."

"No way, Matt. Would you do it?"

"I don't know, Nick. She's so false I can barely stand to be around her for even five minutes, but the kids... Damn, they've got a shitty life there with her and I keep thinking maybe if I move back..."

"Think long and hard, Matt. Don't just do it because Annaleise has this thing going to get you there. Think about it. Suppose you did move back for the kids' sakes and then you just couldn't stand it and it all fell apart again. Think about what that would do to the kids."

"You're right. I've thought about that."

"And, by the way, don't you think it's a little bizarre that she all of a sudden wants you back? I remember when she said she couldn't stand the sight of you, called you a failure and a loser because you weren't making a million bucks like her lover, that old geezer, was. Whatever happened to him? She married him, right?"

"They're getting divorced. He lost a lot of money in some annuity collapse and now he's no longer able to be a sugar daddy."

"Aha! Money. It's always money with her," Nick said.

"So why would she be after me again? I certainly don't have enough to keep her happy."

"I dunno. Maybe she thinks you struck it rich or something. Who knows? I don't trust her, Matt, and I hope you keep your eyes wide open."

"Don't worry, Nick. I am."

"Look," Nick said, "why don't you come stay with me for awhile when they discharge you. That would give you thinking time and it would be a blast for me to have you to hang out with again. It's pretty lonely in the big old house since Barb died. It's been four years and I still can't get used to her not being there. You'd really be doing me a favor if you'd come for awhile."

"Hey, buddy, that sounds like a great idea. You're a godsend once again. That would give me a chance to get my act together. You sure now?"

"Not only sure, but wishing we could get started on it like now."

"Oh—what about Jase and Luke? You won't mind if they come over sometimes?"

"Mind? Hell no. I'll put them to work for Habitat. Lots of good guys their age are going to be working on building a youth house in Trenton. They might like something like that. Do them good to get their hands dirty."

"My God. Can't you just hear Annaleise if that happens?"

They were laughing so hard they didn't hear Annaleise come in.

"If what happens?" She was looking straight at Matthew and ignoring Nick. She'd never liked Nick and all he represented. It had been a humiliation to her that her husband was an alcoholic and had lost his job. In her own warped way of thinking, she blamed Nick for the fact that when Matthew got sober he didn't return to the firm where he'd made a lucrative income.

"Annaleise, Nick just invited me to move in with him for awhile when I get discharged," Matthew said.

"No." She was adamant. "I won't allow it. You're my husband and you belong with me and our children."

"I'm your ex-husband, Annaleise. You're married to someone else now. Do you remember that? Do you remember when you couldn't wait to be rid of me?"

"It's not going to happen." She turned and addressed Nick coldly. "So why don't you just leave now? My husband and I have things to discuss."

"Your ex-, Annaleise. Your ex-." Matt got out of his chair and stood between her and Nick. It was a face off. "And I think you should be the one to leave. Nick and I are the ones who have things to discuss."

"If you do this, you give up your sons—again. I will not allow them to go there to visit you. This man has all sorts of riff-raff hanging around that house all the time." She was livid and in the old days Matthew had thought of her as formidable.

"Not riff-raff, Annaleise. Normal kids who are not riding around in their mother's Mazarati, who are not taking private lessons from the golf pro at the country club. Normal kids, Annaleise, and, yes, they will visit me there and you'll just have to get used to it. Now why don't you go so Nick and I can continue our visit."

"I'll go now and when I come back I'll have a restraining order against you so you can't get near those boys," she said. "And, 'you know what Matthew? This is a huge relief to me. I was dreading putting up with you again. You're such a bore. It was going to be hard finding time to be with my new boyfriend with you hanging around the house all the time. Now I won't have to worry about that. You've made your choice, now live with it. I'll tell your sons you won't be seeing them anymore."

She left and Matthew and Nick just looked at each other.

"She's a sick woman, Matt. A real sick-o," Nick said. "But don't worry about the kids. She can't keep you from seeing them. You've done nothing to harm them and you have that court order from the divorce settlement, remember. She didn't care about them and said you could have them any time you wanted and for as long as you wanted. She was glad to be rid of them whenever you took them."

"Yea, I know, Nick. But why does she have to make everything so fucking hard? God only knows what she'll tell the kids now."

"Don't worry about it. They're not dummies. They know what's going on, probably more than you do. Look, I've got an in with the guidance counselors at the school. Why don't I go there now and tell them the situation and that I need to talk to them before she does. They'll let me and that may soften the blow for the kids. I'll tell them I'll arrange to pick them up whenever they want to come see you and when you're out of here and have your own car you'll be picking them up. That okay with you?"

"What did I tell you before, Nick? You're a Godsend. You really are, buddy. Thanks."

— *Chapter 24* —

ANNALEISE WAS TRUE TO HER words. The visits from his sons stopped abruptly. He called the house but no one picked up the phone. He knew Annaleise had Caller I.D. and he could picture her militantly overseeing it, refusing to let their sons pick up whenever it was Matthew calling.

How can she be such a bitch? And why? He wondered.

Those last days in the hospital were interminable. In the early days he'd been so sick and in pain that time was a blur. Besides, he always had his boys' visits to look forward to. And Katie's.

But Katie had Caller I.D. too and when he'd try calling her the phone rang and rang and no one picked up even though he knew she must be there.

"She's not playing fair either and I don't like it," he said glaring at the phone as he slammed it back down on its holder. His anger at Annaleise started to spread over to Katie and to life in general.

I've been penned up in this place too long. I need to get out of here and get some control of my own life again. Swearing to himself, he got off the edge of the bed and started pacing back and forth. I feel like a goddamn animal in a cage with people poking sticks at me.

He riffled through his closet and pulled out a pair of khakis and a shirt Katie had brought over for him before she left. It felt good to get regular clothes on again, shoes and socks instead of those fucking slippers.

"I'm checking myself out," he told the nurse at the desk.

She looked surprised but kept her cool. "Your doctor's on the floor now as a matter of fact, I'll tell him. He'll see you in your room in a few minutes."

Matthew was cleaning out the drawer of his bedside table, putting notebook, pens, and all the get well cards he'd gotten into his suitcase when Dr. Jameson came in.

"I hear you're sick of this place. Can't say as I blame you." He pulled a chair from the other side of the room and sat down. "I'd like you to stay two more days though. Can you manage that? I'd like you to have some follow-up testing done before you leave to make sure everything's okay. Then, since you're going to be staying in the area for awhile, if all the tests are good, we'll discharge you and you'll just need to come in to see me in my office in a week. What do you think? Can we do it that way?"

Matt sat in the other chair, arms resting on his thighs, head bent, thinking. Finally, "Yeah, I guess I can manage two more days if you're sure that's all it will be."

"I can't promise because if the tests show a problem we may have to keep you, but I really don't expect anything to show up at this point. You've been healing nicely and getting stronger. I'm putting money on your being out of here after two days."

"Okay. I guess that makes sense. At least getting a real time frame makes it more manageable." Matthew leaned back and stretched his legs out in front of him.

The two men talked a few minutes about the Yankees and the Mets and the possibility of a subway series, then, extending his hand, Dr. Jameson said he had to finish his rounds.

⁕

Matthew spent the next two days being wheeled downstairs time and again on a gurney for one test after another. And when he wasn't being poked and prodded, he sat in the chair by the window in his room mulling over his life, trying to make sense of it all.

His thoughts drifted often from his own convoluted predicament to the tragedy of Nancy and Davy's lives in the cabin on Cape Cod. If anything was unfair in this world, it had to be what had happened to them.

To help pass the time, he picked up his notebook and pen and started writing again about what he'd found there in the woods. He felt he knew Nancy, so he began trying to develop what he thought Rev. Heady must have been like. He even drew a few sketches of what he thought the man looked like. Evil. Satanic. But he knew that was probably way off base. Heady probably looked like an ordinary man—hair thinning, maybe a little paunch, but, Matthew was sure, there must have been a look in his eyes that betrayed him for what he was. There must have been something.

He penciled out a word sketch of Davy—tall, muscular, not only because of his whaling family genes, but muscles that had been honed through his trade as a carpenter/builder. He pictured Davy as having curly black hair and the olive skin of his Portuguese ancestors. Dark eyes. And the crooked ready grin he'd seen in the wedding picture in the cabin. From the journal entries, he knew Davy was a gentle man, sensitive.

He saw Nancy clearly in his mind and wrote that he saw her as willowy, tall and slim and small breasted. He saw her as fair skinned with honey-colored hair that she had let grow for years and wore tied back with a ribbon—except for when she let it fall free for her husband.

"She was a gentle woman but one who was strong when she needed to be. A woman who was willing to endure hardships to build a life with her husband and the child she had been so looking forward to birthing," he wrote.

Those last days in the hospital he immersed himself in thoughts about what he would do about the cabin and Nancy's remains when he returned to the Cape.

And there was no doubt in his mind he would return there. He missed Katie more than he'd been admitting to himself. And he was even missing Nell. And his racquetball buddies and the Cape life he'd settled into. He found himself longing for the early sunrises when the world seemed to be opening to a dew-spattered morning; the fishing boats coming into Rock Harbor one after the other at mid tide as they'd probably done for generations. He missed his beach walks and talking one-on-one with the fishermen he met.

But he thought there was no better place to bide his time than with his good friend Nick. Once or twice while in the hospital he'd thought about how nice it would be to crack open a bottle of Jack Daniels and feel that glow creep over him. Being with Nick would safeguard him against that. There was no way he wanted to sink into alcoholism again, no matter how appealing it seemed to him at times.

· ❦ ·

Living together worked right from the start for the two old friends. Nick's house was large enough that they weren't under each other's feet, except when they wanted to be. Matthew kept to his regular physical therapy appointments, his follow-up doctor visits and Nick just went about his business as usual.

"What do you do all day when I'm at work?" Nick asked one night when there was a commercial break between innings in the playoffs.

"I'm doing some writing." Matthew wasn't sure he wanted to open up to Nick about the cabin yet.

"Yeah? What?"

"Just some ideas for a book I might write someday. I'll tell you about it if it all starts to make sense to me. Just getting my head together on it right now."

Paul O'Neill hit a homerun for the Yankees and both men were on their feet cheering. How Matthew spent his days was totally forgotten and he felt relieved. Of late he'd been wondering if he was becoming obsessed by what he'd found in the cabin.

But even with being so engrossed in writing his story, he still longed to spend time with his boys. Knowing they were living just a few miles away was hard for him. He talked about it with Nick one night and they came up with a plan to get the boys' church youth group connected with one of the Habitat houses in Trenton and, that way, Matthew could reconnect with them.

It worked. And before long Matt, his sons, and all the other assorted workers on the project were hanging out regularly, taking breaks together, going for pizza after a day's work.

"I'm going back to Cape Cod pretty soon," he told the boys one day. "You want to come up and spend some time there?"

"Yeah, that'd be way cool, Dad," Luke said. "Let's see if we can get it to work for you guys to come up for Christmas and stay the month-long school break after that," Matthew said.

"There's no way Mom'll let that happen." Jason took off his nail apron and tossed it to his brother who was packing up their tools to go home.

Matthew just said, "Let's give it a try. It may work."

He was planning to be back on the Cape in about a month. He was looking forward to the crisp air, the skies that one day would be leaden gray and the next day would be the bluest blue he could find in his paint box. He wanted to be there and to begin painting again.

He sat back, closed his eyes and pictured the cottage with his easel set up on the porch overlooking the ocean. He pictured his palette and tubes of paint and in his mind began laying out the full spectrum of colors.

He'd been calling the Cape house regularly and had some good long talks with Nell who told him Katie was traveling on assignment.

Then one day when he called, Katie happened to pick up the phone. So surprised to hear her voice, he became speechless. When she heard who was calling, the same thing happened to her. In New Jersey, Matthew sat with the phone to his ear, groping for something casual to say. In Massachusetts, Katie was doing the same thing.

Finally, throwing caution to the winds, he simply said, "Katie, I miss you so much."

There was a long silence on the line and then finally Matthew heard her softly say she missed him too but he was back with his wife and she didn't want to be part of that.

"But Katie, I'm not back with Annaleise. I'm living with Nick. Didn't you know that? Didn't your mom tell you that?"

"No, Matt, I didn't know. The last I heard, Annaleise was taking you home with her and you seemed willing to be going, so I told mom I didn't want to talk to her about you or for her to tell me anything you two talked about when you called."

"Oh, Katie, I was never willing and it never happened. Nick and I have been living here like a couple of old bachelors and that has felt good. We've got a plan in action where I see my boys a couple of times a week at a Habitat for Humanity house we're working on and that's been great. They seem a lot different since Nick has gotten them into this. More just like kids. So, no, Katie, I'm not living with Annaleise, never had any desire to and I'm missing the hell out of you."

Katie was silent on the other end of the phone, not knowing whether to trust what she was hearing or not. She'd been seeing a lot of Ian and lately he'd been talking about their getting married and moving to Boulder, Colorado where he'd been interviewing for a spot in a prestigious law firm. She'd tried to give it serious thought, but couldn't. Matthew kept coming to mind instead.

"I'm coming back soon, Katie. In a few weeks," Matthew said. "Will you be there and can we get past all this and spend time together?"

"I'll be here and, yes, we can spend time together," she replied. "You can help Ma and me. We're going through Granddaddy's things, sending more stuff to the library in Princeton, giving his clothes away, sorting through his old pictures. You know, the things that have to be done now. He's got decades of stuff packed away up in that attic. It's a huge job and we can sure use some help.

"Count on me being there by the 15th," Matthew said. "I'm looking for a car and I'll drive up that Sunday when traffic is a little lighter. I still get tired fast, so I'll probably make a few pit stops along the way, but I should arrive before dark."

After that phone call, they were back to talking every few days. Hesitantly and sometimes shyly, but talking.

And Matthew was suddenly energized. He bought a new Subaru Forester, got it all tagged, registered, and insured. He met several times with Jonas's lawyers who were also acting in his behalf. He bought some new clothes, made appointments for his final checkups with his surgeon and internist, and paid a formal call on Annaleise.

He took advantage of her surprise when she answered the door and stepped inside before she could close it on him.

"I'm leaving for Cape Cod on Sunday and I won't be back for a good long time," he told her.

"I'm glad to hear that." She was still being her nasty self, Matthew observed.

"Annaleise, I don't want to get into an argument. Let's be civil at least." She remained silent, just staring coldly at him and he decided to plunge right in.

"I'd like the boys to come to the Cape for Christmas and for the month they're off from school after the holidays," he said looking her straight in the eye.

"What makes you think they'd want to go?" she asked. "They haven't even mentioned your name since you were in the hospital. They couldn't care less about you, Matthew."

"I know they want to come, Annaleise. We've been seeing each other three days a week ever since I got out of the hospital…"

"That's impossible. I know where they've been every minute and it has not been with you. I've made sure of that."

"…we've been building a house together. Their youth group project, Habitat For Humanity? Are you familiar with that? Do you even know what they're doing when they're out of your sight?"

"I've been quite aware that they've been all embroiled in a youth group project. That was all I needed to know."

"Well they, we, have been building a house for a low-income family in Trenton."

"Trenton? Oh my God."

"Yes, Trenton, Annaleise, and we've been working with kids of other races and other ethnic groups, not just rich white kids who wear designer jeans. And you know what, Annaleise? They've been loving it."

"I'll put an end to it right away."

"Doesn't matter. The house is finished. The moving-in party was yesterday."

"You bastard."

"No, Annaleise, I'm not a bastard. I just love my kids and want them to have a normal life. Come on, let's stop fighting all the time. They're good kids and they really do want to come to Cape Cod for Christmas. It'll do them good. What do you say?"

"Well quite frankly I've been wondering what I was going to do with them for that whole month. William, he's the man I met at the Friends of the Metropolitan Museum soiree in Manhattan last month? Remember? Well we fell in love almost immediately and he says I just have to experience Christmas in the Caribbean. He owns restaurants in St. Kitts, Nevis, and Grenada and has homes on each island. I've been tearing my hair out trying to think of which mothers of their friends would take them in for a whole month. Boys their age can be such a bore and I haven't had anyone agree to do it yet."

"So let them come and be with me, Annaleise. I don't think they're boring at all and they'll be in good hands."

"Well that would certainly free me up wouldn't it?" She walked over and got a cigarette out of the crystal box on the cocktail table. "I guess you can't do them too much harm in a month's time."

"Probably not." Matthew could barely conceal his excitement but he'd be damned if he'd give her the satisfaction of seeing how happy she'd made him so he let sarcasm remain in his voice. "I'll get on line and book their flights from Philly to Boston and get the confirmation numbers to you as soon as possible. Also, be sure to give me phone numbers where you can be reached in the islands—in case they miss you too much and want to say hello."

"I'll give you the numbers, Matthew, but try not to let them call. Just if there's an emergency. William isn't too fond of children."

Oh, that's just great, Matthew thought. Great stepfather material for my sons.

"Don't worry, Annaleise. I'll respect your wishes." He walked out to the door that she was already holding open to him. "In case I don't talk to you before then, Merry Christmas."

It took him less than twenty minutes to get over to the school. It was almost noontime and he got permission to take the boys out for lunch. They opted for Burger King and after they got their Whoppers and found a table, Matthew told them the good news.

Luke let out a whoop and gave his Dad a high five. Jason followed suit grinning and saying over and over, "I don't believe it. I don't believe it. It's too great." Then, "How'd you get her to agree?"

"Don't ask," Matthew told him. "Just behave yourselves and stay out of trouble so she doesn't change her mind."

– *Chapter 25* –

When Matthew's alarm went off at 5:00 Sunday morning he got right out of bed. No snooze button this morning. A quick shower and shave and he was bouncing his suitcase down the back steps to the kitchen in Nick's old house.

"I know you're in a hurry to hit the road but you need to have a good breakfast under your belt," Nick said as he lifted slices of bacon out of the skillet and set them on paper towels to drain. "Sit down and relax. Here, have some O.J."

Matthew tried not to glance at his watch, but when Nick turned back to the skillet to make sure the eggs were scrambling, he took a hurried peek. Not bad. He could take his time eating and still be on the road by 6:15. "I hate to see you go, Matt. It's been a real boost to me having you here," Nick said.

"And you'll never know how much I appreciate it. God, just saving me from Annaleise is something I can never repay."

Nick dished up a pile of scrambled eggs on each of their plates and divvied up the bacon. "No need to. I've gotten connected with Luke and Jason and that's worth a lot to me. We'll be spending a lot of time together now. They want to work on the next Habitat project with me. They've filled a big empty hole in my life, Matt."

"And you in theirs." Matthew looked long at his friend across the table and let his gaze say even more than his words.

Nick nodded, then slapped his palms on the tabletop. "Okay, buddy. 'nuff said. Eat up so you can get out there and head north before traffic starts to build."

Out of habit, Matthew rinsed his plate and coffee mug and put them in the dishwasher, then they walked out together to the car. Before Matthew got behind the wheel they embraced—the kind of hug that had gotten Matthew through a lot of borderline days when he might have so easily started drinking again.

"You know you're welcome up there anytime, Nick. Think about coming, okay?" Matthew said, turning the key to start the car.

"Okay, buddy. I will. Might just do that." Nick stepped back, hands in his jeans pockets, grinning as Matthew pulled out of the driveway and turned the car toward Route One North.

⁂

He'd broken the trip up with a few coffee breaks and a nice leisurely lunch at the same place in Guilford, Connecticut he and Jonas had eaten in on their way south just a matter of weeks before and by the time he crossed the Sagamore Bridge and was making his way up the Mid-Cape Highway, the afternoon was already waning. And when he turned into Singer Lane, early dusk was starting to settle on the dunes.

He'd talked with Katie the night before and she'd told him she was temporarily staying at the house with Nell because her roommate was getting married and they'd decided to sublet their Boston apartment.

"Ma's feeling pretty lonely now that Granddaddy isn't here to badger her so I decided to come and stay while I decided what to do about Ian and me," Katie had told him.

I may be getting back just in the knick of time, Matthew thought as he made his way up the narrow crooked road to the house.

As the car emerged from the trees, he saw every light in the house was on as were the outdoor floods. And his cottage was all lit up and welcoming. Both the big house and the cottage had pots of burgundy and gold chrysanthemums on their porches and big fat orange pumpkins on the steps.

As he slowed to a stop, Katie and Nell burst through the door and came down the steps to welcome him.

"We've been listening for the car and watching for you for the past hour," Katie said as she pulled open the car door.

He got out and immediately they were in a three-way hug. "What a welcome," he said laughing and forcing down a rising lump in his throat.

"Just leave your bags right in there and we'll help you get them to the cottage later." Nell took one arm and Katie the other and they led him up the back steps and into the kitchen he remembered so well. A strong wave of missing Jonas washed over him and at the same time he expected to see the old man come through the door from the front room and ease himself down into his favorite chair at the foot of the table.

Nell had mulled some apple cider and they munched on crackers and a good gorgonzola cheese making small talk about Matt's drive. Was there much traffic? Was he tired? How were the boys?

During one of the awkward pauses, Nell got up to check the oven and stir a pot that was simmering on the stove.

"Supper's almost ready. Why don't you get your stuff settled in the cottage and then come back in about a half hour," she said.

Katie went ahead and opened the cottage door for him as he came up the steps with his suitcase and a box under one arm.

The cottage looked the way it did the day he left it to drive to New Jersey with Jonas. It made him think about the cabin in the woods and how it, too, had remained the way its owners had left it.

He went over and looked at the painting he'd left on the easel—a fragment of sea breaking in on one big rock; barely any sky, no beach, just solid rock and crashing sea. It had all the violence of the fatal crash in Princeton and he wondered now if he'd had a subconscious premonition of what was about to occur.

He took the painting off the easel and stood it against the wall with a bunch of others, but this one he turned face to the wall.

Kate watched. She seemed about to ask a question but finally just said, "I'm going to go back and help Ma set the food out. Come as soon as you're ready." She set the box she'd carried in for him on the table by the door before she left, never noticing it had her name on it.

⁖

Dinner was a typical Nell kind of meal, ample, delicious and satisfying. Afterward the three of them sat long over their coffee and, as they did, their conversation became more relaxed, more like old times.

They talked mostly about Jonas, remembering funny stories about him that the three of them had shared. And Nell told them memories from her childhood and how, though gruff with the outside world, he was so tender and sweet with her mother and with her. She reminisced about how loving he and her mother had been to her when her marriage broke up and she came back home with Katie in tow. Katie chimed in with her own memories of being there with her mom and her grandparents. Matthew knew it had been far from idyllic but now, told in the rosy glow of long-cherished memories, it seemed so.

He grew more quiet as they talked and stifled a yawn now and then. It had been his first long trip since the accident—behind the wheel and in traffic again—and trying not to remember that white box truck bearing down fast on him.

Nell spotted it. "Time for bed for you, Matthew. No excuses. I know it's only 8:30, but forget about the clock and listen to your body. You've been through a lot and you need your sleep. Katie and I freshened up your bed for you this morning with nice clean sheets and we put the down duvet on because it's getting cold here nights now. So just go on with you now. Come back in the morning and I'll make you a good breakfast."

He pulled himself up out of the chair, admitting to himself he just wanted to get under the covers and get to sleep. Katie walked him to the kitchen door and, before he left, she stood up on tiptoes and gave him a brief kiss that she'd aimed for his cheek but fell on his lips when he unexpectedly turned to her.

"Good night, Matthew. And welcome home."

He thought of those words as he drifted off to sleep. "Welcome home." They felt right.

– Chapter 26 –

BRILLIANT SUNSHINE STREAMED THROUGH THE east windows of the little cottage. Matthew yawned and stretched enjoying the sense of returning health and energy. The doctors had told him it would be a long road back, but he could feel his body getting stronger and his mind settling and clearing.

He showered long and did some yoga stretches in the fresh air out on his porch before crossing over to what he still was calling Jonas's house.

Nell had already been down to the harbor and had some kind of fish chowder simmering on the stove. Katie, wearing workout shorts and t-shirt, had just returned from a run on the beach and was doing some cool-down stretches in front of the big window in the living room. Bruce Springsteen's "Glory Days" was coming through a pair of speakers loud and clear and she didn't hear Matthew come in.

"Good morning, Katie," he shouted to be heard over Springsteen. "You're looking bright-eyed and bushy-tailed this morning."

She rewarded him with that dazzling smile he'd dreamed of all those lonely weeks in the hospital. "So are you. What's got you all fired up this morning?"

Following her gesture, Matthew went over and turned the volume down. "Being here. Seeing you first thing in the morning."

Nell came in tying her apron around her middle which, though still ample, looked a bit more trim than before she left on the trip with Katie. "How'd you sleep?"

"I don't know. I was asleep. I don't remember," he said with a teasing grin.

"By the looks of you and your antics this morning I'd say you got a good rest." She was grinning and went over and gave him a squeeze. "So now what can I fix you for breakfast? I've got some of those blueberries left over that didn't fit in last night's pie. You want blueberry pancakes? And a honeydew maybe? How's that? And coffee?"

"Sounds perfect," Matthew said. "You and Katie going to have some too?"

"Katie is, but I ate long ago. Been down to the harbor and back and soon's I get the pancakes made and the sheets out on the line I'll have to be getting the chowder ready to deliver."

"I'll make the pancakes, Ma. And we'll put the sheets out for you too after we eat. You do whatever else you have to do." Katie untied the apron from Nell's waist and put it on her own.

Matthew saw Nell's contented smile and he winked at her behind Katie's back. She winked back and picked up one of the chowder pots to put it in her car.

After breakfast Matt and Katie cleaned up the kitchen, hung the sheets out to dry and then went up into the attic to see how many boxes of Jonas's things were still to be sorted through. They carried two down to the living room where they sat on the floor and worked well into the afternoon putting things in carton boxes which they'd labeled "Princeton," "Family," and "Recycle."

Finally, mid afternoon Matthew sat up straight and stretched his arms over his head. "Ahhh-gggh, let's go for a walk." He got up and grabbed Katie's hand, pulling her up too. They each picked an apple out of the basket on the kitchen table as they passed it and let the screen door slam behind them.

They followed the path behind the dunes down to the deserted beach far below and when they got there they took off their sneakers and both started to run to the water's edge like a pair of playful kids. Splashing where it was only ankle deep, Katie squealed from the icy cold of it and Matthew began chasing her, pretending he was going to dunk her. It didn't take much running for him to catch her and when he did, he kissed her laughing mouth and held her tight to him. She stopped laughing and hungrily kissed him back.

"Ah, it's good to be with you again, Katie." His lips were on her ear and his warm breath sent shivers all over her.

"I'm glad you're here, Matthew," she whispered as his lips found hers again.

They started walking, arms around each other's waist, hips bumping against each other as they moved along.

"So what about your work, Kate? Any assignments on the near horizon?"

"I've got one coming up in about three weeks. I have to check out three new all-inclusive golf resorts, one in Texas and two in Alabama on the Gulf. A 'Golf on the Gulf' kind of thing. And later, one up in British Columbia. I should only be gone about ten days. Then I don't have anything lined up for another few weeks after that."

"And what about Ian, Kate? What's happening with him?"

"I told him a couple of nights ago that I don't want to move to Boulder with him. He wasn't too happy about that. He's used to getting his own way. So he's coming here Thursday so we can talk it through."

"Do I have any input?" Matthew stopped walking and turned her to face him.

"Yes, of course you do."

"Don't go, Katie. Stay here. Give us a chance. It's true we're just getting to know each other, but what I'm feeling for you right now is pretty strong and I'd like us to have some time to see if you feel the same way."

"Right now I do, Matt."

"Then we need time to just get to know each other better and better and to see if we still feel this way a month from now, six months from now. Do you agree?"

"I couldn't agree more," Katie said. "and to tell you the truth, I'm relieved to hear you say that. When I thought you had gone back to Annaleise, I felt awful. She's so gorgeous and sophisticated and she was being so sweet to you. I thought you fell in love with her all over again."

"That will never happen, Katie. Yes, she is beautiful and sophisticated. But she's also cold, calculating, and mean. I couldn't live with her back then and I sure as hell wouldn't be able to now. But I have to tell you, when I heard you were seeing Ian again, I felt awful too. It sounds like he's very successful and has a good future ahead of him and I thought you might be swept off your feet again the way you told me you were the first time around with him."

"At first I was tempted. I thought you were back with Annaleise and Ian was being very attentive and nice. But it didn't take long for his true colors to show again. Matt, he's just too overbearing and self-centered for me. I can't deal with that."

"—So we're going to give us a chance? We're going to find out if we can stand each other for more than a couple of days at a time?"

"You've got it. Let's go for it."

"Yea, babe. Let's go for it—all the way." Matthew threw both arms around her, spun her around, tackled her and they both landed on the sand.

"Now Wait A Minute," she managed to shout as she was laughing and fighting back. "Not so fast, Mister." She played along with him, pretending to fight him off.

"Ohhh, you're taking advantage of a weak man." Matthew lay back pretending to be outdone. "I surrender—for now."

Still laughing and breathless they got up, held hands again and walked on, letting the promise hang in the air, tantalizing them.

They walked far before turning back and when they'd almost reached the steps up to the house that Matthew had climbed with Jonas that first day, he led Katie over to the bench where he'd sat with the old man.

They watched the seagulls riding the waves out beyond the breakers, their earlier exuberance settling into a peaceful and contented companionship.

"Have you been walking in the woods since you returned, Katie?" Matthew asked.

"No. I've thought about it, but I have to admit that I feel kind of creepy when I think of going back in there now." She unconsciously moved closer to him on the bench and his arm went up and around her, resting on her shoulders, his fingers playing with the collar of her shirt.

"I'm going to go back there in a couple of days. Will you go with me?"

"Yes, Matt, it should be easier with you there."

They sat for awhile, each lost in their own thoughts of what lay waiting for them in the cabin, then made their way slowly up the steps to the house and worked again on Jonas's things until it was time to help Nell start supper.

Matthew left them early and went back to the cottage to call Nick. He knew Jason and Luke were going to be there with some other kids discussing a possible Habitat for Humanity trip in July to Appalachia where they'd meet with two adult Habitat groups to help build three houses.

As soon as the phone started to ring, it was answered and he recognized Luke's voice. "Hey, Luke. It's me. Dad."

"Hey, Jase, it's Dad. Hi Dad, how're you doing?" Luke began and then ran on non-stop with every little detail of his life in the two days since Matthew left. Finally he handed the phone over to Jason who, always more laid back than his brother, had a more adult-like conversation with his father.

"Mom's being awful nice lately. She even brought up our trip to Cape Cod," Jason said. "She brought her new boyfriend home last night. Some guy named William. A real nerd. She said since we're going to be leaving her alone over Christmas she was thinking about going to the Caribbean with William for a month or so. She was even talking about getting us new wardrobes to take to the Cape."

Matthew chuckled. "Jase, you don't need wardrobes here. Jeans and sweatshirts and a good warm jacket will do you just fine. Tell her that."

Nick got on the phone after the boys were through and told him, "This house is dead without you, man. Silent. I may have to come up with the boys when they come."

"Hey, Nick, that would be great. Why don't you? What a great idea. You could even save me a bundle by driving them up here. And it would be great having you here for Christmas with us. Do it, buddy. Don't spend Christmas alone in that house or visiting with your sister and that husband of hers and those bratty kids. Come be with real crazy people, not moderately crazy ones."

"You know, I might do that. Let me think on it awhile." Nick stopped talking for a few seconds then said, "Okay. I thought about it. I'm coming."

"Woo-eee. We're going to be jammed up here in this cottage, but it's going to be fun. This old place will need a complete overhaul when we're done. And you've got to plan to stay the month because that's when they're going back."

"Can't do that, buddy," Nick said. "I can't take that much time away from work, but I'll definitely do a week up there with you guys. Then I'll come back up after a month to get them and we can hang out again. How's that?"

"It you can't stay the month, then that's second best." Matthew was already out of his chair pacing the room, planning who would sleep where. "Tell the boys while I'm on the phone."

He heard Nick's rumbling voice and then heard all hell break loose. The kids were thrilled. So was he.

– Chapter 27 –

"Well, looks like we're about finished," Nell said as she wrapped packing tape around the edges of the last boxes lined up on the living room floor. On Wednesday Matthew took three sealed and addressed cartons of Jonas's papers to the post office to be mailed to Princeton. Katie delivered four boxes of his clothes to the Thrift Shop in Harwich and Nell folded the tops in on the boxes marked "Family" and carried them up to the attic.

When Matthew returned from the post office he saw Katie looking cautiously into Jonas's bedroom. When he got closer, he saw Nell was standing in there looking bereft. "I really miss the old grouch," she said, tears filling her eyes. "Hard to believe he's really gone. He was such a presence."

"He sure was that," Katie agreed. "And then some!"

Sitting on the edge of the bed, Nell smiled fondly and Matthew wondered if she was also remembering what a trial Jonas was sometimes.

"Come in both of you," she said. "Sit down. I want to talk something over with you."

Matthew sat off to the side on the window seat and Katie sank into Jonas's old leather recliner and pulled the handle to bring up the footrest. "What's up, Ma?" she asked.

"I've been waiting for the right time to tell you and this seems like it." Nell pulled a tissue from her jeans pocket, dried her eyes and sat up straighter. "Guess it's best to tell you straight out instead of pussy-footing. Tom and I are going to move in together. His place. In Gloucester."

Katie was quiet and Matthew could tell she had never thought of her mother being any place but right there.

"I'm happy for you, Ma, but…"

"But what, Katie m'girl?"

"But…" Tears were threatening. "But why Gloucester? Why doesn't he come down here?"

"We did talk about that, Katie. We did. But he's got a big family and they're all up there. And all his friends and fishing cronies. He's built a good life for himself in Gloucester. And what do I have here, Katie? You sometimes when you're not traveling, but now that Granddaddy is gone, I have no other family. And I don't really call the guys at the harbor or the restaurant cooks my friends. Don't you see, girl? This is my chance to finally have a big family and lots of friends, to have a life."

Katie got out of the chair, went over to the bed and put both arms around her mother. "I'm sorry I reacted that way, Ma. I'm really happy for you and I do understand what you're saying. I want all that for you too and I'm glad you're grabbing at the chance for it. I was just being selfish. All I was thinking about was that you wouldn't be here whenever I want to come and be with you.

"But I'll be about the same distance away from Boston when I'm up there as I am when I'm down here on the Cape. I thought about that too because I want to be able to see you as much as you can get away."

"When is this going to happen, Ma?"

"Soon. I told him I wanted to get everything sorted out here, make decisions about the house and all that. The house is yours, Katie. You know that, don't you?"

"Mine? What do you mean? How come?"

"Well it will be yours about this time next week. Granddaddy left it to me in his Will and I've told the lawyers to make up a new Deed and put it all in your name."

Katie looked overwhelmed. "Why, Ma?"

"I won't be needing it anymore and you're the next generation. Seems only fittin'. What do you think, Matthew? Am I right?

Matthew had been sitting over on the window seat not saying one word, just taking it all in.

"I think it's not going to be the same around here without you, Nell, but I've got to say I'm really happy for you. Tom's a good guy and I'm sure you're going to have a great life with him. And about the house? Yes, I agree with you. You're right that if you have no need of it anymore it should go to Katie. I know Jonas would want it that way. She was the apple of his eye."

Katie, still looking bewildered, was gazing back and forth between them as they spoke. "It's just so much all at once," she said. "You know how much I love this house, Ma. I have to admit I always thought someday, years from now, I would probably inherit it. But never did I dream it would be just given to me, and now while I'm this age and have years to enjoy it. Oh, Ma, I will take such good care of it. You know I will."

"Yes, I know you will." Nell stood and Katie got up with her. They stood looking at each other and then suddenly, it was hard to tell who moved first, they wrapped their arms around each other in a rocking hug, both of them laughing and even crying a little.

When they separated, Katie twirled around, arms outstretched. "My house. This is going to be MY house." She grabbed Matthew's hands and pulled him up. Swinging their arms, she said, "and you're going to be staying in MY cottage! Better watch out, I may turn out to be a wicked old landlady."

"And I may turn out to be an incorrigible old tenant." They all left the bedroom laughing and lighthearted.

"This calls for a celebration," Nell said. "Let's break into granddaddy's stash of single-malt Scotch. You know where he keeps it don't you Matthew? In the linen closet in his bedroom. He used to like what he called 'a nip or two' before he went to bed every night.

"Katie, you get the good glasses down from over the fridge and I'll cut up some of that sharp cheese and get some other stuff."

Now what am I going to do, Matthew wondered. They know I had 'an alcohol problem' but I doubt if 'alcoholic' even enters their minds when they think of me because they've only known me since I've been sober.

He brought the bottle of Glenlivet in from the back of the house, poured three glasses and built a fire in the big fireplace.

The sun was sinking lower in the autumn sky and the fire cast a rosy glow in the room. Nell had been simmering a beef stew all afternoon and the aroma, mixed with the wood smoke, lulled them.

"So why aren't you going to marry Tom instead of just moving in?" Katie asked her mother.

"Don't want to yet. Scared I guess. Scared that tying him to me will make him want to be free of me."

"Ma, he's not Dad Vinerelli. He's Tom and he loves you."

"I know, honey. Maybe someday. Maybe even someday soon. I know his sisters want it to happen. They're already planning a big party for when I come up there. They want to introduce me to everybody. That might be a good time to do it. We'll see. But if I do, I'll plan it for when you're not traveling, that's for sure. And what're you going to do? Stay here for the time being, Katie?"

"For the time being and for all time, Ma. I can work from here just as well as I can in Boston. This is the age of telecommunicating, thank God. I'll be able to sit here in my nightshirt and watch the sun come up in the morning as I write my stories. Can't beat that."

Nell turned to Matthew. "Whatever deal you made with Jonas has been all right with me all along and…"

"And it's all right with me, too," Katie chimed in. "You can stay in the cottage as long as you want to. I'll be glad to have a guy close by for when things need doing—that'll be your rent. Okay?"

"Sounds pretty good to me, but I'll think it over." Matthew picked up the Scotch bottle and topped off Nell and Katie's glasses. No one had noticed he hadn't touched his own.

"Any more of this and we'll all be three sheets to the wind. Better go dish up the stew," Nell said, rising unsteadily aiming for the kitchen.

"This is it for me too," Katie told Matthew as she emptied her glass. I don't want to have a hangover when Ian arrives here tomorrow."

"Oh, damn. I forgot he's coming tomorrow." Matthew put his full glass on the ray next to hers and when Katie looked surprised he said, "I have to keep a clear head in case I have to come over here and rescue you from his clutches."

Supper was a fun time for them that night with Nell revealing some of he details of her romance with Tom, even admitting that the night she'd told Katie she was meeting Tom's sisters in Boston and spending the night with them there, that it was Tom she'd met and spent the night with.

"Oh yea, Ma?" Katie teased. "How was it?"

"None of your business girl," Nell said, trying to look stern but grinning in spite of herself.

They cleaned up the kitchen and when Matthew said he was going to go over to the cottage and spend the evening writing, Katie picked up the garbage and recyclables and walked out the door with him.

He switched on light on when they got inside and went over and put a match to the kindling already laid under the logs in the fireplace.

Katie sat on the hearth to watch the flames and he sat next to her and put his arm around her, pulling her to him. "So you're going to be my landlady, huh?" He was nuzzling her ear and when she turned to get closer to him, they tumbled onto the floor.

"Yup. And are you going to be my handyman?"

"I'll be he handiest man you've ever known," he said moving his hands up under her shirt while he kissed her long, lingering on her lips, her neck, her ears.

"Hmmmmm, sounds like I'm going to be thinking up lots of jobs for you."

"You won't have to think any up. These hands will know just what needs to be done." One hand was rubbing her back and the other he brought slowly around, slipping his fingers inside her bra in search of her nipple.

Their kissing became more passionate. "I want you so bad, Katie," he whispered hoarsely.

"I know. I can feel it." Katie wiggled her hips and pushed her pelvis against him playfully. "But not tonight, Matthew. Not when I've got Ian coming in the morning and am thinking about what I'm going to say to him."

Matthew lay back staring into the fire, trying to make himself focus on the flames licking around the logs instead of the heat in his own body. He turned and saw Katie watching him, saw the desire on her face too.

"I want you too, Matthew. Don't think my body isn't screaming at me right now too." Her voice was husky and she kissed him tenderly on the lips. "But I've got to deal with this Ian thing first. I know you're probably thinking it's crazy, but it's me. It's how I do things. I need to end one thing completely before I can start something new. Please try to understand."

"I'll try, Katie. My head might understand, but there are other parts that I guarantee you will be pissed off—if you'll pardon the pun."

She smacked him on the arm. "You're no better than a teenage boy."

"Yea, a teenage boy with hormones charging all over the place."

"Well put them on hold a couple of days. Give them a rest and I'll re-charge them again really good." She got up, straightened her clothes and ran her fingers through her mop of hair. "Maybe you and I can do an overnight in Boston like Ma and Tom did."

"I was thinking about that. Tom's a good twenty, twenty-five years older than I am and he got lucky before I did. Ain't fair."

"I'll make it up to you in spades." Katie opened the door to leave.

"You'd better, woman." They kissed lightly, he gave her a light smack on her bottom and she left laughing.

Matthew closed the door. "If I'm going to be kidded about being like a teenage boy, I might as well act like one," he said out loud as he headed straight for the bathroom.

– Chapter 28 –

When light finally started creeping around the edges of his bedroom shades the next morning, Matthew sat up, checked his watch, then burrowed down under the covers again. But sleep was going to continue to elude him as it had done most of the night. He got up and started to pull the shade up on his front window but decided against it. He might see Ian. Worse yet, he might see Ian with Katie.

He made coffee, burned his tongue on it and dumped it in the sink. He scoured the kitchen sink within an inch of its life; he gathered up every piled-up newspaper, brochure and magazine he could find and set them ablaze in the fireplace. He tried to write; started sorting through pictures he'd taken looking for something that would inspire him to start a painting. All this with eyes averted from the shade-covered windows.

Finally, he decided to go to work out at the gym. He'd been putting off going there since his return because he didn't feel up to talking about the accident to his racquetball friends.

Damn, if Jonas had been the recluse I thought him to be at the beginning, I wouldn't have to deal with this now, but it was in all the papers and anybody there is going to want all the gory details, he thought as he started rooting around for his gym clothes and stuffing them in his bag. Cursing Jonas for dying, he got undressed and started to get in the shower.

"What the hell am I doing? I shower after I work out, not before." His voice was loud in the little bathroom. He slammed the shower lever to Off and started pulling his boxer shorts back on, pulled them off again, crumpled them in a ball and pitched them hard against the far wall. Yanking the bathroom door open, he went to his gym bag and got out the jockeys he always wore for workout and racquetball.

"I don't give a damn if I open the door and find the two of them out there kissing—or screwing, or whatever. What the fuck do I care? I don't want to get mixed up with another woman now anyway." He realized he was grousing out loud, clamped his mouth shut and grabbed his gym bag.

There was a black MG convertible parked by the house all shiny and sleek. Even though the morning was chilly, the top was down showing the dove gray leather seats and dashboard.

Figures. Of course he'd have a car like that. Of course he'd come tooling in here with the top down so she'd see what a cool guy he is. Matthew got in his dusty Forester, made a fast K-turn and started speeding down Singer Lane. When he reached the first curve, he pulled over and stopped.

I'm acting like a goddamn kid, he thought. First I'm pissed off at Jonas because he didn't survive my driving and now I'm furious with Katie because some other guy is in love with her.

He sat there a long time thinking, trying to convince himself he hadn't fallen in love with her too. He sat there until he thought he heard car doors slamming back at the house and, not wanting to be found there parked and sulking, he took off in a hurry.

As it turned out, three of his racquetball buddies were at the club when he arrived. He braced himself for what was ahead, but they were really good about it. Each welcomed him back with a handshake and a "Sorry to hear what happened" or a pat on the back, but no one asked a question except, "When're you gonna be able to hit the ball around with us again?"

He figured it would be another two or three weeks, but in the meantime he said he'd be there working out on racquetball days.

"Good," Charlie said. "Come and watch us—maybe you'll learn how the pros play." Matt laughed with them as they went into the court and shut the door and he went to the workout room.

He lingered as long as he could at the club, then drove down to Rock Harbor and sat in his car watching people walking their dogs on the rocks, watching the white-haired women in their brightly colored sweat suits out for a brisk walk, watching the gulls circle overhead.

He managed to stay away from the house most of the day by driving o Harwich for lunch at The Stewed Tomato where he used to read the paper and have breakfast every morning and then by stopping in at the Thrift Shop to check out the bookshelves and by visiting with Mrs. Post the nice elderly lady who was his next-door neighbor when he'd lived there in what seemed like a lifetime ago.

Around three o'clock he decided this was nonsense. He'd drive back and if he ran into them, so be it.

The car was still there when he returned, but someone had put the black cloth top up on it. He allowed himself to glimpse at the house but he saw no sign of life. As soon as he got into his cottage he checked the answering machine, saw there were no messages waiting and he went right to the bedroom and got in bed. He was drained—from both the workout and his own inner turmoil.

⁕

When he awoke the cottage was dark. As he pulled down his shades, he could see lights on in the house across the way but he couldn't tell if the car was still there or not. Not wanting to put the outside light on or open his door so he could see, he pulled the rest of the shades down, turned NPR on the radio and tried to concentrate on All Things Considered as he heated up a can of Campbell's tomato soup.

Just as he was about to pour it into a bowl, the phone rang. "I've been waiting for you to wake up over there." It was Katie's voice. "I've been watching for signs of activity. Ma made some good oyster stew today in case Ian stayed for supper, but he left in a snit. How about if I bring it over there? Have you eaten yet?"

"No. Just finished heating up some tomato soup and was about the start on it."

"Good, that can be our appetizer. Shall I come over?"

"Yea, come on. Hurry up." Matthew knew he wouldn't have been able to keep the happiness out of his voice if he tried.

He went out to meet her halfway and took the heavy cast iron stewpot from her. She ran back inside and grabbed the French bread and the bottle of wine she'd set by the kitchen door.

She was last into his cottage and bumped the door closed with her behind. He took the bread and the wine from her and put them on the counter. And they both just stood looking at each other. Even though she'd said Ian left in a snit, he was afraid to ask the questions he needed to have answered, afraid of what the answers might be. So his eyes searched her face for clues in those few seconds of waiting.

"I told him, Matt. I told him it's over and I won't be going with him."

Matthew felt a warm happiness rising up and enveloping him. He reached out for her and they held each other in a wordless embrace for a long loving time.

"I'm so happy to hear that, Kate." He was talking into her hair, holding her almost impossibly tight and they were just rocking side to side.

"And I'm so relieved," she said. "I feel like I've come out from under a massive weight."

He gave her another big squeeze and held her at arm's length grinning from ear to ear. "And now, woman, let's celebrate. Bread, wine, oyster stew and you!"

"And you," she said rising up on tiptoe to kiss him lightly on the lips.

"So do you want to tell me anything about how it went today? Matthew asked as he poured the wine and turned the gas on under the stew to warm it.

"It didn't go well from the minute he arrived." Getting bowls down from the cupboard, Katie paused with one in each hand. "He's just so fake. I don't know why it took me so long to see that. His arrival was so staged—the little sports car, the top down, him wearing a tweed jacket with a muffler wrapped around his neck and that dumb checkered wool cap that he thinks is so British and cool. Ma and I saw him coming and we broke up. He looked so foolish.

Matthew, feeling better all the time, ladled stew into each bowl, Katie cut the bread and they sat across from each other at the little table and began eating.

Katie sipped her wine but Matthew was so intent on drinking in her presence and all she was saying, his glass remained untouched, unnoticed by either of them.

"He didn't want to hang around the house. He doesn't like Ma much. She's a little too "salt of the earth" for his refined tastes. So I took him down to the beach for a walk. Well he didn't like that either. He didn't have sneakers with him and the sand was getting into his tassel loafers. Will you tell me something, Matt? Why would a guy wear good woolen dress pants and tassel loafers when he's coming to spend a day at a beach house?"

She didn't wait for Matthew's answer. "So we came back to the house and I put some decent slacks and a nice sweater on too and suggested we go to Trees Place and a few of the other upscale galleries. In fact, we left right after you did. I was in the kitchen and saw you bolt out of here and take off. Believe me, I had all I could do to not run out, flag you down, and jump in with you.

"So we did the galleries-on-the-Cape thing and then went to Chillingworth's for lunch. He liked that well enough but every time I tried to bring up our relationship he changed the subject. It was as if I would be going with him and he didn't want to have any discussion to the contrary.

"When we got back here he started laying out his plan—that I'd pack what I needed and the rest could be shipped out to us later. I'd drive back with him tonight and we'd leave Saturday morning. He's so damned self centered he never even asked if those arrangements were okay with me. When I told him Ma wouldn't be back until late tonight, he said that would be okay, I could call her from his place to say goodbye. I'm supposed to move hundreds of miles away and say goodbye to my mother in a phone call from his place? Like, 'Hi Ma, I just thought I'd tell you I probably won't be seeing you for several months. I'm moving across the country with Ian. Bye. Have a good life.' I can't believe this guy."

Matthew, listening intently, said nothing.

"So I told him I had no intention of going with him, that I wished him luck with his new life out there but I didn't want to be part of it. He looked shocked. Then I was shocked that he was shocked. But I tried to end it on a friendly note. I asked him to stay for supper and 'you know what he said? 'You don't want to be part of my life and I don't want to be part of any supper you and your *Ma* made.' He was real nasty. He got his hat and scarf from the coat rack in the hall, walked out the door without another word and left. And I felt a wonderful sense of relief."

Matthew reached across the table and put his hand over hers. "And you'll never know how relieved I am too,

Kate," he said. "I've been a mess all day just knowing he was here and wondering what your final decision would be. I kept myself away all day. I even went to have a cup of tea with old Mrs. Post in Harwich so I wouldn't have to come back here. And I went and parked at Rock Harbor…"

"I know," Katie interrupted. "I saw you there. I was trying to fill up the day to make time pass faster and had him drive there thinking he'd like seeing the fishing boats coming in. I saw you sitting in your car. Thought maybe you were sketching."

"No, not sketching. Trying to fill up the day and not think about you. Where were you? I didn't see you."

"When I saw your car I told him the boats were already in and we should just go back to the house. He didn't even notice all the slips were still empty. He didn't like it there anyway."

They'd finished eating and were sitting back sipping the instant coffee Matthew had come up with while she talked.

"Come over here, girl," he said pushing his chair back and patting his thighs.

She settled herself sideways on his lap and put both arms around his neck. They kissed, sweet and soft at first, then more passionately.

"Shall we go back to where we were last night by the fire?" Matt's lips were still on hers.

"Hell no," she said laughing. "The floor's too hard and drafty. I want to get in your bed with you under that wonderful down comforter Ma brought over for you."

"Hmmmmm, I'm glad I had that nap today." Matt was still kissing her—her lips, her eyelids, her ears, her neck.

"Why do you think I let you sleep so long before call-ing you?" She got up and, taking him by the hand, led him into the bedroom.

He undressed her slowly, kissing every part of her body as he took off each piece of clothing. The room was chilly and when he felt her shiver, he threw back the comforter and sheet for her to slip under. His clothes were off in a flash and when they were beside her, pulling the comforter up over both of them. Immediately, they were in each other's arms, legs wrapped around each other, hands bring-ing warmth to places on each other's bodies they admitted later they'd imagined touching. And now at last it was real and there was no holding back. No slow pacing. There would be time enough for that later. There was an urgency now that had a life of its own. Katie reached down, felt his hardness and pulled him over on top of her. She was moist and ready and when he slipped inside her it was like an eruption for both of them.

Still holding tight to each other, legs still entwined and Matthew still inside her, they rolled to the side and lay there smiling contentedly at each other.

"You told me last night I'm like a teenager, but you're as bad as I am, Katie Vinerelli. We didn't even have time to tire each other out."

Katie pushed her pelvis even closer to his and wiggled her hips a little. "That's good, because as soon as you re-cover, we're going to do it all over again, only this time it's going to be 'slow and with feeling' as my piano teacher used to say."

"Can we go so slow it'll last all night and into tomor-row?"

"Mmmmm, definitely all night. I left a note for Ma telling her if she needs me for anything she can call me over here. That's going to make her happy. She's been hoping for this for a long time, even when we were on the cruises. She always talked you up. You won her over right from the start."

"And have I won her daughter over?"

"Right from the start, Matt," Katie said, tenderly kissing his lips.

"I love you, Katie Vinerelli. So much." He smoothed her tousled hair back from her cheek and kissed her where it had been.

"You know when I fell in love with you?" she asked, raising up on one elbow. "The night we talked on the phone when I was in France and you told me what Davy had written in Nancy's journal. I knew then that you're a man capable of deep love like that. I'm that way too and I've wanted to share that kind of love with you ever since."

"We will, Katie my love. We are already."

They lay there talking softly together, sometimes shifting positions slightly, but always in each other's arms. They talked about the first time they met on Singer Lane and as he fondled her breast he told her how good she'd looked in that white t-shirt. She confessed she'd often watched him from her window as he walked away from her because she loved his broad shoulders and "this" she said as she ran her hand over his buttocks. "You've got the sexist bum and it's just as smooth as I pictured it."

"You pictured my bare butt?" It was Matthew's turn to rise up on one elbow and look down at her.

"Yup, that and a few other things." She laughed and pulled him down next to her again.

"I'll be damned—the woman of my dreams!"

They talked and played like that for a good long time. Then Matthew asked, "You hungry? Want a drink of something?" Something to eat?"

He got out of bed and got one of his flannel shirts for her and another for himself. "Sorry I don't have a bathrobe for you."

Their plates were on the table, cold coffee in mugs. On the stove the oyster stew had cooled to room temperature. Matthew got out a jar, poured what was left in it and put it in the refrigerator so they could have it the next day.

Katie put the dishes in the sink, ran cold water over them and left them for morning.

Standing side by side leaning against the counter, they drank cranberry juice and munched on cashews that were still sitting out from earlier. Matthew looked at the Campbell's soup can and the soup gone cold in the pan and thought it looked like it was from another lifetime.

He put his arm around Katie's shoulders. "I'm not even going to ask where we go from here, Katie. This feels like a rest-of-my-life love."

"I know. I feel the same way, Matt. Let's not weight it down with questions, let's just let it soak into us.

He turned her to him, slipping his hands inside her shirt. He held one breast in each hand, looking down at them as if they were priceless gifts. He bent and kissed each nipple tenderly and then let his hands slip down over her hips and held each hand on one round cheek.

"You're not the only one who's been checking out butts, you know. I've been lusting after yours every time you wear those washed out jeans or those little white shorts of yours. Been driving me crazy."

"Oh yeah? Tell me how else I drive you crazy." She was running her tongue across his lips as he talked.

"How about let's get back in bed and I'll show you," he said.

This time they slowly explored each other's bodies, tasting, nibbling as they went. They found new ways of touching, new ways of moving together that delighted them both. Over and over again they spoke of the love welling up between them and of how beautifully tender and yet how powerful it felt. And finally when Matthew entered her they moved together languorously, slowing their movements to savor what was happening until simultaneously, almost by mutual consent, their passion swelled and mounted and they moved together in perfect rhythm to a climax they both said later was even sweeter, more delicious than the last time.

Again, they rolled together to one side and, still entwined, they eventually fell asleep.

– Chapter 29 –

MATTHEW WAS A LITTLE EMBARRASSED but Katie didn't seem to be the next morning when they walked into the kitchen of the main house where Nell was busy working at the stove. But Nell immediately put them all at ease.

"Good morning, you two. Want some breakfast?" She acted as if it were just another ordinary morning.

"No thanks, Ma. We had some Wheaties over at the cottage while we cleaned up from last night's supper," Katie said. "That oyster stew was excellent."

"Thanks, honey. I'm glad you two got to enjoy it. And I'm glad that stuffed shirt is out of the picture. He *is* out of the picture, isn't he? For good?"

"He sure is, Ma."

"Good." Nell poured the last of the clam chowder she'd been making into the container and snapped the lid down tight. "Gotta get this down to Chatham Bars Inn. They wanted all I could give them today. Got some kind of special thing going on with all the big politicians coming to talk about how their campaigns are going. I forget which party they are, but as long as they like the chowder, doesn't matter to me."

Matthew helped her pack the containers in the cases she had built in her SUV where the last seat had been.

"I'll be gone a couple of hours, got some other stuff to tend to too. Don't you two wear yourselves out now," she said with a big grin and her eyes twinkling merrily.

"Ma, come on, we're in our forties, remember? We have to pace ourselves," Katie said.

"Why? Tom and I are in our sixties and we say to hell with pacing, that's for the old people." She shifted into drive and gave them a happy wave as she drove away.

⁂

"Well, Katie, what do you think? Is today the day we go to the cabin together?" They'd been standing side by side, arms around each other's waists as they waved good-bye to Nell.

"Yes, I do, Matt. I want to share that with you and today when all this is so new to us seems to be the right time to do it."

NPR's weather report out of Boston predicted a warmer day than they'd been having with a high nearing sixty by afternoon and the day was already starting to warm up as they started walking toward the woods.

Matthew had gotten out his camp lantern and the sack he'd had with him the last day he was there. In it were the pliers, chisel, some candles, and matches he always took with him.

The woods were a canopy of gold, scarlet, orange, yellow, and green. And in areas where some sun could peek through, bittersweet vines were heavy with the red berries just starting to break through their yellow shells. They walked through the underbrush until they picked up the sound of the brook, then they followed along the stony embankment.

They'd started off talking with one another, but after they found the stream and began following it, neither spoke except for a soft-spoken, "careful here, it's slippery," or "here, duck under this branch."

When they got to the flat rocks that Matthew now knew Davy had laid as steps down to the water for Nancy, Matthew gestured toward them and Katie remembered what he'd told her. She looked around uneasily, remembering also that this is the spot where Rev. Heady had badgered Nancy calling her a heathen. She imagined him in his black coat and hat lurking in the underbrush and then bursting out of it yelling at Nancy when she arrived to wash some clothes.

She shuddered and reached for Matthew's hand.

"You all right?" he asked. "Sure you want to do this today?"

She looked at him wide eyed, nodded and they went on. When they got to the cabin, Katie didn't even see it at first. The vines had covered it and the trees around it were a glorious blaze of color and she thought of nature and life cycles and of how Nancy had blossomed but was never allowed to come to a full ripening.

Standing back, she watched Matthew pry open the boards he'd nailed in place the last time. He pushed on the door and it swing easily into the cabin. He reached out and took her hand, but she stood rooted to the spot.

"It's okay, love. Nothing can hurt you here. I need you to share this with me so together we can decide what to do about it. Please come, Katielove."

Letting his genuineness overcome her fear, Katie stepped inside with him.

The first thing she saw was the poker lying next to the black stain on the floor. Matthew had told her he hadn't altered anything there, but somehow she wasn't prepared for that.

She gasped and took a step back, but Matthew, still holding her hand, led her gently in.

She saw the chairs by the fireplace with the stuffing spilled onto the floor and she walked over to see the sampler that hung there. Matthew took it down off its nail and handed it to her. As she admired the fine needlework and as she looked at the family picture, Matthew took down from the mantle to show her, her eyes kept going to the door on the other side of the room with its broken padlock.

Matthew went with her as she walked around the small room looking at the dishes and pots in the cupboard and then over to the little table by the window where the plates were still set for supper and the journal was lying there.

She opened the journal and seeing Nancy's delicate script faded to brown, reading a few of her words, tears finally came to Katie's eyes. Then she turned the pages forward until she saw Davy's emotional hand. Heavy. Dark. Full of pain. She knew from Matthew what was written there but still she read, "…I brushed my Nancy's hair." "…I held her close to warm her as her body grew cold." "…I go now."

Katie's tears flowed fully and silently and Matthew stood with her, his arm around her shoulders as she leaned over the table and read. She looked up into his eyes.

"I'm ready now," she whispered. And together they went to the bedroom door.

As it swung open, Katie didn't look around at the closet or the far window or the chair next to the bed. Her eyes went right to the bed itself and then as they became adjusted to the dim light, they fell and rested on the skull with the rotting quilt pulled up under its chin.

She turned and looked at Matthew. He was watching her to make sure she was all right. She took her hand from his and went over and stood next to the bed. She was not afraid, not repulsed. She was deeply moved by what she saw and by what, from Davy's words, she'd come to know. She saw the decaying covers on Davy's side of the bed turned back as he'd left them when he arose that next morning and she pictured him lying there through the night whispering words of love to his dead wife.

After experiencing what she did last night and this morning with Matthew, the profound love they shared, she had an understanding of this woman who had been Nancy and her loving young husband that she might not have otherwise had.

Matthew stood silently at her side and when she reached for his hand it was right there. They stood together looking down on the skull that was, to them, not a skull but the remains of what was once a vibrant and lovely young woman.

They stood there quietly, reverently. Then, as if by mutual consent, they stepped back from the bed.

Kate's eyes swept the room and finally rested on a handcrafted cradle on the other side of the bed. Seeing how Nancy and Davy were already preparing for the birth of their child so early in the pregnancy saddened her more than she expected.

"These people were real. They lived. They lived here. They were in love as you and I are now, Matthew," Katie whispered. "We've got to help them put an end to their story."

"How? What can we do?" Matthew also whispered.

They turned and walked quietly from the room. Matthew closed the door and affixed the broken padlock.

Wanting to stay there to discuss the next step, they went over to the little table and sat one on each side much as Davy and Nancy must have sat in their happy days there.

"We need to find where Davy is buried and take Nancy's remains to him," Katie said.

Matthew leaned forward across the table. "Yes, I've been thinking of going to New Bedford to search the records and see if we can find him."

"Let's do it, Matthew. Soon."

"Yes, I feel strongly the time has come to reunite them—and I have this feeling it's my responsibility to do it since I'm the one who stumbled in here."

"Then let's do it as soon as we can." Katie pushed her chair back, got up, went around the table and took his hand. "We'll do this together and that should make it easier," she said.

— *Chapter 30* —

THEY SLEPT CURLED UP IN each other's arms that night, not sexually, but intimately, tenderly, realizing how fragile life is, how easily a loving relationship can be swept away.

And when they awoke in the morning they drew together almost silently, holding each other close, touching, tasting, savoring in a new way, a deeper way, the new love they were beginning. "Just the fact that we're waking up together, alive, healthy, strong, feels like such a precious gift to me," Katie whispered.

"I know, Kate," Matthew said. "a gift Nancy and Davy had torn from them, just ripped away, and for no reason other than one man's crazy obsession."

"What do you think, Matthew, can we drive down to New Bedford today?" Katie asked.

"Yes, I want to. I'll get right on the computer and get some names and places where we can start our search."

As soon as they showered and dressed, they went over to the main house and, while telling Nell about the day before, they poured Corn Flakes into bowls. Katie sliced a banana over each and poured the milk on while Matthew poured coffee into three mugs.

"So we're going to go down to New Bedford today and start searching," Katie told her mother.

"Good," Nell said. "I agree. We can't let that girl lie up there by herself any longer. Suppose someone else finds the cabin? That would be awful. The sooner the better."

❧

It took no time at all for Katie and Matthew to pick up Davy's trail. There was still a whole clan of Nadeaus living in New Bedford and some of the men were still commercial fishermen.

They tracked down the patriarch of the rambling clan, John Nadeau, now eighty-two years old and living alone in the original family homestead. He remembered his mother telling him the sad story of old Uncle Davy who'd died a half dozen years before John was born.

"Some of the old folks knew Uncle Davy. I never did. Born too late," he said. But they'd get to talking about him at family gatherings and I always listened closely to what they said. Always felt kinship to him.

"My mother knew him and always talked about him as hard working, never taking time out to find a woman like the rest of the men did as soon as they got back to port. She said he was married once—a girl from up near Concord or Lexington, but she was killed or something, some real tragedy. He was always sad, my mother said. Never married again.

"Not much else to tell about him. He took care of his father here when the old man was dying. Lingered a long time and Davy took time away from the sea to tend to him. After the old man died, Davy went back to whaling with his brothers and did that until he just couldn't do it anymore. He kept a room here, that room right at the top of the steps there," he said pointing. "That's where he finally died."

Slowly, with a feeling of trust building between them, Matthew told John Nadeau about the cabin and what he found there. He told him about the journal that led them to New Bedford.

"Now it makes sense." John Nadeau shook his head and looked as if something that puzzled him for a long time had just been cleared up.

"He kept a journal every day of his life. Strange for a man. Some women do that, but not a man. Not a whaling man anyway. But he wrote in his journal 'most every night." He got up and pulled a carton box from a closet. "Here they are."

Matthew and Katie were speechless. There were more written words, Davy's words, to complete the story that had just begun to reveal itself to them.

"May we look through them?" Matthew asked.

"Hell, you can take them back with you. Too many to go through here. Just make sure you get them back to me when you're done with them. I've read every word, but maybe someday one of the young Nadeaus may take an interest in them and I want them to stay in the family."

"Of course. We'll respect them and get them back to you." Matthew began tucking the flaps of the cardboard box in and around each other. "But now, can you tell us where Davy's buried?"

"Sure can." John Nadeau opened the door of the wood stove and poked some of the dying embers. "He's in the big family plot in Sacred Heart Cemetery over on Mt. Pleasant Street. His grave is marked. A headstone with a whale on it like his father's and his brothers'. Can't miss his though. It's clearly marked."

Matthew and Katie thanked the old man and, taking the carton of journals with them, they promised to return in a month.

It was a circuitous drive from old John Nadeau's house to the cemetery but, after a few bad turns and two stops at a 7-11 and a gas station for directions, they finally got there. Finding the Nadeau plot was another challenge, but finding Davy's grave was not.

"It makes it all so real." Katie's voice was hushed as they stood reading the headstone.

"David Nadeau, loving husband of Nancy Titus Nadeau," it read and the dates, "Born August 30, 1838. Died June 24, 1913."

"Now I understand the cliché 'carved in stone,'" Matthew said. "Being here, seeing his name and the dates literally carved in stone make it even more real than finding Nancy or reading his entries in her journal. This seems to make it official somehow."

"I agree." Katie took his hand. "And for me, it makes it more imperative to reunite them and put closure on their story."

They left the cemetery and drove back to the Cape and talked over their plan with Nell. She agreed with every step of it.

Matthew made himself wait until 9:30 the next morning to put in a call to Bill Mason, his attorney back in Jersey. After a long catch-up conversation, he outlined what he'd found and what he hoped to do. Bill recommended a Massachusetts attorney, Nathan Haggerty, who'd know the ins and outs of Massachusetts laws.

"He's good," Bill told Matthew. "It sounds like what you plan to do is straightforward, but each state has its own peculiarities about opening graves and Nate'll be able to walk you through the whole thing.

Nathan Haggerty had a slot open a few days later. Katie and Matthew drove to Hyannis to meet with him and by the end of the session they already had things in motion. They took home papers for Nell, as the current property owner, to sign for the removal of Nancy's remains. And they faxed Releases to open the grave in the Nadeau plot to John Nadeau at his son Frank's office.

They heard nothing for a few days and Matthew called John Nadeau to ask if there was a problem.

"Wish you'd never faxed the Release to my son." John Nadeau sounded frustrated. "If he and that wife of his think there might be money made in anything, their antennas go up. He's saying you're a scammer and he's getting a buddy who's a cop to run a check on you."

Matthew slammed his fist against the wall so hard the glasses in the cabinet rattled. "Damn. What can we do, John?"

"Don't worry. Don't worry," John said. "It's a pain in the ass, but he can't stop anything. I own the cemetery plots and I have the final say. Besides, nobody in the family has any time for Louise, that wife of his, and they're pissed at Frankie for bringing her into the family. They'll back me up."

"Well that helps, but now the whole story will get out and the press will have a field day."

"Give me some credit, will you?" John fired back. "Do you think I told him *why* you want to open the grave? Stop and think. The Release doesn't state the reason, just the fact that you want it opened and that there has been full disclosure of intent between both parties and their lawyers."

"And he never asked you why we want to do it?"

"Sure he did."

"What'd you tell him?"

"Told him you're writing a book about whaling out of New Bedford and you came across something that says the real David Nadeau was murdered in a bar fight on the Boston waterfront in 1850 and his killer came here pretending he was Davy because everybody knew the family was making good money whaling. Told him you want to get DNA to prove the story's right."

"That doesn't make sense." Matthew interrupted him. "The brothers would spot the guy as an imposter right away. They'd know he wasn't their brother. The father would know it wasn't his son."

"I know. I know. Give me a chance. I covered all that. Told Frankie that Davy never came home after the War because he was shot up pretty bad in the face and the family knew that. Wasn't true, Davy was never even in the War, but Frankie doesn't know that. Told him you found out this guy was all scarred up in the face too and kind of looked like Davy, built like him too, people said—and he knew a lot about the family and that Davy didn't talk much. So he figured he'd give it a try. Told Frankie the stuff you found about it all said it worked."

"You're quite a storyteller, John. What'd you do, write this all out ahead of time so you'd keep it straight?"

"Didn't need to," John said. "It all just kept coming as I told it."

"Did he buy it?"

"Not at first, but you've gotta understand, Frank's not too smart. And he's greedy. I told him we should let you get the DNA because that'll prove it's Uncle Davy and you'll be on your way. Told him otherwise people might start claiming to be descendants of the imposter and start suing to get some of the family money. Knew that would stop him short. And it did."

"So where do we stand?"

"To appease him I told him to go ahead and check you out. Told him that was good thinking on his part."

"He's not going to find anything," Matthew said tersely.

"I know that. Stick with me. My son may not be too smart, but I am." John Nadeau chuckled. "Told you I read every one of those journals, right? Davy wrote a lot over the years about how Nancy died and how he left her. What you told me matched exactly and there was no way you could have known all those details if you hadn't actually been there and found everything the way he left it. Do you think I'd have let you take the box of journals if I didn't know you were telling the truth? So I figured, let Frank do all the investigating he wants to. It'll keep him busy while we're doing what we have to and, in the end, he'll fell like he covered all bases."

"Gotcha," Matthew said. "So what's next?"

"What's next is to move as quickly as we can to get this done. That Louise'll gnaw at it like a dog with a bone, but if we can satisfy Frankie, he'll get sick of it and tell her to shut up and she'll go off in the corner and sulk for awhile. She'll call her sisters and whine and they'll all agree she made a bad marriage and finally it'll all die down."

"I hope." Matthew shifted the phone to his other ear.

"Don't worry. I know these people—unfortunately," John Nadeau said and they both hung up.

⁂

John Nadeau signed the Release and his lawyers filed the Petitions. If there were no objections filed, the grave could be opened sometime in the next week.

In the meantime, Katie called her friend, Peter Addison, an undertaker in Orleans. When he heard the story, he agreed to remove Nancy's remains from the cabin and inter them in New Bedford as soon as possible.

The judge handed down her decision the next week and the date was set with Peter Addison and the cemetery director. November 28.

Matthew called John Nadeau as soon as he got the word. "How are things there?"

"Well Frankie came by last night with the rundown on you. Biggest thing he found out is you're an alcoholic…"

"Recovering alcoholic. Been through AA and I've been sober for almost three years now," Matthew jumped right in.

"The report showed pretty much that," John said. "They found nothing else against you except a divorce and the fact that you were driving a car when some bigwig got killed down in Princeton. Report showed you were cleared of any wrongdoing."

"All that is right," Matthew said. "So what's your Frank doing with that information?"

"Nothing it seems. He's just quiet about it. I guess he feels kind of sheepish that you didn't turn out to be some fly-by-night scammer."

"Good," Matthew said.

"Well—could be good. I won't rest easy 'til it's a done deed though. With that Louise of his pushing in the background, you never know with him. Can we move fast and get it done?"

"It's set for November 28th. Can you keep him occupied until after that?"

"You know what? I have my annual physical scheduled for that day. Was going to just drive myself to it, but what I'll do is tell him I'm feeling sick and need to talk over some things with the doctor that have been worrying me and wonder if he can be with me. He'll think maybe I'm getting ready to croak and he'll want to go and get the big news first hand. That ought to keep his mind occupied for days before and definitely on that day. After that, who cares, right?"

"Right. Good deal, John. Thanks." Matthew sat and stared into space after he hung up. Two more days....

~ Chapter 31 ~

Peter Addison arrived in his gray Toyota SUV at eight a.m. on a day that was gray and overcast. Not unusual for late autumn on the Cape. They'd discussed logistics beforehand and came to the conclusion that because the cabin was so secluded back in the woods, the only way they could bring Nancy's remains out would be by carrying her in a body bag to Peter's vehicle parked by Jonas's house.

Matthew and Katie led the way for Peter. When they got to the cabin, Matthew pried open the boards he always nailed in place when leaving and he opened the lock as he had been doing each time, but this time he was fighting down strong feelings about the intrusion of this stranger. Peter had wanted to bring an assistant, but Matthew insisted he come alone and that Matthew would assist him.

Fortunately, Peter was a professional and acted like one. It was obvious he was curious, but he asked no questions and that really helped.

Matthew removed the broken padlock from the bedroom door and the three of them entered quietly.

With gestures and only a few words, Peter indicated to Matthew and Katie what they could do to help.

Matthew took hold of the top edge of the quilt on one side and Katie did the same on the other. As they raised it to pull it back, some of it disintegrated into powder. And as they pulled it back, the bones of Nancy's skeleton were revealed, mostly disconnected, but lying in place as Davy had left her. Her legs were turned slightly to the right side, Davy's side of the bed. Her torso was slightly turned also and Matthew and Katie both remembered Davy's written words about having held her through the night.

They watched as Peter meticulously gathered Nancy's bones, making indications in a notebook as he did so. Finally her bones were in the body bag and they watched as Peter gently lifted her skull and placed it in the bag.

The bed was empty.

I know we're doing the right thing, but somehow this feels like a violation, Matthew thought. He looked across the bed at Katie and she looked like she was thinking the same thing.

Without any of them speaking a word, they left the cabin. Matthew boarded it up again and they slowly made their way upstream to Jonas's house and to Peter's waiting vehicle.

Nell came out and stood on the porch as they arrived. Matthew and Katie joined her and silently they watched as Peter put the body bag in the back of the SUV.

They'd picked out a coffin earlier—a white one, child size because that was all that was needed for Nancy's few remains.

Two days later, Matthew, Katie and Nell followed Peter to the New Bedford cemetery. This time Peter was driving a hearse and they could see the casket riding in the back.

Early in their search for Davy, Matthew and Katie had contacted descendants of Nancy's family in Concord. One great-great-niece, Nancy Titus Foster, a great granddaughter of Nancy's sister Priscilla, was very moved by the story of her namesake and asked to be present at the burial. Hers was the third car in the procession. Driving was her husband Joseph and their three-week-old son, David.

The little procession made its way to the gravesite where the grave lay open. John Nadeau had cancelled his doctor's appointment when his son said he couldn't go with him. The old man stood with the others. They had chosen to have no clergy present but, instead, Matthew read excerpts from Nancy's journal in which she'd written about her love of her family and her tender love of Davy.

A car came slowly creeping up the lane and stopped by the small gathering at the gravesite.

"It's Frankie and Louise," John Nadeau whispered to Katie who was standing next to him. "Now I know why he said he couldn't go with me to the doctor's. Don't know how he got wind of this."

Matthew continued his reading, choosing to let Nancy's words dominate her burial scene rather than allow the intrusion of present-day people who didn't know her and had no compassion for how her life had ended.

Matthew read Nancy's last written words and then turned to those of Davy. He ended with Davy's, "I go now."

There were tears in the eyes of those assembled and heads bowed in reverence.

Frank and Louise who obviously had no clue as to what was going on were, luckily, shocked to silence.

Matthew ended the closing ritual hurriedly because of their presence and did so resentfully.

Frank, acting like a significant player in his wife's presence, blustered up to his father.

"What's all this?"

"It's a family burial and it's going to be kept within the family," John Nadeau said.

"A family burial? Who? What family?"

"Quiet now, son. This is not the place. Come back to the house and we'll talk." John Nadeau walked resolutely to the car.

Frank walked up to Matthew and pushed his face in close. "I'm going to get to the bottom of this. Now." He strode angrily to his car with Louise marching right behind him, her spike heels ramming into the soft sod of Nadeau graves.

"If I didn't like John Nadeau so much, I'd get a good laugh out of that performance. They're like comic strip characters," Matthew said.

❦

Matthew Katie, Nell and Nancy's great-great niece and her family decided to go to the diner down on the highway near John Nadeau's house to give him time alone with his son. When they saw Frank and Louise's car pull out into the highway when it left John's house, Matthew paid the check and they left.

"Well you won't have any more trouble from them." John Nadeau answered their knock with a smile. "I told him if he started anything, he was out of the Will. That's talking a language they both understand."

John welcomed them in and they sat comfortably in his living room. "I gave him the true story though, Matthew. Thought it better that way now that the deed is done. Told him Uncle Davy's wife's body was found and I wanted her buried with him. That's all there is to it. Told him I didn't let on to him earlier because I knew he and Louise would turn it into some money-grabbing fiasco and for Uncle Davy's sake I didn't want that. Nor will I abide it after the fact. Told them it's done now and there's been no skin off their backs, no money out of their pockets. Told them there's not to be one word of it beyond this family and, if there is, he's out of my Will. Then I told him to take his wife and run along, that I needed to have them away from me today. When he heard the big "W" word mentioned, he told Louise to shut up, pulled her out of the chair and out the door so fast…!"

"But I need to remind you that I'm in the process of writing a book about Davy and Nancy," Matthew said quickly.

"I know. I know you are. But I know you'll tell their whole story and tell it with some understanding of them as real people and compassion for what happened. I'd like to have their story told that way, and I hope I'll still be alive to read it. I just don't want it doled out in bits and uninformed pieces to the press.

"Thanks. I won't let you down." Matthew rose and offered his hand to John Nadeau who by-passed it and took him into an embrace instead.

– Chapter 32 –

"We contacted the headstone carver," Katie told her mother a few days later. "He's going to go there tomorrow and add Nancy's name to Davy's headstone. Matthew and I are going to drive down on Saturday. Do you want to come with us?

"Nell said she did want to and asked if Tom could go too. He was coming on Thursday to help Nell pack and they'd be leaving for Gloucester on Sunday.

Katie and Nell had met with the lawyers earlier in the week to transfer title to the house. Everything was neatly tied up, freeing Nell to leave on the weekend to begin her new life with Tom.

Katie had been staying in the main house with her mother all week. "We'll have all the time we want to be together after Ma leaves," she told Matthew, "but for now I want to spend as much time as I can with her. I'm going to miss her so much."

When she awoke the next morning at 5 a.m., Katie went over to Matthew's cabin and slipped into bed with him.

"G'mornin' sleepyhead," she whispered, her lips breathing warmth into his ear. "Any chance a girl can get some sweet lovin' this early in the morning?"

"Do you think there's any chance she wouldn't when she comes in here under my covers and presses her sexy bod up against me?" He was already rolling over on top of her, smiling down into her eyes.

He always slept naked and she'd taken off her nightshirt as she approached the bed. She opened her legs and he slipped inside her. What began as simply a loving coupling quickly escalated into a passion that released the buildup of their several days' abstinence.

Afterward they lay together talking about the day ahead and finally they got up and showered together. Katie, once again in her nightshirt, dashed across to the main house to dress for the trip to New Bedford.

"Well starting tomorrow night you won't have to do all this middle of the night scuttling back and forth." Nell greeted her with a smile as she came in through the kitchen door. "Is he going to move over from the cabin?"

"No, actually, Ma, we've talked about it and we both like having our own space. This way we can be together as much as we want and when either or both of us needs alone time, we're set up for that too. Best of both worlds, huh?"

"Sounds like a good plan, honey. In fact, I'm a little worried about Tom and me living in his little house. I'm so used to being independent…"

"When you need a break, come back here, Ma. I'd love that." Katie filled both their mugs with coffee that had just finished perking. "And a lot of the time I'll be away on assignment and you'll have the place to yourself—like old times."

"We'll see Katie dear. I may not need to do it at all, but it's good to know I can if it comes to that."

They heard Matthew's footsteps on the porch and Nell opened the door for him. "I'm going to miss seeing you everyday." She gave him a big good-morning hug.

"No you won't," Matthew said with a laugh and a wink at Katie. "You'll be seeing handsome Tom every day and you won't give one thought to good old Matt."

"You know what? You're probably right," Nell quipped. "Tom IS much cuter than you, so…"

"Hey, hold on there, Ma," Katie jumped in, "cute is in the eye of the beholder. I think my guy has yours beat by a mile."

"Or at least by twenty years," Nell said laughing.

✤

"Ma's like a schoolgirl," Katie said to Matthew with a smile as they were relaxing by the fire in his cabin the night Tom arrived. They'd been with Nell all afternoon helping her put things she was taking into boxes and as the sun started to set they couldn't help but notice her glances out the window watching for his car. When he pulled in, her face broke into a big smile and she immediately went out to greet him with one of her all-enveloping Nell hugs.

"They almost couldn't wait for the two of us to come over here." Matt was reading the newspaper and Katie pushed her head under his extended arm and snuggled in closer.

"I almost couldn't wait for it either," Matthew said as he let the paper fall to the floor. "Come over here, girl, and tell me you're going to spend the night in my bed with me. You are, aren't you? We owe it to your mom."

"Of course I am. Can you imagine how welcome my presence would be over there tonight?"

They both laughed and then talked about how happy they were for Nell and Tom.

⁕

All four of them were lighthearted the next morning when they left for New Bedford. It seemed like reuniting Nancy and Davy had lifted a heavy shadow from all their lives and now they could move on to whatever was coming next.

They stopped by John Nadeau's house and picked him up on their way to the cemetery.

"What's happening with Frank and Louise?" Matthew asked him.

"Oh they're all sentimental about the whole thing now," he told them. "Cowtowing to me like you wouldn't believe. Probably because when I went for my physical the doctor ordered a stress test. Says my old ticker ain't what it used to be. Frankie's smelling inheritance money. I could murder the Pope right now and he'd say, 'It's okay, dear old Dad.'"

"Have you had the stress test yet? How are things?" Matthew asked.

"I had it yesterday. Waiting for the official results, but when I was alone in the room with the doctor, he told me everything checked out okay. There's no way I'm going to tell Frankie that though. If this is a way I can keep him quiet and reasonably peaceful, so be it. Just wish I'd thought of it years ago."

They reached the cemetery gates and drove slowly to the Nadeau gravesite. The grave still looked raw. Sod had been placed where they'd opened the ground for Nancy, but it would probably not fuse and blend until next Spring.

But the new words on Davy's headstone looked like they'd been there all along. The stonecarver had done an excellent job. It now read:

David Nadeau
Loving husband of Nancy Titus Nadeau
Born August 30, 1824
Died June 24, 1897

~Reunited Here With~

Nancy Titus Nadeau and their unborn child
Born October 20, 1826
Died July 2, 1847
Interred here November 28, 2001

"We did the right thing, Matthew." Katie finally broke the silence.

"Yes. This feels right," Matthew said. "There were times I had no idea what I should do. Call the police? Tell no one and just board the place up and never go back? I'm glad we went this route with it, Kate. Thanks for helping me."

They stayed a few minutes longer and then, just before leaving, Katie bent down and placed at the foot of the headstone the bouquet of hers and wildflowers she'd had the florist on Route 6 in Wellfleet put together for her. "Rest in peace with your Davy now, Nancy," she whispered.

They all said their silent goodbyes and walked quietly to Matthew's car.

"I haven't had a chance yet to even open the first of Davy's journals," Matthew told John Nadeau.

"Don't worry about it. Keep them as long as you need to." They'd accepted John's offer for coffee and donuts back at his house and now they were getting ready to leave. "I know you'll get them back here in due time."

"What I'm going to do is, when I'm done with them I'm going to come down to get you and bring you to the Cape to stay with us for awhile. Then I'll drive you and the journals back here when you're ready to leave. How's that?" Matthew was helping Katie into her black suede coat.

"Sounds real fine to me. Get it done by next summer. I'd like to spend some time on the Cape in the summer. Do some fishing. I'll look forward to that."

"Consider it a done deal, then," Matthew said. The two men shook hands and smiled affectionately at each other.

⁂

"A nice man," Nell said once they'd gotten back in Matt's car and were heading east on I-195. "How could a nice guy like that have such a dick for a son?"

They all laughed at the appropriateness of Nell's remark and Tom reached over and pulled her closer in a hug. "That's my girl. She tells it like it is," he said.

They were still in a lighthearted mood as they crossed the Sagamore Bridge and returned to Cape Cod. But the as they got closer and closer to Singer Lane on Route 6, the whole mood of the car changed. They got quieter, each realizing the time had come when Nell would be leaving the place she'd called home for most of her life. She and Katie wouldn't be seeing each other every day anymore.

The December days were getting shorter and all was dark as they drove up the lane and parked by the main house. Trying to recapture some of the upbeat mood of earlier in the day, Matthew ran up, unlocked the door and turned all the outside lights on and those in the kitchen. He went through the house flipping switches on, turning the thermostat up and before they even had their coats off he'd put a match to the fire Nell had laid before they left.

"I think we're going to get right back on the road," Tom said. "It's a few hours to Gloucester and if we just keep moving we'll get there before it's too late."

"Are you sure you don't want to spend the night and get a fresh start in the morning?" Katie asked her mom.

Nell looked like she probably would like to do just that, but one glance at Tom told her he was anxious now to leave.

"No, Katie dear, I think it's best we go now. It'll be nice to wake up there tomorrow morning and be ready to start fresh and rested. We'll be down for Christmas though and that's only a few weeks away."

"Your room will always be ready for the two of you."

Katie's words were louder than she intended and Nell could see her bottom lip quivering some. It was the Katie, "I be brave" face that Nell had seen so many times when Kate was a little girl facing some kind of traumatic event or another.

She went over and gave Katie a big hug, rocking her as she'd done so many times over the years.

"Remember what it says on our favorite coffee mugs— "Our love will keep us together." I packed my mug and yours is right over there on the counter. Make yourself a hot toddy in it tonight and you'll be fine," she said.

Nell brushed Katie's tears away with her fingertips, kissed her on the cheek one more time and then followed Tom out the door. As Matthew closed the car door after helping her in, she stuck her head out the window and said, "Take good care of my girl, Matthew."

"I will, Nell. I promise." He leaned down and kissed her gently on her cheek just as Tom put the car into gear and slowly started away.

– *Chapter 33* –

By the time Nell called the next morning to say they'd arrived safely and were already settling in, Matt and Katie had been up, been for a brisk beach walk and were already rearranging things in the bedrooms, setting them up for when Nick, Luke, and Jason would arrive.

The plan was they'd drive up the weekend before Christmas and that wasn't far off. There was plenty of room in Katie's house for them to stay there and Katie and Matt even decided to set aside a room for Matthew for the duration of the visit. It just happened to be the room next to Katie's and it just happened to be connected through a shared master bathroom.

"Good plan, woman," Matthew had said when she proposed the idea. "I knew you were my kind of woman right from the start."

They spent that first day "playing house" as Katie called it and in the days that followed they were busy Christmas shopping, planning some special things to do when the boys came.

They set aside alone time every day so they could both keep up with their work. Katie had press trip invitations and needed to contact editors to get story assignments. And she still had to do some rewriting on the European riverboat cruise guides that she'd written after she and Nell had returned from their trip.

One day as they walked the beach at sundown, Matthew told Katie, "Davy's first entry in his own journal was that first day out when he left Nancy in the cabin. He was on his way to Concord to tell her family what had happened. He said he missed the stagecoach and had to wait for the next one to arrive and spent an overnight in the shell of a house he'd been building in Eastham. He said he was writing while he still had enough light."

They walked along quietly. The waves slurping around their bare feet making the only sound.

"I'm not going to do any more writing until I've read through all Davy's journals," Matthew said. "I want to get to know him."

⁕

During those weeks, Matthew's unfinished paintings stood propped against walls waiting to be completed. He'd sit there in the silence studying them, thinking about picking up a brush and adding color here, a shape there, but then his mind would wander back to the journals or he'd look at the clock and realize it was time to go back over to the house and help Katie start their supper.

They talked a lot about the cabin and what they should do with it now that it was vacant. One morning, Matthew suggested they take a walk up there again. The sun had just risen above the tips of the red oak branches and the pine trees. It was cold but crackling clear. The stream sparkled in the clear sunlight. Ice glazed the rocks and clung to some of the reeds and grasses that rose up from the water and as they left the stream and followed by now-known path to the cabin, their feet crunched on ice-frosted leaves and ground cover.

Once inside, Matthew, for the first time, thought of lighting a fire in the old fireplace. Logs and kindling laid all those years ago by either Nancy or Davy, were still there waiting to be ignited. It was all mostly rotten and turned to sawdust, but there was still some intact and that, along with some almost-dry sticks Katie had gathered in the dooryard, was enough to get a nice blaze going.

"How strange to know we're burning logs that either Nancy or Davy laid," Matthew said.

"I know. It feels weird to me, and yet it doesn't. I feel like I know them and they'll probably come home any minute." Katie was stirring the kindling with a branch she'd brought in, avoiding the poker that still lay on the floor by the large black stain.

Matthew bent, picked up the poker and stood it by the hearth. "It's time we get past the tragedy that happened here. We've done what we could to make the situation as right as it ever will be, Kate. Let's give this little cabin a new life. What do you think?"

Katie, still engrossed in stirring the ashes with the tip of the branch, didn't answer at first. "I'm not as quick to move on as you are, Matt. Maybe it's a girl thing, but I'm feeling like I don't want to just come in here now and throw open windows and scrub floors to erase every trace of them. I'm needing to just be here with the place for awhile to find my own comfort zone with it and it with me."

She threw the branch in the fire and it popped and sparked to life.

"But I could make new curtains easily enough," she said as she took the shredded remnants of Nancy's once-calico curtains down from the window over the table. It was impossible to tell what colors they might have been when Nancy had hung them, but the print was still faintly visible on some of the shards of rotting fabric. "I'll take this in to a place I know in Boston and see if I can find something close to what these must have been."

"I understand how you feel, but I'd like to do something here. To fix this place up for us," Matt said. "I'll wait until you're ready, but then I'll bring down a broom, some mops, a pan and scrub brush and get to work on this wood floor. I doubt if I can get the black stain out of the wood, but maybe we can get a rug to put over it."

They picked up and examined the few pots and crockery on the shelves. Although there were few, they noted they were quality and worthy of a good cleaning and restoration.

They opened the door to the bedroom and decided to keep the door open from then on to let light from each room to flow into the other.

"This bed is so beautifully crafted, let's see if we can clean the years off the wood and oil it so it shines as it must have when Davy made it," Matthew said.

"And we need to get a new mattress and some good linens and a nice quilt for it." Katie was removing the remains of the rotten quilt from it and trying to bundle it for later removal.

As she did so, her eye went to the wooden cradle next to the bed and then to a low blanket chest she didn't notice when she'd been there before. She went over and lifted the lid. In it were the remains of bed linens and what must have been the beginnings of a layette for the baby. Carefully placed between layers of what must have been tissue paper, were powdery remains of booties, a sweater and cap, two nightgowns and a tiny blanket.

Under those, in a flat wooden box, was a yellowed dress. Katie lifted it out and let it unfold. It was clear it must have been white at one time, but now the delicate yellowed fabric was speckled here and there with faint brown mottling. There was lace on the bodice and tiny pearl buttons and at the neck and wrists, a narrow ribbon that sill held traces of blue had been woven through the lace. As Katie lifted the dress from the box, Matthew saw a piece of paper fall to the floor. He picked it up and, still surprisingly clear were the words written in ink that was now brown, "My wedding dress. March 11, 1846."

Katie held the dress in front of her and felt a real kinship to Nancy when she realized they were probably about the same size women.

She and Matt carefully folded the dress and when they lifted out the wooden box to put the dress back in it, they saw about six or eight notebooks that had been laid flat underneath it. They stopped and just looked at each other, not daring to hope, but hoping still. "Could it be?" Matthew wondered.

"Do you think…?" Katie asked. She lifted one out and opened it and just inside on page one was the same inscription that was in the journal that had been left on the table: "This Journal Belongs to: Nancy Titus." It gave a beginning and an ending date. And there were seven others just like it.

Matthew and Katie sank to the floor and began leafing through the books, reading entries here and there, sometimes just to themselves and sometimes out loud to each other.

Davy's journals began after the tragedy, but Nancy's began when she was a girl growing up in Concord. The first entry in the first one read, "Today is my 12th birthday…"

"What shall we do with them? Katie watched a daddy-long-legs spider climb up the stack of journals then down the other side and off to its obscure destination under the bed.

"I think it would be okay to take them back to the house with us," Matthew said. "We have Davy's journals there and we can keep them together. I'd like to read them all before I get back to writing their story."

"I'd like to read them all too and it will be just so much easier if we have them all up at the house with us."

They dug deeper into the chest and found a few daguerreotypes labeled with Nadeau names. There was an old primer with Davy's name carefully written on the fly-leaf in a young boy's hand. And there were three packets of letters, yellowed and crackly, each tied with what may have once been a ribbon. Two of the packets were from Nancy's family in Concord. The smaller packet, just about six or seven short letters, were signed "Mama" and on a few of the envelopes the name Maria and something, maybe Aguillera-Nadeau was barely visible.

They packed the letters and journals in the backpack they'd used to bring Matthew's camp lantern and their lunch down with them. The lantern and some of the hand tools could stay there now. They boarded up the place when they left but now, especially with winter coming on and especially now that Nancy was no longer there, they weren't concerned about intruders.

As the days passed and it got closer to Christmas they had less time to spend reading the journals and letters and one day Matthew suggested they pack them away until after the holidays, after the boys and Nick left. "That way we won't be distracted and we'll be able to start fresh with them in January," he said.

– *Chapter 34* –

CHRISTMAS WAS ON A WEDNESDAY that year and Nick and the boys came tromping in the Sunday before. Their spirits were high, their voices exuberant and there was a lot of laughter and kibitzing. Katie, being the only female in the midst of four males who all acted the same age—about 14, she decided—reveled in their teasing.

The day after they arrived, they all trudged through the woods in search of the perfect Christmas tree. The boys discovered the stream and started following it but Matthew and Katie, with glances at each other, steered them in another direction where Katie remembered from her childhood a stand of Douglas firs. When they finally agreed that they'd found the right one, Jason and Luke did the sawing and Nick and Matthew hauled it on the long trek back to the house where Katie, who had gone ahead once they found the tree, had hot chocolate with mounds of whipped cream on top waiting for them.

"Trying for Norman Rockwell scene, guys," she told them and they agreed it came pretty close.

Nell and Tom arrived on Christmas morning looking for all the world a good ten years younger than when they'd left just a few weeks before. Tom's family always celebrated Christmas after midnight mass the night before and kept Christmas day low key. When they said they were going to the Cape, Tom's teenage grandson and granddaughter begged to go with then to meet "the cool guys from Princeton."

It was a full house. There wasn't a lot of gift giving, agreed upon ahead of time. Just token stuff and joke gifts. But there was a lot of good food and more laughter than that old house had heard in many years.

"It's like this place is coming alive," Nell thought as she looked around at everybody having a good time.

The kids hit it off. Tim and Colleen regaled the group with tales about Grandpop Tom and it was easy to see right from the beginning that Jason was mesmerized by Colleen's long straight blond hair, green eyes and freckles.

The Gloucester group stayed three days and, by the time they left, Luke and Tim had made plans to meet there again during Spring Break and Jason and Colleen had covered all bases with email addresses, snail mail addresses, and phone numbers.

"It's not as hard for me to see Ma go now because she looks so happy," Katie told Matthew.

"They both do. And Tom told me they're talking seriously about getting married. He said we shouldn't make any big plans to be away around the end of April."

The week whizzed by and before anyone knew what was happening, it was time for Nick to head back to New Jersey. They'd done almost none of the special things Matt and Katie had planned for them. Instead, the days had mostly been spent with all of them playing card games, Scrabble and Monopoly, beach walking, doing a 1,000-

piece jigsaw puzzle and sprawling by the fire talking, talking, talking.

Matt and Katie told them about the cabin and told them the long involved tale of finding Nancy, Davy's journal, and finally, the reuniting of them in New Bedford.

Right away Luke wanted to go see the cabin, but Matthew declared it off limits. "Next time you guys come, we'll go," he told them.

Nick left on Sunday and with him gone and the Gloucester group gone, Jason and Luke tried to keep up the holiday tempo, but their jokes fell flat, their banter seemed edgy rather than fun.

"It's going to be a long three weeks," Luke said as he and his brother got ready for bed that first night.

"Yea, but it's better than being shoved off on some of mom's friends back in Jersey so she can go island hopping with that creep."

Jason pulled back the covers, punched his pillow into shape and got in bed. When he turned to face the wall, Luke turned out the light and did the same thing.

Matt took them to the gym with him the next morning. They swam and worked out and then he started teaching them racquetball. Luke, a natural athlete, took to it right away. Jason decided he preferred the pool and the steam room.

As they were leaving the gym, Matthew's friend, Steve, was coming in and they stopped to catch up on things. Steve, a commercial fisherman, ran a charter boat all summer out of Rock Harbor.

"Doin' a lot of work on the interior of the boat this winter," he told Matthew. "A hell of a lot of work—scraping, sanding, refinishing. If you hear of anybody who wants to earn a few bucks doing grunt work, let me know."

"You guys interested?" Matt turned to Luke and Jason. "Want to earn some money while you're here and put some of your house-building skills that Nick's taught you to good use?"

They didn't look all that excited about doing grunt work on their vacation.

"They've been doing a lot of Habitat for Humanity work on houses back in Jersey with my friend Nick," Matthew told Steve.

"I could use the help. Even just a few hours a couple of days a week," Steve said. "Why don't you come down later today and have a look at the boat and see what needs to be done, guys? I'll pay you a fair wage and as a bonus you get to get away from your old man for a few hours a day."

Steve picked up his gym bag, gave them each a high five and strode off. Matt, Luke, and Jason looked at each other blankly, then Luke shrugged and they started walking out to Matt's car.

"You don't have to do it if you don't want to," he told them. "We'll go have a look this afternoon and it'll be entirely up to you."

The boys were quiet all the way back to the house and while they ate their lunch.

Might as well deal with this as soon as possible, Matthew thought as he was loading the dishes in the dishwasher. "Come on, guys, let's go and get this over with. And remember what I told you. It's your choice."

Steve's Golden Retriever came running out of the boat shed to greet them as they got out of the car. She had a beat up stuffed bear in her mouth and kept jumping first on

Luke and then on Jason, trying to get them to play. Steve corralled her and put her in the fenced yard then led the way to where the boat was in the shed.

He told the boys to climb up on her and look around and, as they did, he showed them what he needed to have done. It was going to be grunt work all right—sanding and scraping—but then, Jason saw, the satisfying part would come when they'd rub the wood with oil and then put on the coats of spar varnish to bring it up to a nice finish and to protect it from the weather. Luke, on the other hand, was more intrigued with the motor and all the controls. They'd gone there expecting a beat-up old fishing boat and what they found was an impressive seaworthy vessel.

"What do you think, guys? Want to help me some?" Steve asked. "Earn some bucks instead of hanging out with the old man all day?"

"Yeah, man." Luke was sitting at the controls, the wheel in his hands.

Jason said, "Sure, might as well. It's a really nice boat."

– Chapter 35 –

"STEVE NEEDING HELP ON THE boat was a Godsend. The kids would have been climbing the walls without that job. And so would we." Katie, folding her black sweater, laid it in her suitcase on top of her black moleskin pans. "Without that, they would never have met Steve's regular mate—what is name? Mike?" She wedged a couple of pairs of pantyhose in next to the sweater and made room for the pouch that held her jewelry.

"Yea, that made all the difference. Nice of Mike to invite them on that bus trip to see the Bruins. That was the ice breaker—if you'll pardon the pun," Matthew said. "They love hockey."

"And it seems like a nice bunch of kids they got in with on that trip," Katie said. "What do you think of their idea that they spend the whole summer here this coming year?"

"I think it's great, but the real question is, what do you think, Kate? This is your house." Matthew was sprawled in the recliner by the windows in Katie's bedroom watching her pack for her trip to British Columbia on a story assignment.

"I like having them around. They're good kids," Katie said. "My only hesitation is that a whole summer is a lot longer than a four-week Christmas break. Would they get bored? Would we wish we had the place to ourselves?"

"Well we don't need to decide right now. Annaleise told me she'd agree to finish out the school year with them and that was all anybody should expect from her because, after all, she's had them since they were born and enough is enough. She has her own life to live now." Katie could hear the bitterness in Matthew's voice. "She's a real devoted mama," Katie said and gave Matthew a look of understanding. "But you're right. They'll be with her for these months finishing out the school year and when the time gets closer, we'll talk with them again about it. Just play it by ear."

Matthew drove Katie to Logan Airport the next morning. It was the first time they would be separated since he returned to the Cape after the accident last Fall. Matthew had taken advantage of their adjoining rooms the night before, as he had been doing more and more regularly of late, and they made love when they first went to bed, fell asleep in each other's arms and then made love again sometime around three a.m. when they both seemed to awaken simultaneously with the same need to keep each other close.

"I'll only be gone a week but it seems like it's going to be forever." Katie was resting her hand on Matthew's thigh as he maneuvered the car in the almost-gridlock traffic around Boston's Big Dig. They'd agreed with all the new security regulations since 9/11, he wouldn't be able to go to the gate with her anyway so he'd just drop her at the terminal. It was a hurried goodbye and airport traffic was so heavy he couldn't even sit behind he wheel and watch her until she disappeared into the crowd.

He was tempted to drive over to the art museum and spend some time with the John Singer Sargent paintings, but Nick was scheduled to arrive that afternoon and the next day Nick and the boys would head back to New Jersey. In fact, traffic was so tied up he arrived home only an hour before Nick got there.

⁕

"So, Dad," Luke said, "Is it all set? We'll come up here in June when school lets out and stay for the summer?"

Jason was digging around in the refrigerator for something to eat but Matthew could tell he was all ears.

"Let's hang loose, guys. You may change your minds by then, but if you still want to, we'll work something out."

"Way cool." Luke gave his dad a high five and Jason backed out of the fridge smiling.

"I may also need you to help me with a project I've started working on for Habitat in Puerto Rico," Nick said as he came back into the room from a trip to the bathroom. "That would probably be two or three weeks at least. So you've got choices. Wait and see what feels right."

Matthew shot Nick a grateful glance. He wanted to have his sons with him but until he found a place of his own he didn't feel he could make any definite commitments. He felt so at home where he was, but he had to keep reminding himself it was Katie's house and he couldn't just assume anything. Not yet.

The boys were all packed and it was a good thing because the phone kept ringing all evening—their new friends calling to make sure they had their email addresses.

"I don't know how you guys are ever going to get schoolwork done. Seems like you're going to be on email most of the time," Nick chided.

But it was good. They were leaving on a happy note. And more than that, Matthew could see changes in their attitudes. Little by little the snobbery he'd seen in them a year or so ago was disappearing. And he gave Nick most of the credit for that. Nick and the projects he'd gotten them involved in. They were becoming regular kids with a good sense of values. Matthew's only hope was that Annaleise coming back into their lives wouldn't change all that.

⁘

Early the next morning Matthew stood out on the porch waving and looking after the car long after it got swallowed up in the woods as Singer Lane curved down to Route 6.

It was the first time he was alone on the Singer property and he shivered with a sense of foreboding as his eyes swept the leaden sky and the surf down below that was crashing in at high tide. The big house felt empty, desolate. He went to the cottage, pulled a few canvasses out, and sat looking at them trying to get motivated to paint. It didn't come. He checked through his paints and made a list of colors he was low on and finally called in an order from his favorite catalog. He made a promise to himself he'd come back over later and stretch a few canvases and get them gessoed and ready.

By the time he went back across the yard to the main house, an icy wind was coming in off the ocean. He checked the Weather Channel and found a major winter nor'easter was coming right at the Cape. Checking to make sure there were enough food staples, firewood, and kindling in case power went out, he felt reassured that he was well stocked with everything. There was even a good supply of safety matches and oil for the lamps.

The day continued to darken and then the pounding rain started. One of the dozens of times he looked out the windows he saw Calley, the little feral cat, crouched in a corner of the porch. He opened the door and, much to his surprise, she came in. She cowered under a chair but he figured at least she was warm and dry.

Around mid day Katie called to say she was in Victoria and all settled in. It was a pretty day there and she was off to do some interviews. As they talked, the phone line crackled, the power flickered and then went off completely.

"Damn," Katie said. "I wish I were there with you. I love storms on the Cape and we'd be there alone together…"

Matthew was just about to tell her what he knew they'd be doing if… when the phone crackled again and died.

There was still some light but he went around and lit a few of the oil lamps just to ward off some of the gloom. He started a fire and put some water on to boil for a cup of instant coffee.

I guess this is as good a time as any to get back to the journals, he thought. At least there won't be any interruptions.

He pulled the quilt off Katie's bed and settled himself in Jonas's favorite lounge chair by the fire. Deciding to start back at the beginning and work up to facts he already knew, he began reading Nancy's journal that she began on her 12th birthday. He had a notebook and pen with him in the chair and made notes as he read long.

The initial entries were typical of a twelve-year old girl. She wrote about the farm, about helping her mother in the kitchen, about her siblings and about her girlfriends. She mentioned a Henry Gibbs whom she thought was cute and hoped he'd be at the feed store with his father when she accompanied her dad there later that day.

"Ordinary nice girl," Matthew wrote in his notes. "And very smart," he wrote after reading about her good grades and about the fact her teacher was working hard to convince Nancy and her family that she should go off to college when she graduated a few years hence.

One whole section of that first journal was devoted to drawings and plans for an herb garden she was beginning in the dooryard of her parents' house. She listed about a dozen herbs, their description and their medicinal qualities. And she had a long list of herbs she wanted to plant and wanted to learn about.

Nearing the end of that first journal she wrote that she and her mother had had "that mother-daughter talk." Apparently, Nancy had gotten her first period that day and she wrote about it with a mixture of embarrassment as well as a sense of awe.

"I had to tell mama," she wrote. "But if she tells Daddy or even Prissy, I'll just die. I know I will. Mama gave me some flannel cloths she'd been saving for this and showed me how to make a pad of them

_and fasten them in my bloomers. And the whole time
she talked to me about how babies are made—as if
I didn't know, growing up here on the farm and all.
But how strange to know now I'm capable of having a
child. I want lots of them when I get married."_

Matthew laid the book down on his knees and thought
about the cradle beside the bed in the cabin. And the remains of tiny clothes Nancy had been making for her first
child.

The wind howled outside his window and when he got
up to make sure it was fastened tightly, he saw the rain had
changed to snow and it was so dense he could no longer see
the ocean below. He tried to scratch CalleyCat behind her
ears to let her know she was welcome there but she darted
off and hid behind the sofa.

He spent the next several hours reading, taking notes,
thinking about the girl named Nancy Titus. At one point
he turned to a fresh page in his notebook and began sketching what he thought she must have looked like at the time
based on the daguerreotypes he'd seen and, even more so,
on the girl he found so alive in her journal entries. He
drew her with long braids that he knew would have been
the color of wheat, each tied with a ribbon. He gave her
a mischievous look and an endearing smile. He body was
slight but looked strong and healthy. He drew her holding a fragile herb as if she were about to plant it in a clay
pot Matthew conveniently drew from a one on a nearby
windowsill.

For hours he read and took notes, sketched and dozed
off thinking about how things must have been back then.
A bitter cold chill awakened him. The house was dark and
the wind was whistling in through any crack it could find.

He got the fire going again and re-lit the oil lamps that had burned out while he dozed. He took one over to the window and saw the snow was piling up fast.

There were leftovers from last night's lasagna dinner and he was grateful the stove was gas. No matter how bad the storm got, he'd have hot food and hot coffee. He put down a bowl of crumpled up Wheaties moistened with warm milk for CalleyCat. She'd come out of her hiding place and was watching him warily from across the room. When he settled at the table to eat his meal, she cautiously crept over and then practically vacuumed hers up. He gave her a refill and she did the same with that then went back behind the couch.

Checking his watch, he decided Nick and the boys must have made it home by then even if they were slowed by the storm. He took a chance and dialed on his cell phone. They were there. "Thank you, God," he whispered.

"Hey Jase, how was the ride down?" Jason had answered on the first ring.

"It was awful. We drove right into the storm. Took us eight hours to get home. It's pouring rain here, but we saw on the Weather Channel you're getting heavy snow. Is that right? Man, I wish we were there. That would be so cool."

"It's not only cool, it's downright cold," Matthew made like he was shivering and his teeth were chattering.

He talked to Luke and then to Nick. He reassured them all that he was doing fine and enjoying the storm, then they hung up.

He left the cell phone on in the hope if Katie found out the house phone wasn't working, she'd try the cell. He was right. Around ten she called. She, too, had checked out the

Weather Channel and saw the big glob of bright pink sitting right on top of Cape Cod indicating twelve to sixteen inches of snow expected along with gale force winds.

Matt wanted to tell her what he'd read in the journal, but there was a lot of static and they cut the conversation short with a series of I love yous and I miss you so muches. He settled back into reading and was still at it when the old grandfather clock struck two.

This kid is a good little writer," Matthew said out loud. He was well into journal number three and his interest had not flagged one bit. In fact, as Nancy grew up, he became more engrossed in her story.

Finally, by journal five, he came to the place where she and Davy met.

Prissy and I went to Youth Group tonight, she had written. It was pumpkin carving and we were helping the young ones so they wouldn't cut themselves when I looked up and the handsomest boy in the world came in. Guess I shouldn't call him a boy. He must be twenty years old. David is his name. David Nadeau. He's here visiting Jonathan Evans. Jonathan ran away at sixteen to go whaling and they met on the docks down in New Bedford. They came tonight to help Jonathan's little brother and sister carve.

When I looked up and saw David, my heart started flipping and flopping all over the place. I must have been blushing because he caught my eye and just stared at me. I was so embarrassed. I kept trying to keep busy but every time I looked up to see if he was still there, he caught me looking right at him.

Later, when we all took a break for cider and ginger cookies, he came over and introduced himself to me. I could barely tell him my name I was so nervous. I saw Prissy and our girlfriends looking at me and they were giggling, but I didn't care. He is just the sweetest boy I've ever met. He started carving a big pumpkin right there at our table where I was carving mine. I don't know whose turned out worse, his or mine. At least mine has a scary mouth, not a lopsided grin like his does. When everybody was done, we all carried them out to the Green. David put his right down next to mine. It was like they belonged together. He lit his candle and when I was having trouble with mine, he lit mine from his. I could see the candle light shining in his big dark eyes and I wanted to never have to stop looking into those beautiful eyes for the rest of my life. But Prissy and the other girls came over to look at our jack-o-lanterns and to tease us about how 'funny looking they were and pretty soon it was time to go home.

I'll probably never see him again as long as I live, but I'll always remember how sweet he is—and those beautiful eyes.

Matthew remembered reading in Nancy's last journal some of her memories from that time of her life. He remembered she wrote in that last journal that both she and Davy swore they fell in love that very first night they met when he lit her candle from his.

⁘

It was late and bone-chilling cold in the house when the clock struck again. The cat was curled up in the quilt where one part of it had slipped to the floor. He stepped carefully over her and left her sleeping there as he went off to try to get warm in his bed.

Oh how I'd love to have Katie's warm body under these cold covers with me, he thought as he finally drifted toward sleep.

The rest of the week was sunny and bright. The cold air was crisp but not penetrating as it had been the day of the storm, but it was a day and a half before electric was restored to that part of the Cape. Consequently, there had been no way to charge Matthew's cell phone and it eventually went dead. The phone lines remained down for several more days and it wasn't until the third day that the Samson brothers who fixed cars and did all sorts of odd jobs managed to come up Singer Lane with their plow. They said their phones were working and Katie had called them from British Columbia to tell them Matthew was snowed in.

Matt didn't really care though. He had more than enough food and firewood. He had the journals to read and he had little CalleyCat to keep him company. They were becoming wary friends. She sat in a sunny window and watched him as he shoveled a path from the main house to his cottage and when he came back inside, stomping the snow off his boots onto the old rug by the kitchen door, she didn't run and hide but cautiously crept over to investigate those strange white chunks that quickly turned to water.

On one trip over to his cottage a day or two after the storm, Matthew brought back all the fresh vegetables that were in his refrigerator and, putting them together with some that Katie had on hand, he made a big pot of vegetable soup. He liked having one of Nell's soup kettles on the back burner. Just seeing it brought back nice memories and, smelling the soup as it simmered put him in a mellow mood.

Throwing more logs on the fire, he did a few yoga stretches and then settled in for more reading. There were two more of Nancy's journals left.

He'd fallen into the habit of sketching her as he saw her in his mind's eye as she grew and matured. When he read her account of making applesauce with her mother and Prissy, he sketched her wearing an apron over her long housedress, her thick hair, no longer in girlish braids, pulled back in a bun. He sketched her singing in her church choir when he read her comments about how much she loved singing the joyous Easter hymns. And he sketched her smiling brightly, eyes sparkling as she snuggled down under the heavy lap robes on one of the many sleigh rides she wrote about having taken with her Davy. (And he noticed how her entries about the handsome David were now about a sweet Davy.)

When he opened that next-to-the-last book, Matthew was surprised to see it looked different from the others. Nancy had bordered the flyleaf with drawings of vines and wildflowers. Her script was more bold with her name and date ending in curlicues and flourishes.

When Matthew turned the page he understood why. *"We're Going To Get Married"* was written across the top, surrounded with a wreath of hearts and more wildflowers. And just below that she tried on what her new name would be: *"Mrs. David Nadeau, Mrs. Nancy Nadeau, Nancy Titus Nadeau, Nan Nadeau."*

Matthew smiled picturing the happiness she must have been feeling as she wrote. He read on:

> We went for a walk through town tonight and took the side trip all the other couples take here in Concord—we walked up the hill into the Old Burial Grounds. And there, of all places, Davy asked me to be his wife. He said he felt badly that he didn't have a fancy engagement ring for me, but he offered me a ring, if I'd accept it, that was, to me, more beautiful than any precious stone could ever be. It was a ring he carved out of a piece of whalebone he'd carried in his pocket during the long months at sea. It was from a whale he, his father and his brothers had brought in. He'd shaped it to a size he thought would fit my finger and on the face of it he carved a Portuguese knot, the symbol of love. I've always loved scrimshaw and now I know why. I must have known someday my love would inscribe his love for me in that delicate way.

Matthew was totally engrossed reading a young woman's journaling about her betrothal and preparing for her wedding. Never before had he been so privy to a woman's innermost thoughts. Page after page was filled with what seemed to him to be every word Davy spoke to her, every gesture he made, every touch, every kiss, every sexual awakening happening within her. He understood how Davy had given his heart so completely to this lovely young woman.

The storm had enveloped Matthew in a pocket of timelessness that was exactly what he'd needed. It had allowed him to slowly get to know Nancy through her words and when he'd read the last of her journals he turned to those Davy had written.

Now the sun was out, but the wind still howled and whistled and battered the old house hunkered down on the dunes. At one point Matthew lowered the journal he was reading and he listened to the silence inside the house that only happens when there is no electricity. No modern age whirrings, rumblings and beepings.

The only sounds were the logs snapping and crackling in the fireplace. He thought of the little cabin up there in the woods and what it might have been like to have weathered a storm like this in that tiny place. He could easily put himself in Davy's place and imagine how he would have wanted to protect his wife and unborn child.

Although all of Davy's journals John Nadeau had lent Matthew to read were written after he'd returned to New Bedford, they were full of reflections of the few too-short years he'd spent loving his Nancy. Reading them, Matthew got a picture of a couple who liked to have fun together. Davy reminisced on the pages about how he'd liked to tease Nancy to make her blush. He wrote that her laughter *sparkled*. He wrote about *spinning her round and round* in the cabin while he *sang like a troubadour*. Matthew smiled as he read Davy's reminiscence of the summer midnight the two of them walked through the woods, *Nan in her summer nightshift that was not more than a handkerchief.* They'd found their way to a rock promontory overlooking the Atlantic. (Maybe right here where this house is now, he thought) and picked their way through the dune grasses down to the beach. Matthew could almost feel Davy smiling as he wrote and remembered Nancy modestly at first and then *almost wantonly* taking off her shift and running naked into the surf. *She was like a sea nymph, so natural and so beautiful and my heart almost broke for loving her so much,* he had written.

Reading between the lines and doing some quick calculations in his head, Matthew suspected that may have been the night Nancy conceived.

Davy's journals were a mix of reportage about sea journeys and storms, stories about the lives of his father and brothers and other seamen, and they went on for pages and pages about the life he'd led on Cape Cod. It seemed to Matthew that for the rest of his life Davy lived in two worlds: the real world of men and the sea and the world of his memories. And it was clear that Davy was most alive when he wrote about Nancy and the life they had shared.

※

The wind was abating now and the background music was the drip, drip, dripping of the snow melting off the eaves. CalleyCat, settled on what was now her favorite windowsill, watched every drip and every bird and squirrel that came to the feeder. And still Matthew read on and jotted down notes that later, when the power came back on, he'd feed into the computer. He did some sketching of Davy too as he read. Mostly, though, he was unable to portray a joyful and happy Davy, much as he wanted to. There was always a sadness in Davy's eyes, always a sense of tragedy looming. Even when he tried sketching the two of them together, Nancy was happy and carefree but, though Davy had a broad smile, there was also a poignant look in his eyes.

Matthew had thought when he finished reading the journals he'd have to just back off and digest it all before he could start writing. But that wasn't so. He barely closed the last one when he picked up his pen and started filling page after page in his notebook with their story.

By the time Katie returned, he'd written well into the story and was going full steam ahead.

⁂

She'd gotten in late the night before and Matthew picked her up at Logan Airport. They drove straight back to the Cape and almost immediately fell into a deep contented sleep in each other's arms.

The next morning, however, was an entirely different story. As soon as light edged the shades on the east windows, Katie's eyes were wide open. When she turned to look at Matthew, he was looking right at her and grinning. "Ready?" he said and rolled right over on top of her. They started off laughing and nuzzling, but it wasn't long before they were making love in a hungry frenzy. Then, when they were both finally and fully satisfied, they lay there sticky, naked, and content.

They talked about Katie's trip to Victoria where she'd gone to do a story on the old steam locomotive that had just started running up the mountain, through all the little villages and back down again through breathtaking landscapes.

They talked about Nick and the boys and they talked about what Matthew had been reading in the journals and what he'd been writing.

As they got up and poured bowls of cereal for breakfast, Matthew read out loud the last several pages he'd written.

They discussed the story line, where he wanted it to go, how much he wanted to tell.

"How would you feel if I talked to Sam Madden about it?" Katie asked, tossing clothes from her suitcase into a laundry basket. "He's a really sharp agent and he could give you some input on how to get the manuscript onto a publisher's desk instead of a slush pile in a corner for months."

"I'm not ready for that yet, Kate. I've got a lot written, but there's a long way to go with it and I don't want other people to see it yet. If they started making suggestions, those things would stick in my head and the story might take a different track, have a different feel. I want it to be my story. My voice that tells it. The time will come when I'll have to put it in an editor's hands and I'll have to make changes, but the whole thing will be written by then. It will be the story as I've told it. Does all that make sense to you, Kate?"

"Yea, it does. I'm that way with my articles too. I usually keep them close to my chest until they're finished and then I'm okay about working with an editor."

"Close to your chest, huh? Any chance I can get close to your chest right now?"

She threw a sock at him. "You're such a 'guy' sometimes, Matthew Joseph Callahan, always looking for a little action even when you had some just a couple of hours ago. Get off your duff and help me clean up this kitchen."

— Chapter 36 —

"Hey, Kate, I'm going to set up shop back in the cottage again. You okay with that?" Matthew asked a few days later. "No offense. It's just that I think it's good for you to have your space and I have mine so we're not in each other's hip pocket all the time."

Katie looked relieved. "Yeah, I need a lot of alone time and I've been worried about how I was going to bring that up to you."

"Well don't worry anymore. I need alone time too. More so when I'm writing than when I'm painting, but I'm planning to do a lot of both those things now."

"We'll be falling into a routine like you and Granddaddy had," Katie said.

"Except he and I didn't cozy up together every evening like we do, reading and watching movies on tv. And I had to go out in the cold to my cottage every night. Now I get to curl up with you in bed under your mom's quilts.

Some nights they drove out to Provincetown for dinner and to hit a gallery or two. Or when a new movie that looked interesting was playing at the Wellfleet Cinema or down in Harwich they drove in for the early show and stopped for pizza afterward.

And some Friday nights when they could no longer resist the temptation, they went for big platters of cholesterol-killer fish and chips at the Elks Club in Eastham.

"I like going there," Matthew said. "The food's good and it's fun to eat family style with the locals."

Katie nodded and smiled. "It's always like we're the tough ones sticking out the winter—the real Cape Codders.

Going there, they'd gotten to know some other couples and pretty soon they were getting together with them on Saturday nights to play cards and swap stories or go to a play or a concert.

Katie talked to their new friends about her travel writing, but when they found out Matthew was writing too and asked him about it, he shrugged it off and talked about his painting.

❧

The winter broke records as the coldest in twenty-two years. And when they talked about fixing up the cabin, Matthew said it would be too cold there.

"Come on, wimp," Katie said elbowing him in the ribs as they stood side by side looking out the window down onto the beach where the surf was crashing in. "Nancy and Davy lived there through two winters and they survived."

"Next week," Matthew said with a shiver. "It's supposed to warm up some—the January thaw."

"Wimp," Katie said again as she turned in closer and wrapped both arms around his waist.

"In the meantime…" Matthew said moving his hands up slowly under her sweatshirt.

The temperatures did rise as predicted a few days later and the thermometer on the deck read above freezing for the first time in more than a week.

"Let's go today." Katie was sitting on the edge of the bed pulling her long silk underwear on to wear under her jeans. It'll be cold in there but we can get the fireplace going and we've got that leftover potato soup from last night that I'll put in the big jug thermos."

Matthew was less enthusiastic about the whole thing than she was, but he finally agreed to go. "I've hit a dry spell and maybe going there will help," he said and reluctantly got out of the warm bed.

The temperature was hovering just above the freezing mark and strong winds were blowing in off the ocean as they trudged along the edge of the brook. "Imagine if Nancy had gone full term and delivered their baby and then had to care for an infant during a winter as harsh as this one," Katie said. She was huffing and puffing trying to keep up with him through snow that was sometimes drifted knee deep.

"It must have been hard for them," Matthew agreed. "And to come through a winter like this and get to spring and then have someone like Reverend Heady stalking you. They were really up against it."

Matthew had brought a snow shovel along and now he made a narrow path from the brook to the door of the cabin where it had drifted.

They stepped inside and saw the room was as they'd left it, but this time it was bitter cold in there. Matthew lit the logs and kindling he'd piled up there the last time.

The fire caught and blazed up quickly, but still it was only warm right up close.

Katie pulled the two old slipcovered chairs up close to the hearth and sat on the edge of one, arms wrapped tightly around her chest, clouds of breath hovering in the air whenever she spoke.

"Okay, I agree with you, Matt. It's too cold to work here now. But why don't we at least check out these old chairs and see if they can be salvaged. And I'll take measurements in the bedroom for curtains, a rug, and a quilt. Then we'll go."

They turned over the fireplace chairs and Katie poked, pushed, and wiggled legs and seats. "They're sturdy and well made. We can get them reupholstered and they'll do us just fine."

The fireplace was doing its job and slowly the little cabin was becoming more comfortable. Katie went into the bedroom and Matthew followed to hold the other end of the measuring tape.

"We need to get rid of this mattress, Kate," he said.

"Yes, but we'll have to get one this size so it fits on the bed frame. I hope what was standard size then is standard size now," Katie said as she started measuring. "I can still check to see if one of mom's quilts will fit one this size. And I can start looking for sheets and a summer blanket for later."

Matthew pulled back the tatters of the rotting quilt that was still there from when Nancy had lain in the bed for so long. Parts of it crumbled into dust as he did so.

"'You know, Katie, this might be a good time to get this old mattress outside and burn it, with the snow and all," he said.

Katie agreed and they decided to drag it outdoors to the clearing where Nancy had had her herb garden. Together they pulled it off the bed, gathering the rotting linens with it. They got almost to the bedroom door when they heard something that sounded metallic hit the floor and roll for a bit.

Both looked puzzled, then set the mattress down and went back to look for what it had been. At first they saw nothing, but then Matthew spotted something white that had rolled almost under the cradle. He went over and, picking it up, saw it was a ring. A scrimshaw ring with an intricate design inscribed on its face.

He held it in his hand and he and Katie just stared at it. "Nancy's engagement and wedding ring," Matthew said. "The one Davy carved from the old whalebone."

"It must have fallen off her finger when we moved her," Katie said. "How sad."

"But how wonderful we found it." Matthew closed his hand around it as if to protect it. "I wish we'd have found it in time to bury her with it."

"You're right," Katie said. "But maybe we can find some way to keep it here with their other things in the cabin." She took a small portion of the quilt that was still in reasonably good condition, wrapped the ring in it and tucked it into a corner of the cradle.

The mattress and bedding burned quickly and when the fire burned down it was easy to smother in the snow and make sure it was out.

While Matthew checked the floors, walls, and ceiling, making notes about what they needed to do to stabilize the cabin that was now sagging in places, Katie poured the potato soup from the jug thermos into the two Tupperware bowls she'd brought from home. She unwrapped a chunk of cheese, peeled an orange and set it out on paper towel placemats.

"This is going to make a nice little getaway spot for us." Matthew was sipping his soup and looking around the room. "I wish we could keep it just for ourselves and not let anyone else know it's here."

"Matthew, you know that's going to be impossible," Katie said. "Once your book comes out…"

"If it ever really does. Who says anybody is even going to want to publish it?"

"I say." Katie was adamant and perfectly sure of what she was saying. "It will be published. And we may even be sorry some day."

⁕

They spent the afternoon planning, talking about how they might keep the restoration as close to what Nancy and Davy must have had as possible.

Matthew was busy sweeping out the fragments of mattress and bedclothes that had fallen when they dragged the mattress out of the bedroom.

"We're going to have to get a vacuum cleaner down here," he called out to Katie in the next room.

She didn't answer.

"Do you hear me? I said we're going to have to get a vacuum cleaner down here," he repeated, never thinking there was no electricity.

When she didn't respond the second time, he walked over and looked through the doorway. She was bent over a book at the little wooden table and when she still didn't look up, he went and looked over her shoulder. It was a recipe notebook. Part of the cover and the edges of all the pages had been chewed by mice and some of the pages were stuck together and mildew stained, but much of the writing was still legible.

"I found this in that shelf behind the curtain over by the work counter," she said. "It's full of recipes for soups and stews and that kind of stuff, but, look, there's all kinds of recipes for herbal remedies too. This is what that Heady guy was so pissed off about. And, look, Matt, she's even got notes here about who she gave potions to and for what—and in some cases whether it helped or didn't. Usually it did."

They turned page after brittle page intrigued by Nancy's meticulous notes about planting, growing, and harvesting the herbs and their uses.

"I'm going to take this back to the house so I can spend time studying it," Katie said. She closed the book and as she started to stand up, a packet of brown papers slipped out from the torn back binding. She sat back down and opened it.

"Now look at this," she said with wonder. "Somebody—I can't tell whether it was Nancy or Davy—drew sketches of this cabin with all its measurements and the kinds of wood used. Here's an inventory of all the supplies and what each board and nail cost."

They read through the short list. It didn't take much to build a little cabin of that size. Then they turned to the following pages and saw the same person had drawn sketches of the room they were now sitting in and the bedroom. There was also a sketch of what looked to be a proposed room that would have been built beyond the main room on the other side from the bedroom. Very faintly they could read, "Baby's Room."

All of the interior drawings had detailed notations about things like window measurements, yardage used to make the curtains and even a description, including colors, of the curtain fabric. The same was true for the slipcovered chairs and even the pads on the wooden chairs on which they were now sitting.

"Matthew, this is wonderful. It's a perfect guide for the restoration. It's almost as if they knew, isn't it?"

"No, Katie. Don't go there. They didn't know. They had no idea. They just loved this little place so much they wanted to make it perfect."

Armed with the new information, they finally put the fire out, boarded the door once again and left.

— Chapter 37 —

A COUPLE OF WEEKS LATER, Matthew walked across to Katie's house for breakfast with printed sheets in his hand. He'd been working almost non stop since that last visit to the cabin. "I think I've got a synopsis down pat, Kate. Read it over when you get a chance and tell me if you think it's ready to have Sam Madden look at it."

Katie turned away to hide her surprise. She knew the story was pouring out of him these last weeks and that it was bound to come to this point, but she thought she was going to have to prod him to get him to show it to an agent.

Later that morning when he went to play racquetball, she settled into Jonas's leather lounger and read what Matthew had written. It was a good synopsis. Clear, direct, to the point, but still carrying all the varying emotions that played into the story.

"It's good," she told him when he returned. "Let's give Sam a call."

Matthew agreed. "I guess I'm about ready to let it go public," he said, but not without trepidation.

Madden asked to see the synopsis and all Matthew had written so far. They faxed the synopsis down to him, made copies of the manuscript and sent those regular mail. Days passed and then it was two weeks from when they'd faxed it. Not even an acknowledgement of receipt came to them.

Matthew called to ask what was happening with it and was told Mr. Madden was not available but that, yes, the materials had been received and they would hear Madden's opinion in due time.

"So now we wait." Matthew was pacing. Katie was poring over fabric samples for curtains for the cabin.

The phone rang and, knowing it wouldn't be Madden calling just a few minutes after Matthew's call to him, Katie picked it up.

It was Nell. "Got some news for you Katie-my-girl. We're getting married." Nell was never one for preamble.

"Wow, Ma. That's great news. When? Where?" then with a teasing laugh, "Who's the lucky guy?"

"In Gloucester. April 3rd. To some guy I picked up on the waterfront," Nell joked back. "Can you be my maid of honor?"

"Oh Ma, I'd love to be. This is so great. Matthew, Ma and Tom are getting married April 3rd. Ma, I want to see you. I want to hug you. I'm so happy for you."

"Well you're going to get a chance to see me and hug me very soon. Can you meet me in Boston and help me pick out my wedding dress and what you'll wear?"

They made plans to meet that Friday and spend the weekend in town shopping and doing girl stuff.

Now with the manuscript just about finished, Matthew was spending more time with his paints. He was still just going through his morgue of ideas, ordering colors he needed, stretching and gessoing canvases, but he was feeling a strong desire to get back to it full tilt and knew the upcoming weekend alone would be well spent.

※

Katie and Nell were propped up with pillows in each of the queen-sized beds in their hotel room.

"I'm exhausted. You wore me out today, Ma. And to think we hit all those shops and neither one of us found anything we like." Katie was fiddling with the tv remote, surfing continually.

"You're driving me nuts with that, Katie. Either find something or shut it off." Nell had been doing the crossword puzzle in the Boston Globe and trying to ignore Katie's restlessness. Finally she gave up, folded the newspaper and laid it on the bedside table. What's up girl?" she asked.

Katie kept surfing.

"You were fine all day, but since you talked to Matthew a little while ago you've been in another world. Want to talk about it?"

Katie turned the television off and tossed the remote over onto her mother's bed.

"I've fallen in love with him, Ma," she said plaintively.

"So? That's bad? Sounds pretty nifty to me."

"That's the trouble, Ma. It *is* 'nifty,'" she said accenting her mother's word. "It's almost too nifty."

"How can it be too nifty? --Unless you're afraid of something."

Katie slumped down in the mound of pillows and was quiet for awhile. I'm afraid of losing my independence," she said finally. "Being able to take off at the drop of a hat, being answerable to no one. I've lived like that for so long now and I love it."

"Has Matthew been trying to rein you in and tether you?"

"No, but suppose he starts to?" Katie was picking at her blanket the way she used to when she was a kid and had something heavy on her mind.

"Well if he starts to, at the first sign of it you sit down and have a talk. Matthew's a sensible man. And he loves you. That's sure plain as day."

"How's that working out with you, Ma? Living up there with Tom and all his family, I mean. You two are together all the time. Does it ever get to you?"

"My situation's different from yours, Kate. I never really had the independence you've had. Women just didn't when I was your age. And now that I'm older, I like being part of a big family. And Tom's such a good companion. Actually, honey, I feel like a schoolgirl again. It's great to be in love if you just don't worry about the "what ifs" and let yourself enjoy it."

"I know you're right, Ma. It's just that I've been single for so long and sometimes I get scared thinking about those big "C" words like Commitment and Confinement."

"How about Contentment? Try that one on for size." Nell got out of her bed, leaned over and kissed her daughter on top of her head, and padded off to the bathroom.

By the time she came back out, Katie had turned her light off too and was snuggled down under her covers. Nell bent and kissed her lightly one more time.

"Goodnight, sweet girl," she whispered.

"'night, Ma," Katie whispered back and smiled up at her mother.

⁓⁕⁓

Two days later they were in the hotel's parking garage loading their overnight bags, department store shopping bags and shoe boxes into the trunks of their cars that were parked side by side. A garment bag was laid carefully on the back seat of each car. They closed their trunk lids and then spontaneously hugged each other.

"I love your dress, Ma," Katie said. "You are going to be one beautiful bride."

"I'm just glad we finally found things. I was beginning to wonder," Nell replied tossing her purse onto the front seat of her car. I like our choices. That emerald green is the perfect color for you. Always has been. Wait'll Matthew sees you in that. We'll be having another wedding in the family before too long."

Katie laughed happily. "One at a time, Ma. One at a time."

They hugged again and kissed goodbye. "Safe home," Nell said, getting behind the wheel.

"You too, Ma. It's been so much fun. Let's do it again soon."

"Yeah, we'll meet right here to shop for your wedding dress—soon." Nell was laughing she backed out of her parking space.

Katie watched her round the bend in the parking garage and then got in her car and headed out into Boston traffic following signs to Cape Cod.

— *Chapter 38* —

Matthew was on a painting roll. He painted straight through the weekend Katie was in Boston with her mother and the spurt continued for another week or so. Then he was painted out.

"It's just what happens," he told Katie when she asked if anything had happened to bring it all to a screeching halt. "Over the years I've learned to respect it. I just do other things for awhile and when I've been replenished, I start to feel it again."

"I have that in my writing too," Katie said. "I'll go like a house on fire and then I don't even want to think about it for a few days. Then I'm at it again."

But she knew there was more to it this time for Matthew. And she knew what it was. He still had heard nothing from Sam Madden about his story. She noticed he'd go right for the answering machine as soon as he came in the door. And he was always the first one out to the mailbox as soon as the mailman came. She knew the signs. She'd been there often herself. But what she didn't know was whether to bring the subject up with him or not.

She didn't.

Then a few days later the call came. They'd been out shopping for Nell and Tom's wedding gift and found exactly what they wanted at Snow's in Orleans. They came home all excited about their purchase of a copper weathervane—a gorgeous leaping fish.

Matthew was so intent on getting it out of the box to admire it anew he didn't check the answering machine.

"The light's blinking," Katie said. "On the phone machine. You get it while I get a knife to cut this box open."

Matt pushed the button. "Sam Madden here. Give me a call."

After waiting so long for the call, Matthew was taken unaware when it finally came.

Katie had heard it being played back and she, too, stopped in her tracks. They just looked at each other.

"What do you make of it? I couldn't tell anything from his voice," Matthew said.

"No, I couldn't either." Katie laid the knife down next to the weathervane box and went over to check Caller I.D. "We only missed his call by ten minutes. He's probably still in the office."

"Okay. I'll call him right now," Matthew said running his palms down the sides of his jeans as if they were sweaty. "Wish me luck."

"Luck," Katie said, kissed him on the cheek and left the room to give him privacy.

❧

"Hey Matt. Thanks for calling me back," Sam Madden said. "I've got good news for you. Walton Publishing likes what you sent me. They want it. They've assigned an editor to you, a guy named Ben Fabriano. He'll be calling you."

Matthew was silent.

"You there? You hear me, Matt?" Sam asked.

"Yeah. I hear you, Sam. It's just taking a while to sink in."

"Well look, Matt, you caught me just going out the door. I've got a meeting across town and I'm running late. I'll call you in the morning. Wanted to give you a heads up in case Fabriano called you right away. I just found out. Congratulations, by the way."

"Sam, thanks. I don't know how to thank you enough. I..." Matthew was starting to unthaw and get words again.

"Look Matt, I've gotta run. Talk to you tomorrow," Sam said and hung up.

Matthew slowly put the phone back on the holder. He stood thinking for a few seconds and then bellowed: "Katie? Katie? Where are you?"

She same out of the bedroom looking apprehensive. She couldn't tell by looking at him which way the conversation had gone. He looked stunned and that could mean good news or bad.

He stood behind the desk and just looked at her. "It's going to be published." His voice was so soft she wasn't sure she'd heard him right.

Then all of a sudden he slammed both hands down on the desktop, raised them again and came at her with open arms. "It's going to be published! It's going to be published and I love you," he said sweeping her up and spinning her around.

They were both laughing and Katie was also crying with happiness for him. "Oh I love you too, Matthew, so much. And I'm so so happy for you."

They spun around some more then collapsed on the couch under the big window, just missing CallyCat who had been snoozing in a shaft of sunshine.

"So tell me, what did he say?" Katie asked.

"Just that Walton Publishing wants it, their editor, a guy named Fabriano, is going to call me, and Sam will call me back in the morning. He had to go someplace in a big hurry now."

"Oh my God, this is so wonderful." Katie was still laughing and crying at the same time. She jumped up. "I've got to call Ma and tell her."

"Wait, hon." Matthew reached up and took her hand. "Do you mind if I call my mom first? I want her to be the first one, after you, that I tell. She's always been so supportive and she's had a long hard haul with me."

He kept his arm around Katie while he talked with his mother. She could hear his mother's excited voice when he told her the news. And she heard the tenderness in his voice when just before he hung up he said, "Thanks for believing in me all this time, Mom."

He hung up and wrapped both arms around Katie and said, "And you too, Katie my love. Thanks for believing in me."

Katie reached up and softly kissed the tear that was running down his cheek. She said nothing, just held him closer and rested her cheek against his chest.

❧

Sam Madden's phone call didn't come until after the editor's the next morning. Never having been in that position before, Matthew didn't know what to say and felt like he was bumbling. But Ben Fabriano was used to the nervousness of first-time authors and quickly took control of the conversation.

"First," he said, "You should come down here to New York so we can meet and I'll explain the process to you. "Can you come down next Wednesday? Meet me here in my office say around ten a.m.?"

"I'll be there," Matthew said.

"Good. And bring another clean copy of your manuscript, okay? We'll get started on it right away."

"Okay, I'll do that. Sounds good. See you then," Matthew said and they both hung up.

"Whew!" Matthew ran his hand over his eyes. "How come I never got this nervous in my p.r. work? I used to close some big deals and I never lost my cool."

"Maybe because this is more important to you than the big p.r. deals were?" Katie asked.

"You've got it." Matthew leaned back in the desk chair. "It's hard to explain but because, after all those years, I was the one who stumbled into Nancy and Davy's lives, it's felt like I've been given their story to tell. And I want to tell it in a way that will make anyone who reads it feel the love they had for each other—and to feel the atrocity of the heinous thing that creature Heady did to them. This is far more important to me than any p.r. deal ever was or could be."

⁘

Matthew left Sunday for Princeton so he could have a couple of days with Nick and the boys before his Wednesday meeting with the editor in New York.

Luke and Jason sounded happy for him when he told them he was going to have a book published, but it was Nick whose hearty kudos resounded. Matthew hadn't let the news leak when he talked to them on the phone. He wanted to tell them in person and when he did there were a lot of high-fives and "way to goes."

He stopped in briefly to see Annaleise on Monday when he and Nick went to pick up the boys for the big Princeton-Penn basketball game. The Ivy League Championship was at stake and Luke and Jason were anxious to get to Jadwin Gym to see the warm-ups. Matthew could see his visit to Annaleise was poorly timed. She was seated at the far end of the long dining table and he new fiancé William was at the other end glowering at the interruption of his meal and at the boys' exuberance. That gave Matthew the opportunity to only exchange pleasantries and be off. He could discuss the boys' summer vacation plans with Annaleise another time when Winsome Willie wasn't present.

The next day he drove past the house where he'd grown up. His parents still hadn't put the house on the market even though they'd been in Florida more than a year now. He'd come to the conclusion his mother was still hoping she could convince his dad they didn't have to actually move down there. They could just winter there the way all the other elderly snowbirds did. The house looked cold and empty. He knew he could probably dig his hand into the corner of the flower box closest to the front door, retrieve the key and go inside, but decided to save that for a time when his parents would be there. He didn't want to feel the cold emptiness, the passage of time without the warmth of shared memories.

❧

The meeting with Ben Fabriano went well on Wednesday morning despite Matthew's worries, fears and premonitions. It turned out to be just a getting-to-know-each-other meeting. Fabriano took him around to meet some of the staff, people he'd be talking to on the phone and working with. He explained the editing process and gave Matthew some materials about the publishing house to take home and read. They went to lunch at a Mexican restaurant that boasted real Tex-Mex cooking and found they had a lot in common—most importantly, they were both Mets fans. Matthew came away feeling like maybe this was going to be a good experience after all.

"Ben says this is usually a long process," Matthew told Katie when he returned. "He's going to get started reading and editing right away and will feed chapters back to me with his comments, but he warned there will be times I'll feel frustrated with how long it's taking."

"Do you think you will be, Matt? With everything else that's going to be going on with the wedding and with your painting and the boys coming up for the summer? Maybe it's good that you won't be feeling pressured."

"It'll probably be some of both—glad to not be pressured, but wanting to see it finished." Matthew was lying across the bed petting CalleyCat who had jumped up to sniff and make sure who she was about to snuggle up to. "In the meantime, sexy lady, why don't you come over here and welcome me back home?"

She went over and lay in the crook of his arm, snuggling as close as possible. CalleyCat, with an attitude of not wanting to be part of any of this nonsense, left the room, tail straight up and eyes straight ahead.

"Poor Calley. I think she thinks female humans should be spayed too so we won't have to put up with the likes of you tomcats." Katie was laughing as she dove under the covers Matthew was holding open for her. The room was chilly, but he was warm and anxious to make her that way too.

— *Chapter 39* —

THE DAY OF NELL'S WEDDING dawned bright and sunny. Katie and Matthew woke to a full chorus of birds singing happily in the big oak trees outside their window and the screeching of gulls circling the waterfront a block away.

Tom's house had been built by a sea captain in 1810 and there were broad views of the ocean from the top two stories and the widow's walk that could be reached by stairs from the master bedroom. Bay windows looked out over a small park across the street and a waterfront walk that led to the docks where the fishing boats came in.

"How perfect for Ma to be so near the docks. No wonder she feels at home here." Kate was sitting on the window seat, knees drawn up with her cheek resting on them as she looked out.

"This is a great room. It's been fun being right here in their house with them." Matt yawned, stretched, and smiled over at her invitingly.

Nell had asked them to come up a couple of days before the wedding not only to give a hand with the preparations, but also to give the four of them a chance for time together.

"Yeah, it's been nice," Katie said going over to get back in bed with him. "I've liked Tom since day one, but being here in his home with him I feel I know him so much better. Mom's getting a really good guy. A real gentle man."

Gathering Katie in with a contented sigh, Matthew started to agree but was interrupted by a soft knock at the door and Nell's voice asking, "You awake in there?"

Pulling the quilt up to her chin so her mother wouldn't see she was naked underneath, Katie called out, "Yeah, Ma, c'mon in."

Nell stepped a half step into the room asking if they'd like breakfast any time soon. "Tom's doing some scrambled eggs, Vermont sausage, fried apples, and biscuits. You guys hungry?"

"We are now," Katie said looking at Matthew to see if he agreed. "We'll be down in a minute.

The wedding, scheduled for 4 p.m., was far enough away it gave them all time to linger long over breakfast and take a brisk walk along the waterfront.

"I can see you're going to be happy living here, Ma," Katie told Nell. "And nothing could make me happier."

"And nothing would make your old mom happier than to see you just as contented as I am now."

"I will be, Ma. I can feel it happening. I'm learning a lot about acceptance and the big C word from you. I'm learning to go with my instinct and trust it." Katie looked at her mother intently then took a step closer and put both arms around her. The two women stood for a minute or two rocking and murmuring words their men couldn't hear and didn't even try to. It was a mother-daughter time and they knew it.

Tom and Matthew went to Tom's brother Bill's place for the afternoon to give the women the run of the house.

When it came time to dress for the formalities, Kate stayed up in her room instinctively getting ready a little early, leaving time to spare just in case... And it turned out she was right. At about 3:45 Nell called her on her cell phone.

"Katie, can you come hook my necklace? When it comes to this, a woman alone is helpless."

Knowing her mother was never helpless, Katie gathered up her stole and purse and closed the bedroom door behind her.

When she got to Nell's room, she found, as she'd expected, Nell had managed to hook her antique necklace around her neck and was fastening the earrings Tom had given her as an engagement gift.

"Ma, you're gorgeous," Katie said softly.

"And so are you," her mother answered as she reached up and tucked stray auburn curls back under the band of delicate English ivy Katie had entwined in her hair.

Margaret, Tom's oldest sister, stuck her head in the door. "It's time, she said. "And Tom's as nervous as a jig line. He's jittering all over the place looking for you."

Nell laughed. "And I'm the fish that's about to be caught on that line. I'm one of those the fishermen laugh about and said were so easy to catch they jumped up onto the hook."

Katie laughed and hugged her mom. "That's the best thing a daughter could her on her mom's wedding day."

They wrapped their arms around each other's waists, squeezed through the bedroom door side by side laughing, out into the upstairs hallway and onto the landing. Then

Katie started down the broad staircase feeling surrounded by the music being played on the piano in the living room. When she got downstairs and took her place next to Tom, Jr., she turned and looked at her mother who was slowly making her way down the stairs.

Nell wore a simple dress of ivory silk that was accented only by the garnet necklace and earrings that had been Tom's grandmother's and that he had ceremoniously passed down to her one night shortly after she came to live with him. She carried a small bouquet of early spring roses in the same garnet tones. Ivy trained down from the bouquet and matched the tiny leaves and miniature roses entwined in her French twist.

The ceremony was not really a ceremony. It was, instead, more Quaker-like with friends speaking in turns about the couple they knew and loved. The Unitarian pastor spoke of the sanctity of marriage and the fact that the bonds were not really bonds but were the assurances of love and total acceptance, thus freeing each partner to be all she or he could be.

Then Tom spoke of his love for Nell and his wish to spend the rest of his days knowing the joy of her. And, finally, Nell said just a few words about how happy she was with Tom and his family and how much it meant to her that at last she'd found a partner who had come to love her Katie in a way that told her he would always be there for her daughter as well as for herself.

Katie wept silent tears and when she glanced over at Matthew she saw he was doing the same thing.

Tom's friend, Charlie Goudeck, who ran the town's biggest scallop operation and who was also a Justice of the Peace, invoked the laws of the commonwealth. The formalities were over and the party began.

It started off with a dignified tea for the bridal party and invited guests. Then it opened up for anybody and everybody in town to come by to share a sumptuous feast, to raise a glass in toast of the marriage and to dance a few dances with their friends. "In other words," Katie and Matt said later, "It became a free-for-all in the best New England style!"

— Chapter 40 —

AN OKAY-LET'S-GET-THINGS-DONE ATTITUDE GRIPPED KATIE when they got back after the wedding. She researched textiles that had been produced in the mills of New England and went on line to find experts who might tell her how to find the closest match in today's materials to what might have been available in 1852. One day she drove to a mill outlet in Lynn and bought upholstery material she learned was the closest to what the fireside chairs had probably been covered with initially. Research suggested the chairs may have been 25 or 30 years old when Nancy and Davy had them slipcovered.

"I wonder if Nancy's family passed them down to her when she and Davy set up housekeeping," Katie mused. "They may have been in her home as she was growing up and were a little worse for wear having been sat in by a family of six."

The same mill outlet in Lynn had the closest match on the slipcover material too and, happily, it was a pattern Katie liked. It had narrow blue stripes on a creamy background and between the stripes there were multi-color wildflowers.

She never did find an exact match in the curtain fabric, but she learned there was a lightweight cotton blue and white striped pillow ticking that was widely used back then for curtains. When she finally found a modern-day version of it at a remnant outlet in Boston, she laid her fragments on it and it did look awfully close. She found two remnants that gave her even more than she needed. She bought them both.

Armed with Nell's old sewing machine and what she remembered from her ninth grade home-ec sewing class, she set up shop and started making curtains for the cabin.

"I'm mightily impressed." Matthew was toasting a bagel to go with his morning coffee as he watched Katie ironing the hems on the finished curtains to knife-edge precision. "Not only can the woman make a mean linguini with clam sauce, she can sew too! I may have to marry you someday just to make sure nobody else gets hold of such a domestic diva."

"I not only can cook and sew, I can.."

"I know, and you do that extremely well too," Matt interrupted.

They both laughed. "Is that all you ever think about, Matthew Callahan?"

"Yup. You have a problem with that?"

"Go butter your bagel," she said giving him a playful shove as he came behind the ironing board and tried to nuzzle the back of her neck. As soon as I get these all ironed I'm going to take them up there and hang them."

"Wait 'till I finish reading the paper and I'll come with you and hang the rods we bought."

They'd been going to the cabin once or twice a week now that the weather had broken and summer had actually settled in for good. Matthew worked outside clearing vines that had worked their way under roof shingles and in every crack and crevice in the siding. Roof repair went rather quickly but the siding and foundation repairs were time consuming.

They'd found Katie's old Radio Flyer wagon in the basement of Jonas's house and started using it to haul things back and forth. They took a battery-operated dust buster and Katie filled it up time and again with mouse droppings and other unidentifiable detritus that had accumulated in the past 150 years.

"I'm excited about fixing this place up to be our getaway in the woods," she said as she stacked Nancy's few pots, pans, dishes, and crockery in the wagon so she could run them through the dishwasher at home. Not having running water in the cabin was getting to be a real challenge.

"Can you imagine how Nancy would have reacted to the thought of her pots being washed in hot, soapy water in a machine instead of water hauled up from the brook and warmed in the fireplace?"

One day they trudged through the woods with the wagon full of scrub buckets, rags, two mops, an assortment of cleansers, both liquid and dry, and disinfectants. By the end of the day and two more just like it, the little cabin seemed to sparkle in the sunlight streaming in through the squeaky clean windows. They tried but couldn't completely remove the black stain on the floor near the fireplace.

"I guess it's fitting," Katie decided. "It's part of the history of this little place."

The detailed notes they'd found about the cabin said Nancy had braided four small rugs from strips her mother had gathered from her neighbors and sent along. Matt and Katie had found what they believed to be the remains of two of them in the bedroom, one on each side of the bed and a small one near the cupboard shelf they late learned had served as the area where Nancy prepared their food. Mildew, mice, and time had left only unusable fragments of them. And they never did find any sign of the largest one that Nancy had noted was placed by the fireplace between the two chairs. They speculated about what might have happened to it, but never came up with a satisfactory answer. It was one of the mysteries of the cabin that would never be resolved.

Katie remembered her grandmother Bridget making braided rugs and how she'd loved recognizing strips from her favorite dresses braided into them. Matthew teased her that she acted like she struck gold one day when he heard her whooping and cheering up in the attic. She'd found seven of the old rugs packed neatly in a steamer trunk, brought all seven of them downstairs, and laid them throughout the house so they could see them in varying lights and decide which ones to take to the cabin. There were also four chair pads and she brought two of them downstairs too.

"I like the idea that Grandma Bridget's rugs will be there. She was scared to death of the place, but now that we're giving it a new life it's like grandma's rugs will add to the peacefulness there. Katie was sitting cross-legged in the middle of the largest one running her hand across its textured surface. They chose that one and two small ovals that would go on each side of the bed.

"I remember this one," Katie said about the one they decided would go in the food prep area. "It used to be in front of my toy box and I used to run my matchbox cars around the braids."

"Matchbox cars?" I thought little girls only played with dolls," Matthew said pretending to be aghast.

"I was an only child, so I got to be both girl and boy whenever I wanted."

"I'm glad you ended up girl."

Matthew patted her bottom and she gave him a wilting look. She rolled the little rugs inside the larger one and they took them to the cabin later that day. The largest one covered the black stain in front of the hearth.

⁂

Now, two weeks later, they had curtains hanging on all the freshly washed windows and, with the rugs in place, the cabin was beginning to take on a homey look."But how are we going to get the fireside chairs to an upholsterer? They're too cumbersome to carry through the woods to the car and I'm not ready to let anybody else know about this place, are you?" Matt was leaning his folded arms on the backrest of one chair watching Katie tie the new chair pads on one of the scrubbed and polished wooden chairs that stood by the table.

It took awhile, but Katie finally solved the dilemma in what Matthew later told Nick was typical Katie style. She got books out of the library and learned all she could about reupholstering. Then she removed the rotten slip-covers, the upholstery fabric and stuffing underneath and set about doing the job herself. "And she did a really decent job of it," Matthew told Nick without even a hint of surprise in his voice. "The chairs actually look so good we decided to deal with slipcovers later."

⁘

Restoring the cabin time was wedged in between the writing they both were doing. Matthew had sent a copy of the whole first draft down to Ben right away, but now he was feeding the first few cleaned-up chapters as he worked on them.

On second reading, he saw some things he knew should have been cut the first time around—areas where the story spun its wheels and went nowhere. And he saw other places where a little more background was needed to answer questions the reader might have.

It turned out he was right. Ben called him late one evening. I'm reading what you wrote about Nancy when she was a girl growing up in Concord and I'm starting to get a feel for her but not enough. I'm wanting to know what the farm looked like, where it was in relation to the town, to the church they went to. Were they poor folk? Wealthy farmers? Did she know Emerson, Alcott, Thoreau? What did she leave behind when she took off with this Davy guy from New Bedford?"

"Now that I'm working on the second draft I've been feeling some of the same things," Matthew responded. "I'm thinking I'd better spend a couple of days in Concord and see what I can come up with."

"Good idea, Matt. You've got a good handle on Davy and New Bedford because you've been there a few times and talked to some of his descendants, but you're a little weak on Nancy and the Concord connection. It doesn't need a lot more words, just something to put her in that family in that place when handsome Davy came and swept her off her feet. See what you can do with that and get back to me."

⁘

Matt and Katie had been watching an old video of "Camelot" on VCR in Matthew's cabin because it worked better than the vintage one Jonas had over in the main house.

"Was that Ben?" she asked yawning. She always dozed off just when movies were getting to the good part. He could never understand that.

"Yes. He picked up too on just what I was telling you about, that my story gets weak when I talk about Nancy's growing up in Concord. I'm going to go spend a few days there this week poking around. I'd like to see if I can actually find the farm."

"Can I come too? I love that little town. Would I be a distraction?"

"You sure would be. But I like your kind of distracting. When should we go?'

"How about tomorrow?" Katie, now fully awake was stretching and turning he upper body from side to side.

"Move like that and we might not get out of here until next week." Matthew, too, leaned back in his chair and stretched his arms over his head. "I want to read farther along with it and to make notes on things I want to check on. How about if we go day after tomorrow?"

– *Chapter 41* –

KATIE DID SOME RESEARCH THE next day in prep for their excursion to Concord. A genealogy search turned up Grammy Fuller who had given Nancy her herb remedy recipes. And, in a search of real estate records, she found two farms, one of which might possibly have been the farm where Nancy grew up. She located the address of the church Nancy and her family had attended and she even downloaded a map of the Old Burial Ground.

They got an early start and when they made the turn off I-95, the sun was still not very high in the sky. After driving past Minute Man State Park and promising themselves a visit there later in the day, they went to the Visitor's Center in town right near the Emerson manse, picked up a self-guided walking tour map and another map that showed historic sites in the outlying areas. Another map showing current roads also had notations designating farms known as the old Allen Farnsworth Farm, the Joseph Baedecker Farm, and one that was noted as the Titus Farm. They lost no time in heading in that direction.

"I don't know—we can't just go knock on the door and say did Nancy Titus live here 150 years ago? They'll think we're crazy." Matthew pulled the car off to he side of the road and they sat looking across the fields to the trim white farmhouse that stood at the end of the lane.

"So what? We know that already," Katie said. "Come on. Let's do it. This is the right place. I can feel it in my bones."

They pulled up under one of the massive oak trees that threw leafy shadows dancing on the gleaming white clapboards of the house and before they even got out of the car a young woman in jeans, carrying a toddler on her hip came out onto the porch to greet them.

"Can I help ya?" she asked with broad New England inflection in your voice.

"Yes—well-do you know if a Nanc…"

Katie jumped in to Matt's rescue. "We're doing research for a book and at the Historical Society in town we saw this listed as the old Titus farm. We're researching a Nancy Titus."

"You've got the right place," the young woman said. "What kind of book are you writing? We get a lot of historians come through Concord and Lexington as you can imagine. Are you writing history?"

"Actually, I guess you could call it an historical novel," Matthew answered. "We're from Cape Cod and Nancy Titus lived on Katie here's family property after she got married…"

"To a Davy somebody." The young woman's eyes lit up and Matthew and Katie looked at each other dumbfounded.

"David Nadeau," Matthew said. "But how…"

"There's stuff in an old trunk up in the attic from the original Titus family. My mother-in-law loved this farm and did a whole genealogical study of all the families who've lived here. We'd sit for hours in the wintertime and she'd tell me story after story about them all. Nancy and Davy were always my favorites, maybe because it was all so tragic for them."

The woman stepped back into the oak shade so she wouldn't have to keep squinting while she talked. "I'm dying to hear about your book and maybe be able to help you some. Why don't you come in. I'll make us some tea and I'll tell you what I know.

"I'm Elizabeth, Liz, by the way. Liz Freeman." She set the child down in the grass and offered her hand to Katie and Matthew as they got out of the car. "and this is Timothy. He's two. A little afraid of strangers these days. He doesn't usually wrap his arms around my legs in a death grip like this."

Extricating herself, she leaned down to the child, "It's okay, Tim. They're nice people. Let's go make tea."

Tim was up on the porch and through the screen door in a flash with his mom right on his heels.

"Gotta catch him," she called. "To him, tea means cookies and he's figured out how to climb up to get them. C'mon in."

The door opened into a large and typical farm kitchen in the middle of which stood a round oak table surrounded by an assortment of ladder back chairs. And Liz was right. Timothy had already pulled a chair over and was climbing up to reach the cookie tin in the cupboard.

"I love this old house," Liz said later as they were sipping their tea and enjoying oatmeal cookies she'd made the day before.

"Dunk," Tim directed them. "Dunk, dunk, dunk."

Katie dunked and so did Liz. Pretty soon Matthew did too and, much to Tim's delight, they were all enjoying tea and soggy cookies.

"My husband, Jake, his name is, he grew up here. So did his parents and grandparents on his father's side. The Freemans. They're all dead now," Liz said as she wiped off Timothy's face and hands. "Jake and I moved in with his folks right after we got married. He grew up farming the land with his father and we found out real quick it would just be easier on all of us if we lived right here instead of Jake having to drive out from town and back all the time.

"Want to look around on your own outside while I get this little cookie monster down for a nap? I'll show you around inside when you get back."

⟡

As soon as they were around the side of the house and knew they couldn't be seen, Matthew and Katie simultaneously slapped each other high fives. "Yesss! I'm glad we listened to your bones Katie-my-girl," Matt said with a huge grin.

"She's a delight isn't she? A chatterbox but I'll bet she's a wealth of information. Which way shall we go?"

Grabbing her hand, Matthew started walking toward the main barn. There were chicken coops and a kennel midway. Two beagles jumped down from the roof of their house and came over to the fence to be petted.

Katie stepped into the dimness of the barn with Matthew close behind her. They stopped and stood silently just taking it all in—the smells, the shafts of sunlight filtering in through the high windows.

Katie's eyes went to the hayloft. "Do you think this might be the original barn, Matt? Could it be Nancy and her sister and little brothers played up there?"

"Looks old. But well kept," Matthew said. "Liz will be able to tell us."

They walked back out into the sunshine and as they were about to turn the corner of the building, Matthew saw the cornerstone. 1801. "I guess we have our answer," he said.

Going around back, they saw the property opened up to fields where the crops were just starting to show green. Off in one of the fields they could see a figure on a tractor. "Probably Jake," Katie said and then, turning her gaze over to the tree line, she asked Matthew, "Does that look like a bunch of headstones over there? Like a cemetery?"

"Yeah, I think so." Taking her hand again, Matthew led her onto a narrow footpath which they followed until they got to two stone pillars covered with blue morning glories. "There must have been a gate here," Matthew said.

There were a dozen or so headstones and most were leaning toward each other as if even in death those buried there were still reaching for each other to give or receive comfort. They were white alabaster markers and all bore the rust stains of many years. Although the entry gate was missing, everything else was neatly tended. The graves were covered with an evenly cut and trimmed blanket of grass and on each grave an assortment of perennials was in various stages of bloom.

"Somebody really cares about this place," Katie said. "I'll bet it's Liz."

"Come here, Katie. Look at this." Matthew reached out for her hand. A pair of tall headstones stood side by side: Mother. Father. Mother was Abigail Fuller Titus and Father was John Titus. According to their birth dates, they would have been the right ages to be Nancy's parents.

"Look, Matt, Abigail died not much more than a year after Nancy was murdered. And John lived to be ninety-one—and apparently never remarried." Katie stood next to Abigail's marker resting her hand gently on the sun-warmed stone. "She must have died of a broken heart. And how sad for John to have lost both is daughter and his wife in such a short time."

They spent quite a while in that quiet place going from grave to grave seeing names they'd read in Nancy's journals. Her sister Priscilla who'd married her first beau, Ethan Kimmel. She was there along with her husband, their infant son and their five-year old daughter Nancy Titus Kimmel born four years after Nancy's death.

Bees buzzed in the violets blooming on the edge of the tree line. A pair of finches darted by and off in the distance they heard the rumble of Jake's tractor turning the earth for a new round of planting.

They made their way quietly back toward the stone pillars where they'd entered. There, unnoticed by them when they entered, was a low monument in the shape of a wave about to crest. On it was inscribed, "William Fuller Titus, Age 19. Lost at Sea, 1860."

"One of Nancy's little twin brothers. How sad. This family certainly knew a lot of tragedy," Katie said.

Matthew just nodded as they started back on the footpath.

"Oh there you are. Timmy's asleep. Let me show you around then we'll have some lunch." Liz held the screen door open for them as they came up the steps onto the porch. "How about some lemonade first though?"

As Matthew started to protest, she interrupted him with a wave of her hand. "No trouble at all. Much as I love this house, I don't get near enough company what with living way out here."

Filling three glasses with ice and lemonade, she said, "So this is the kitchen" and then gave a little laugh at the obviousness of what she'd said. "The only things the same here are the cook-in fireplace, the walls, windows, and floor—and, oh, this big old table and some of the chairs. I'm told old John Titus's father built the table for John and Abigail as a housewarming gift when they built this house. Did I tell you the land was owned and farmed by John Titus's father and mother, Nancy Titus's grandparents? They lived in a little house back over the rise. You'll be able to see it if you drive out the back lane. Christopher Kimmel, Pricilla's grandson, restored the little place. We keep it up and open it once a year for tourists.

"Anyway," Liz continued with hardly a break in between, "this is the original table. Lots of Tituses have sat around it through the years."

Going from room to room, Liz Freeman pointed out what was original to the house and described in minute detail all the changes that had been made.

Later Katie and Matthew said Nancy had captured the spirit of the place so well in her journals that, despite Liz's chatter, they'd each felt like they could almost hear the voices of Nancy and her siblings growing up there.

"And when Liz took us in the bedroom Nancy and Priscilla had shared, I could really picture a young girl lying on that twin bed dreaming of her handsome young Davy," Katie said later.

"Mmmmm," Matthew nodded. "Me too."

Liz had taken them up into the attic and moved some things to get to the Titus trunk before going downstairs to check on Timmy. When they opened it, there were some carefully wrapped locks of golden curls each marked with a child's name and age; one pair of high-top shoes with a label that read, "first shoes, Nancy and Priscilla." And tucked under them was a box on whose lid someone had written, "Christening Dress, Nancy Fuller Titus, April 28, 1827 and Priscilla McDonald Titus, November 6, 1829."

There were also two faded sepia pictures in the trunk and there was Nancy, a happy pigtailed little girl with a hint of mischief in her eyes.

Packets of letters were neatly tied with twine and Katie lifted out a slim packet—this one tied with a faded blue ribbon. "Nancy's letters home," she said. So few of them."

Matthew weighed them in the palm of his hand. "So little left of her," he said taking the pictures from Katie and placing them where they'd found them, under the box that held the Christening dress.

As he settled them into place, he noticed another, larger envelope. Thinking and hoping it held more pictures, he opened it. Inside were brittle and yellowed newspaper clippings.

Katie came closer and, resting a hand on his shoulder, read the first clipping silently as he did. When they finished, they just looked at each other, speechless.

"Oh my God," Katie said as she read it again—out loud this time as if to convince herself it was true.

"Plimouth," she read, "Eli Heady, the perpetrator of the heinous crime on Cape Cod, killer of young wife Nancy Titus Nadeau, broke free of his leg irons as he was being transferred to the jail here yesterday. He hied down into the woods by Saunders Creek. Dogs and men are search-ing for him still All people should keep doors fastened and allow no intercourse with anyone from away. Heady is evil and desperate."

"Oh Matthew, I wonder if they ever caught him. How awful if he got away without being punished for what he did," Katie said. "This makes me feel sick."

"He didn't get away, Katie. Read this." Matthew hand-ed her a second yellowed clipping, this one from a Concord paper, dated more than a year later.

With a sharp intake of breath and another "Oh my God," Katie whispered the boldface headline: 'MURDER." Then, voice hushed, she read on, "Early Tuesday morning, a beggar came knocking at the back door of the Titus farm. Mrs. Abigail Fuller Titus took him in and fed him fruit and oatmeal. Priscilla Titus heard him asking her mother questions about her herb garden. When her mother told him to just finish his stewed apples and be on his way, he became angry and demanded to see the book of Fuller cure recipes and Mrs. Titus saw who he was. She screamed that he was the evil person who had killed her Nancy. He picked up the bread cutting knife and plunged it into her chest two times. Mr. John Titus was haying in the barn and heard the fracas.

He ran into the kitchen and tried to beat the attacker off with his hayfork, driving him out to the dooryard. Eli Heady was wild.

He tried to take hold of the hayfork, the farmer knocked him down with it and then plunged t into his back. The killer bled to death face down in Mrs. Titus's herb garden. He was buried by nightfall in the potter's section of the graveyard on the hill. Mr. Titus has been absolved of any crime being as he was trying to save his good wife. Mrs. Titus will be buried tomorrow in the family graveyard at the farm."

While Katie was reading, Liz had come quietly up the attic stairs so as not to awaken Timmy.

"I thought you knew how it all ended," she said. "I'm sorry. I wouldn't have let you find out this way had I known."

"No, we just never knew," Katie said. "But I don't understand, how did he get here from Plymouth and did he know he was at Nancy's parents' farm? Did he do that purposely? I suppose we'll never know."

"We do know." Liz dug deeper in the trunk and lifted out a small cloth-covered book. "Priscilla's journal from that time," she said. "It's a lot of grieving, a lot of anger and despair. I've read it and I can tell you, yes he did know. He did come here purposely. Priscilla wrote that after it was in the paper about what happened, letters came about Eli Heady. They're in here too," she said pointing down into the trunk. "Stories were passed along to neighbors by their relatives from away, and one traveling tinker man came through town, verified them all to be true and added some of his own.

"Some of the stories told of Heady coming out of the woods and stealing clothes off clotheslines, pies that were left to cool on windowsills, vegetables growing in backyard patches. They said he kept moving west and, when he got far enough away, people didn't know who he was. They said he got hired for odd jobs, working on farms always kept on working his way toward Concord. People didn't know then who he was, but when they heard about this, they remembered him telling people he was a doctor who had fallen on bad luck. He told them he could cure their illnesses with his own secret herbal portions once he found his recipe book that was stolen from him. They said he always had a weird look about him when he talked about it. He'd say he had to get to Concord to get his recipe book back. They said he was strange and people got scared of him. And when he'd disappear and they heard he'd moved on to the next town, they were relieved.

Katie and Matthew stared at Liz as if they could hardly believe what she was saying.

"After the killings, people said he was possessed by the devil. Some people wanted him dug up and removed from the cemetery but that never happened. They never put a marker over him though and now nobody has any clue about where his grave is. But there is a patch covered by deadly nightshade and baneberry. Locals say he's under there and that's the poison coming up out of him. They leave that spot alone. Nobody goes near it except kids sometimes hiding up there at night behind headstones watching to see if he appears and scaring themselves silly."

Liz stopped talking and thought awhile. "Strange isn't it how one person can be so evil and cause so much sadness and suffering? Doesn't seem like it should be allowed to happen."

They packed things back into the trunk, closed the lid, and made their way downstairs, tiptoeing past Timmy's room.

As Liz walked them to their car, she took them on a short detour.

"I want to show you the herb garden," she said. "I have some of Nancy's original plans for it where she wrote that her father had tilled it to get her started and her grandmother Fuller had told her what to plant and when. I even have some of her grandmother's letters. In Nancy's last letter home she asked her mother to send the plans and letters to her but I guess she died before her mother could. My mother-in-law said the garden was all overgrown when she came here and it took her several seasons to get it thriving again. I learned a lot from her and I'm enjoying keeping it going."

"That and the burial ground, right?" Matthew said with a smile.

"Right. I love being up there. I feel like I know all those good people."

The sun was lowering when they said they had better head for home. Jake still hadn't come in from the fields and Liz extracted a promise from them to return soon to meet him.

– Chapter 42 –

THE NEXT MORNING MATTHEW WAS holding his coffee mug in one hand and scribbling notes in a notebook with the other. He wrote with new enthusiasm and kept at it for days. He rewrote and tightened and tightened and rewrote, working his deepened vision of Nancy into the pages.

He kept going on it all summer while Katie went off on travel assignments. He allowed himself to follow his impulses between writing and painting and found if he didn't try to be too regimented, it flowed easily.

Jason and Luke came to visit awhile and stayed for weeks, crewing for the commercial fishermen and hanging out with their friends until it was time to leave with Nick on another Habitat project. Life settled into a comfortable routine.

And then it threatened to fall apart.

Suddenly Matt was being called to meetings with the publishers in New York so often he took to flying out of Hyannis and back in the same day and that began eating into his finances as well as his stamina which still hadn't gotten back to what it was before the accident.

It went on for weeks that way and it was wearing him down.

"I don't know if I'll make it through to the end of this rewrite," he told Katie one midnight when he'd been writing for hours without a break. "Ben said I might get frustrated because it's such a slow process, but with them wanting it to be in the bookstores sometime this Fall, I feel like I can't do anything else but plug away at it."

Katie had come over to his cottage with him after dinner hoping for an evening like they used to have with both of them working companionably together. She was filing tear sheets of some of her recent travel stories, but the only times he paused at the computer were to grumble and swear.

"Maybe you need to get away from it for a day. When I do that I always come back to it refreshed," she said.

"I don't want to take a day away from it, Kate. I want to get the damned thing done."

Putting a sheaf of papers down, she went over to him and stood behind his chair massaging his neck and shoulders. "Is the end in sight?" she asked.

"NO." Matthew had never raised his voice to her before and that one terse syllable hung in the air reverberating.

Katie ended the silence with the words that had been going around in her head for a couple of weeks. "If this is how you behave under pressure, I don't want any damned part of it."

"And I don't want to hear about how you get away for a day and come back refreshed." Matthew whipped around in his chair and glared at her. "Maybe your travel stories don't get under your skin the way this story does."

Katie gathered up her files and, without looking at him, went to the door. "Screw you."

In a burst of frustration, Matthew threw his pen at the door moments after she slammed it shut and with one fell swoop scattered manuscript pages all over the floor.

"Fuck it," he shouted into the silence. "I ask for a little sympathy and Miss High and Mighty stalks off in a huff."

I'm in over my head and this woman I was thinking I wanted to spend the rest of my life with comes at me with this get-a-life-attitude. I sure as hell don't need her crap on top of everything else. I'm not even sure I want to publish this goddamn story. What right do I have to lay open the lives of these two people from their century to this crappy one? I'm not feeling good about this whole goddamn thing.

What he hadn't said to Katie and didn't even then admit to himself was in the past few weeks he'd been wanting a drink. Something good and strong to obliterate all the built-up tensions. He'd had a couple of beers now and then with a pizza or sometimes when he met Ben for lunch. Beer had never been his problem, beer or a glass of wine with dinner. But he found himself longing for Jonas's single malt scotch—a tall one with no ice—and that was scaring him. He'd been planning to talk to Katie about it but now he'd be damned if he would.

Instead, he got in his car and drove down to Gulley's Tavern in Wellfleet. When the bartender slid in front of him the four fingers of Glenlivit he ordered, he grabbed it with a shaking hand. Hunched over it, the aroma filled his head with memories of how good it felt going down. Looking down into the amber glow that shimmered as his hand on the glass shook, he also remembered losing his job, his wife, his friends and almost losing his sons.

"To hell with it," he thought. "This one drink won't put me back there. I'm smarter than that now. I just need it to help me through this night."

The bartender came over, picked up Matthew's twenty dollar bill and slapped down the change. "Drink up, man," he said. "Shutting down early tonight. The wife and kids and I are taking off first thing in the morning for Ohio. Going to see our families." He started emptying dishes of peanuts back into canisters and wiping down the bar.

"Mom," Matthew thought as he still gazed down into the shimmering booze. "And Dad. I can't put them through that again."

"You gonna drink that or not? I gotta close up."

"Do you have a plastic cup with a snap-on lid?" Matthew asked. "I'll take it with me."

"You okay? Sick or something? You need help of some kind?" The bartender leaned on the bar and examined Matthew's face. "You know I can't send you out of here with booze in a plastic cup. Something happens and I'm up the creek. Lose my license."

"Then sell me a bottle from your package store next door." Matthew pushed the glass toward the bartender and got up.

"Sure, if that's what you want."

Katie's house was dark when Matthew pulled in except for what he knew was the little reading lamp on her bedside table. He didn't want to see her. He'd driven into the parking area as quietly as possible, parking lights only. Now with the bottle of Scotch tucked inside his windbreaker, he closed the car door, hardly making a sound, and quickly went inside.

"I'll limit myself to two drinks," he thought as he broke the seal—just enough to take the edge off. I've been sober so long now I know I won't slip back into all that again."

He poured a water tumbler half full and set it along with the bottle on the table next to his recliner. Picking up pages he'd thrown all over the floor, he put them back in order, then settled into the chair and tried to read. But he couldn't. The half-full glass an arm's reach away was a presence.

He sat looking at it a long time remembering the smooth taste, the slow warming and relaxing that only a few sips could bring. But with those memories also came the clear and vivid memories of how he'd come to crave that escape and how it took over his whole life causing him to lose the respect of his colleagues, his family, and friends.

"What am I, crazy?" he said out loud. "Did I pull myself back out of that hell only to jump back in again when I get stressed out?"

He swirled the amber liquid around in the glass staring at its welcoming warmth, smelling its aroma. Who says I'm jumping back in? I've got a handle on this. Who says I can't enjoy a little drink or two to help me relax like anybody else can?

He swirled some more and let his memory take its lead. The morning-after shame, the cold stares of people he cared about. Dragging himself to that first AA meeting and the humiliation of saying, 'My name is Matthew and I'm an alcoholic."

That's when his memory took a shift and he heard Nick talking to him, endlessly talking to him at midnight, two a.m., three in the afternoon: "Stay with it, buddy. You can do it. I know you can, now you just have to know it for yourself."

He sat there swirling, thinking, remembering for a very long time then slowly he got out of the chair and took his glass and bottle to the sink. He stood there watching as the amber liquid swirled around the drain and disappeared.

He left the bottle sitting on the counter, no longer significant enough to even take it right out to the recycle bin. Then he got in bed, turned out the light and settled in thinking of ways to apologize to Katie and make it up to her for his loss of temper.

⁂

As it turned out, he didn't have to. She arrived around seven a.m. and crept under the covers with him full of apologies for not understanding how tired and stressed he'd been.

They made love tenderly and as they lay close afterward, Matthew slowly told her all he'd done the night before. He looked over at the empty still standing on the counter and Katie's gaze followed his.

"It's always going to be a struggle to some degree, Katie. You've got to know that before you sign on permanently with me. But I think last night was a big test for me and I passed it."

"I'm not sure the struggle is always going to be this tough for you, Matt," she said. "I think you proved something to yourself last night. It's like you had to come to this to know it for yourself."

"Yeah, you're right. I think I have a better grip on it, and on who I am and where I'm going." Matt got out of bed, picked up the bottle and without any fanfare, started walking across the room to the recycle container. Then he paused and looked directly at her.

"And now, Katie-my-girl, now that I know who I am and where I'm going—will you go with me? Will you marry me?"

"Well Matthew," Katie said laughing, "when I was a little girl and pictured my knight in shining armor proposing, I have to say I never pictured him standing naked before me with an empty Scotch bottle in his hand."

She laughed and stood to embrace him. "Yes, Matthew. I'll marry you. If I don't, Granddaddy's ghost will badger me the rest of my life. Besides, I love you, crazy man."

– Chapter 43 –

MATTHEW GRABBED ONTO THE NEW sense of peace flooding into his life and, riding on it, he wrapped up the manuscript and delivered it in person to Ben.

Katie flew to Manhattan with him regularly and, to keep the safety valve open, they coupled the publisher's meetings with Broadway plays, fun lunches down in TriBeCa or across the river in Hoboken and a nice dinner or two in some of Manhattan's finest restaurants. There were more revisions and there was editing to pare down and tighten, tighten, tighten. But finally, one late August afternoon, the word came.

"Looks like we're ready to go," Ben said as soon as Matthew answered the phone. "I'd like you to come in and talk to our publicist as soon as you can so we can start the promotion program."

"Promotion program?" Matthew couldn't keep the apprehension out of his voice. "What's that going to entail?"

"Bookstore signings, print interviews, as many as you can line up. Maybe a couple of talk shows if I can snag them. Maybe a tour. Olympia over in Promotions will assign someone to you and they'll get you all lined up. See if you can get Tina. She's a dynamo. Call Olympia at extension 356. Do it asap, okay, Matt?"

"Yeah, okay Ben. I'll call her tomorrow." Katie came in, her arms full of laundry from the line that ran between two trees on the edge of the dune.

"Hey, honey, how come you're looking so down?" she asked, dumping sox, underwear, jeans, and t-shirts on the couch where she sat to start folding them.

"Promotion."

"What?"

"Promotion. The book's ready to go and now I have to go and meet with the promotion people. I didn't figure on this. Didn't think enough ahead, I guess."

"Matthew! The book's ready to go?" Katie's eyes lit up and she broke into a wide grin. Matt, that's so great. No more rewrites."

"Right. No more rewrites, but now I have to go sit at a table in some Barnes and Noble for hours writing my name."

"Part of the business, sweetie." Katie added another t-shirt to the stack.

"But I want to paint. I'm thinking of approaching Abington Gallery and I need to build a body of work before I can do that." Matt was trying to keep his voice reasonable instead of whining, but even he could hear the whine in it.

"It won't last forever, hon. Besides, I'll go with you as much as I can and we'll find some fun stuff to do wherever we go. We always do. By winter that part of it will be over and we can hole up here and you can paint and I can catch up on my writing. But come on, Matt," she said getting up and reaching her hand out to him. "Your book's going to press and we're going to celebrate."

She pulled him out of his chair and gave him a big happy hug. "C'mon sweetie pie. Get your best duds on while I make us a reservation at the Chatham Bars Inn. My treat. I've been planning this all along. You are going to have the dinner of your fondest epicurean dreams."

❧

The Labor Day weekend was upon them. Nick, Jason and Luke had just gotten back from their Habitat project and they were due to arrive on Cape Sunday and spend part of the next week. They'd be stopping in New Bedford on the way picking up John Nadeau and bringing him along for a few days of fishing. Nell and Tom were planning to drive down from Gloucester Sunday and they were all going to have a clambake on the beach below the dune.

Matt and Katie decided during their celebration dinner to wait and break the news to the family when they were all together.

It turned out to be a raucous group that gathered at the old Singer place that weekend. Several of Luke and Jason's friends they'd mated with on the fishing boats earlier in the summer showed up to say hi and were invited to stay. Katie had invited a few of their couples friends they'd gotten to know at the racquetball club. Nell and Tom brought Tom's sister and her husband with them. The weather was perfect all day and, as the sun started to lower in the west, the fire was ready for the clams. Beer cooled in a small tidal pool, corn roasted and chowder simmered in a big cast iron pot on the log fire Tom was tending. They ate, played a vigorous game of volleyball and even ran a race or two from one jetty to another.

It was when the sun was hovering just above the horizon and they were drinking Nell's excellent coffee that Katie started clanking her spoon against the side of her granddaddy Jonas's favorite pewter tankard.

"Hey guys, come on up here. Matt has something to tell you."

"Okay, okay. I can tell by the big grins on all your faces you have a pretty good idea what I'm going to tell you. But I'm going to tell you anyway, so act like you didn't guess ahead of time, all right?" Matthew said. "Are you ready for this now? It's a done deal. The book goes to press Tuesday."

"Way to go, Dad," Luke shouted and Jason loped over to give his dad a high five. There was a lot of hand clapping, some cat whistling and even a whoop or two.

The teenagers kept the party going into the wee hours, the young parents and old folks said goodnight soon after sundown, and sometime in between Matthew and Katie slipped away.

As planned, they stopped at the big house to pick up an overnight bag and a basket of breakfast. Then, with flashlights in hand, they made their way to what they still called Nancy and Davy's cabin to celebrate in a different way.

The cabin had become their private hideaway and they cherished their hours of joint solitude there. It was cozy and cheerful and always welcoming—and they carefully protected the secret of its existence.

The next morning with the sun streaming in through the last of the wild pink roses at the open window, Katie stretched and yawned.

"Wake up, sleepyhead, we've got a houseful of company down below and I want a little more of my man before we go."

She reached down under the sheet and fondled him, limp and warm and already beginning to swell.

They made leisurely love and afterward lay together talking about how right and lovely it had been the night before to steal away from the others and come here where it had all begun.

Katie pulled a sweatshirt over her nakedness to ward off the chill of the Cape Cod morning and brought the picnic basket up onto the bed between them. She poured still hot coffee from the thermos and unwrapped the cranberry nut muffins she'd baked the day before the clambake. Matthew pulled out a banana for each of them and peeled the thick yellow skins back.

"So how are we going to keep this place secret once the book is out there?" Katie asked as she reached for the banana he held out to her.

"Just post a 'Private Road' sign down at the entrance to Singer Lane."

"C'mon Matt. Do you think that's going to stop the curious?"

"Now you 'come on' Katie," Matt said almost spilling coffee in his naked lap. Do you really think this book is going to create a curious public? It might get read by some locals, but we can deal with them."

"I think it's going to get more attention than you expect and it would be good for you to prepare for that." Katie was slowly picking muffin crumbs off the checkered tablecloth she'd spread over the bed quilt. One by one, studying each one thoughtfully before putting it in her paper napkin.

Matthew knew she wasn't thinking about muffin crumbs.

"What's up, Kate?" He rested a hand on her knee. "What're you thinking? You look a little sad."

"I'm feeling like this wonderful part of our life together is coming to an end—your finding this place and sharing it with me, our discovering Nancy and Davy's love for each other—our love. I just don't want to let the world in, that's all. I'm scared we've unleashed a dragon who's going to slurp us and this sweet place of ours up on his big greedy tongue."

"I don't see it happening, Katie, but if it does, we'll protect what we have in any way and every way we can." Matthew put his coffee mug on the little bedside table and reached for her, burying his lips in her hair. "There's no way I'm going to let us lose this, Kate. Trust me," he murmured.

⁕

By the time they made it back to the main house it was late morning and Nick and the boys were loading the car for their trip back to New Jersey. The others had gone out for breakfast and pulled into the parking area just about the same time Katie and Matthew walked out of the woods.

We're going to have to take off right after the bridge party," Nick said as he stuffed the last duffle bag into a wedge of space in the trunk. We want to get John back to New Bedford in good time and then we have a long drive after that.

Nell and Tom joined them and said they'd be leaving right after that too. "It'll take forever just to get off Cape so we figure we might as well join the exodus at a decent time," Tom said.

"You boys probably weren't here for Labor Day last year," he added when he saw Luke and Jason exchange what's-the-big-deal-about-some-traffic glances. "It's fun. The people who live here year round give the summer people a real send off."

"Here are two of last year's banners." The screen door slammed behind Katie, her arms too full to catch it. "Everybody goes up on the overpass bridges all down Route 6 right down to the Sagamore Bridge and we all hang banners and signs over the sides. Here, look."

She spread an old sheet on the ground that read, "Goodbye For Now. Come Again" and another that said, "We'll Miss you."

"It's tongue in cheek but it's all in fun, she said. "Every summer they come and clog up our roads and fill our beaches—and I have to admit it does get annoying—but, hey, what're you going to do? Might as well have some fun with it."

Luke and Jason liked the idea. Anything for a party. Their buddies had already brought banners of their own and tossed one to Luke. "Come Back Next Year—All Is Forgiven" it said and as soon as they got to the first overpass just beyond the Eastham rotary, they flung it over the rail. No sooner had the banner settled than car horns started beeping. The summer people waved through their windshields and out their windows. Luke and Jason and all the others on the bridge waved and held up their beer bottles in a farewell salute.

Knowing the exodus would go on all day, Nell and Tom were the first to say they'd better get their car into the creeping phalanx. Nick said they had a long drive ahead and they'd better join the deserters too.

"I feel kind of sad that summer's over and at the same time it's like there's an excitement in the air about what's ahead," Matthew said as they watched the tail lights of the last car disappear down Singer Lane.

"Probably a holdover from back-to-school days," Katie said. "But now comes the good time. Now we can take a book and a sand chair down to the beach and it'll be almost deserted. We'll have the warm September sun almost to ourselves."

"It's a great night for a walk," Matthew said grabbing Katie's hand and leading her down over the dunes to the beach below. They walked on the wet sand with the edge of the waves rippling in over their toes and walked, almost silently, up to the rocks where Matthew had walked the day he found Nancy's skeleton in the bed. Then they turned and walked slowly back and finally settled on the bench where Matthew had sat the first day he met Jonas.

Katie pulled her feet up onto Matt's lap and sighed deeply as he began massaging them toe by toe.

"You're distant tonight, Matt, what's happening?"

Matthew didn't answer. Instead, he just kept kneading her toes, looking down at them pensively.

"Matt?"

Still he kept kneading.

Katie pulled her feet from his lap. Sitting lotus style next to him on the bench, she asked again, "Tell me what's on your mind, Matthew. You're brooding over something and I can't deal with that."

"Ben told me the other day there's talk Hollywood has gotten wind of the story and they're interested in doing something with it. It's even gotten to the point where names like Keanu Reeves and Gwynneth Paltrow are mentioned for lead roles."

Katie was quiet for a long while. Then, "I'm impressed, Matt. But not surprised. It's a good story and you told it well. And it's got all the angles Hollywood likes."

"But I don't like the idea Hollywood likes it." Matthew stood up, hands in his pockets, and walked down to the water's edge. He was quiet a long time and Katie instinctively gave him the space to be.

"I can't do it, Katie," he finally said. "I know we'd make big bucks and we'd never have to think about money again, but I just can't do it. I can't make a sideshow of all that happened."

Katie began rubbing her own toes, thinking, feeling, trying to bypass her own reactions and tune in to his. She waited, listened to what he was saying and what was going to follow.

"I'm realizing I didn't write the book for everybody out there to read. I wrote it—well I just wrote it because it was in me and I needed to put it into some form. I've done that now and that's enough," he said still staring out over the water. "I really don't want to be sitting on a plane someday and see some guy across the aisle reading what Davy wrote in Nancy's journal that day. I don't want some book discussion group talking about how he bathed her, brushed her hair, held her all night. I just can't do it, Katie. It's become too real to me. Too much a part of us in some way. You and me."

They were both quiet a long time, Matthew jiggling the change in his pants pocket as he looked down at the foam quietly dissipating as each ripple ran back out to sea. Katie sat there rubbing her toes, over and over and over.

Finally they looked up at each other and both knew they'd reached a turning point.

"I'm going to call Ben tomorrow morning and tell him. I dread doing it, but I have to," Matthew almost whispered. This is the last chance I have to stop it and I'm going to do it. I'm going to break the contract. What do you think, Kate? Do you agree?"

"Think long and hard before you do it, Matt. It will be the end of any hope of you ever having a literary career. No agent or publisher will get near you after you do something like that. Make sure it's what you really want to do, Matt. Make real sure."

"I'm sure," he said quietly.

She got up, went over to him and took both his hands in hers. "I'm sorry and I'm glad, Matt," she said. "Sorry you won't get the recognition you deserve for such a good story, but I'm so moved that you're the kind of man who's not seeing dollar signs all over the place."

Matthew drew her in and held her close, running the palm of his hand down over her springy red curls for the next several minutes. Then he put his fingers under her chin and tipped her lips up for a gentle kiss.

"Thanks, Kate," was all he said and she knew how much those words meant. They went back to the bench and both stretched their legs out in front of them digging their feet in the sand that still held the warmth of the day's sun. They were quiet, thinking.

"What about maybe just donating the manuscript to the Wellfleet Library if they want it so people who learn of the story and really care enough about it can go there and read it?" Katie said after a bit.

Her words hung softly in the air and felt right to both of them.

"You know, that might be exactly the right thing to do," Matthew said. "God only knows what's going to happen when I call Ben and tell him, but I never took an advance; no money has changed hands. It's still my story."

"You're right, Matt, that's the bottom line and they have no recourse but to ultimately accept that."

Matthew threw his head back, raised his arms way up over his head and stretched energetically. "You know how good this makes me feel? I've been carrying that weight for a long time. That and my wanting to get back to painting full time. The gallery in Orleans wants paintings and now I won't have a book tour looming over me."

He turned to her, pulled her into his arms and, wrapping one leg over her hips growled into the hollow of her neck, "Now why don't you come back up to my place with me, woman? I want to show you my latest painting of this beach at night, and then…".

<hr/>

They drove down to New York together on Thursday. Katie planned to make an appearance at two of the magazines she was writing for while Matthew met with Sam Madden to face the music with him before talking to Ben.

He soon learned the music he faced was not slow and easy as he'd hoped. Sam hit the roof and before Matthew knew what was happening they were in a cab together heading for Walton Publishing.

"You're gonna tell them yourself," Sam shouted over the traffic noise on Sixth Avenue. "You know what this makes me look like? You know what this will do to my reputation? I'm your agent. They're going to be pissed that I brought them some amateur who's now gone all soft and scared to face the big time."

"I feel like shit putting you in this spot," Mathew said.

"You should."

When the cab pulled up in front of the Walton office building, Sam got out without even looking over his shoulder while Matthew dug into his pocket to pay the fare. Katie met him at the door of the hotel room when he got there several hours later.

"My God, Matthew, you look awful," she said as she closed the door behind him and he lowered himself into a chair, a dazed look on his face. "What happened?"

He shook his head, didn't say anything, and leaned forward resting his arms on his knees, staring at the floor. After awhile he said quietly, "Next week. I have to meet with their lawyers next week."

Katie was silent. It had been her worst fear.

"They say even though they never gave me an advance, they invested behind the scenes money in salaries—and their valuable time. They brought out the contract I signed and said they have the right to go forward. When I protested, they just said they'll set up a date with their lawyers and call me. They all got up, even Sam, and it was clear the meeting was over. They opened the door and I walked out alone."

"Oh my God," Katie whispered. She knelt beside him and tried to take him in her arms but he just sat there.

They cancelled plans to drive down to Princeton to see Nick and the boys and drove back home.

⁂

A pall hung over the house that had only a week before been filled with laughter. If Matthew wasn't pacing from room to room in the big house, he was over in the cottage brooding silently. The meetings with the Walton people and their lawyers and the lawyers Matthew hired to defend him got so numerous he finally let Katie talk him into flying down to New York with Joe Fallon, the husband of one of Katie's friends who kept his plane on Hinckley Pond in Harwich and flew into Teeterboro Airport in New Jersey on a regular basis.

"You've got to let me pay you a regular fare," Matthew said as Joe pulled out of the airport road and into the heavy traffic going into New York. "Buy me dinner sometime," Joe said. "I like having the company. Making this commute all the time gets old fast."

Negotiations with Walton and the lawyers were not going well. Matthew dug his heels in and was more sure than ever he didn't want the book to see the light of day. Ben ranted and raved and Sam ranted and raved. And Matthew dug in deeper.

His lawyers began talking settlement and Katie agreed. "Matthew, just paying the legal fees is going to eat up any savings you have," she said. "Buy it back. Offer them an amount to cover what they've spent and see if they'll agree."

"They won't."

"Think about it, Matthew. Just give it a try."

He talked to his lawyers and they didn't think it would fly either.

Then Matthew got a break. The film company in Hollywood sent the manuscript back saying "maybe in the future but not right now."

"You can feel them losing interest in the project," Katie said. "Now's the time to make the offer. They may be glad to just get the whole thing over with."

And they were.

They can't get me out of there fast enough now, Matthew thought as he left Sam's office. They were all fired up about the book a couple of weeks ago and now it's like just get out of here, we're too busy for this. But, oh, what a relief!

— *Chapter 44* —

"How about the dinner I owe you? You up for that?"
Joe's plane had leveled off at 10,000 feet and they were relaxing as they watched Long Island slip by beneath them.
"I have to come in next Wednesday to sign all the papers.
I'll set it up for late afternoon and we can meet someplace
down by your office before we head home. What do you
think?"

"I think I'll take you up on that. I know a good steak
place on Lexington. We'll meet there."

⸙

Matthew had called Katie as he left the Walton building to tell her the good news and when she saw his car come
out of the woods and pull into the clearing, she ran out to
greet him. "We're going to be free of all this mess, Kate.
The story's going to be mine again. We can start getting
back to normal—whatever that is."

They were laughing and talking again. They were
dancing and making love. The week flew by and before
they knew it, it was Tuesday night.

Katie pulled her jeans off and tossed them on the chair. "I wish you hadn't made plans to take Joe Fallon out to dinner tomorrow night," she said. "It would have been nice for us to do something to celebrate."

"We can do that right now." Matthew grabbed her and tumbled her onto the bed with him. She pretended to fight him off and when he pulled her t-shirt up over her head he twisted it around her arms and pinned her to the bed. She wrapped her long legs around his middle. "Okay, big tough guy. Now what're you going to do? You can't get away."

"Who says I want to?" Matthew was nibbling her neck and ear right where he knew she liked it. "You think I'm a fool? I don't ever want to get away."

"Good," she said, pulling him down on top of her, "because you wouldn't stand a chance. I've got you in a lock grip and I'm not letting you go."

"Marry me, Katie," Matthew's lips were on hers softly mouthing the words. "Marry me soon now, Kate. I love you so much and I want the world to know it. I want you to be my wife."

His lips felt hers saying, "Yes. Soon." And in the aftermath of their love making they lay wrapped around each other making plans. "Thanksgiving," Katie said. "What better day. We have so much to be thankful for."

"But that's a month away. I'd like it to be tomorrow. Or the day after at the latest." Matthew's hand was brushing her tousled hair off her face.

"Me too in a way, but you know we want mom and Tom to come and the boys and Nick and some of our friends. We have to give them all some time to make plans. And we have to plan a celebration—the biggest Thanksgiving dinner Cape Cod has seen since the feast at Plymouth."

They talked and planned until they both drifted off to sleep and overslept in the morning. It was a mad dash for Matthew to get dressed and get down to Joe Fallon's plane in Harwich. "I'll be thinking about you all day," Katie told him as she hugged him goodbye. Don't linger long over dinner. I don't like it when you guys have to come in on the pond after dark. And I thought maybe we could call the boys and mom and Tom tonight and tell them our Thanksgiving plans. I can hardly wait to tell them. And we have some other things to talk about too, lots of plans to be made.

"I'll be back before dark, mama, don't fret." Matthew teased her sometimes about how she worried about him. "I'm a big boy now. And when I get home I'll even prove it to you-----again."

She laughed, gave him a quick kiss, and pushed him to the door. "Go. Joe'll be buzzing the house looking for you if you don't get going. Be safe. I love you, sweet man."

"I love you too and don't you ever forget that," he said just before he closed the car door and was off.

Katie stood on the porch listening to the sound of the car motor disappear into the bird songs and the rustling of tree leaves. She'd been thinking of telling him last night of her suspicions but then they started making love and then all the wedding talk and she decided she'd wait and talk with him about it tonight. She'd go out and buy the pregnancy kit today and they could do the test when he got home. What better way to celebrate the end of the Walton publishing fiasco.

– Chapter 45 –

THE LATE AFTERNOON HEAT HIT Matthew in the face when he emerged from the air-conditioned Walton building after the meeting. Everything was signed, sealed and delivered and he came away feeling it ended up a pretty fair deal, considering.

He had more than an hour before he had to meet Joe at the restaurant. Plenty of time to get down to Tiffany's.

He'd been looking at rings on some of his other trips in to the city and he decided last night that tomorrow morning he'd find some reason to get her to go with him to the cabin where he'd give her the one he'd finally chosen, a simple and elegant opal set in platinum. It was ready and waiting where he'd left it last week on the mantel next to Nancy and Davy's wedding picture. Today he'd look at Tiffany's wedding bands just to get some idea of what they might like and next week he'd bring her in and they'd find the right one to go with the opal. It had to be elegantly simple too. He was glad Katie wasn't a diamonds and glitz girl. So different from Annaliese. They'd have a good life together.

The streets and sidewalks were wet when Matthew and Joe left the restaurant. They could hear distant rumbles of thunder, but the sky was clearing and it was obvious the storm had passed through. They ran through puddles to get to Joe's car and had to use the wipers all the way to Teeterboro but that was just to clear the kick-up spray off the windshield.

Always mindful of the weather, Joe checked the reports at the airport and checked with the tower before take-off. "The thunderstorms rolled south and it's clear straight through to Hyannis. Might be some light fog coming in from the ocean but nothing to worry about," he was told.

They took off and Matthew, as always enjoyed the sight of Manhattan getting smaller and smaller and then following the coastline north. The sky was clean of clouds and they could see for miles. Little boats leaving v-shaped wakes, even the movement of the waves coming onshore.

"I'll be glad to not have to make this trip on a regular basis any more, but I'll kind of miss it too," Matthew said. "There's really nothing more relaxing than being up here--it's the ultimate 'getting away from it all,'" he added with a laugh.

"Yea, and I'm going to miss your company. But don't forget, any time you need a ride down, just give me a call. Katie too. Maybe some weekend we can make it a foursome, go to a show and dinner. Something like that," Joe said.

They were coming near the Cape and Joe stopped chatting to focus on what he had to do to get them down safely. Matthew liked that about him, that he knew when to cut the banter and be serious. They began their descent and Matthew noticed thin wisps of fog trailing across their windshield and down the sides of the plane. "Nothing to worry about," he told himself. "Just what the tower in Jersey told us about."

But the wisps got thicker. Matthew glanced at Joe and thought he could see tension building on his face. "Everything okay, Joe?" he asked.

"Hope so," was all Joe answered.

Matthew could see by the instruments they were pretty low now. He was reassured when the fog broke enough for them to see familiar landmarks below. Hyannis airport, Route 6, Patriot's Square, the shopping center in Dennis. And Hinckley Pond. "Ah, thank you God," Matthew whispered a silent prayer.

⁙

Kate was trying not to worry when it got later than she thought Matthew would arrive home. She tried not to look out the window because the fog worried her. It wasn't the socked-in heavy stuff, but still it worried her. Then she heard a car come out of the woods and park by the back door.

She opened the door with a big happy smile for Matthew, only to see two men in uniform getting out of a police car. She froze. "Are you Kate Vinerelli?" one of the men asked.

Kate couldn't speak and he repeated the question.

"Yes. Is it Matthew? Has something happened to Matthew?" she asked.

The policemen were up on the porch with her by then. "May we come inside?" the taller of the two asked.

"No. Just tell me. Has something happened to Matthew? I mean, yes, come in, but tell me, is he okay?"

"A small plane crashed down on Hinckley Pond in Harwich, ma'am. We're told two passengers were in it. It was registered to Mr. Joseph Fallon and his wife said the other passenger was most likely Matthew Callahan. Do you agree that might be so? She said he lived here with you."

Kate was trembling. Her teeth were chattering. She was cold. So cold. "What do you mean "*was*" Matthew Callahan? He's okay isn't he?"

"No ma'am. I'm afraid not," the officer said. "The plane overshot the pond and crashed into the woods on the far side. It burst into flames when it hit. There's nothing left of it but charred metal parts. The woods down at the end of Dogwood Lane are still burning.

"I've got to go there. I've got to go find him. He may have gotten out and he's hurt someplace down there." Katie started looking for her car keys.

"Do you have someone who can drive you? Family here or a close friend?" the other officer asked. "You can't go there alone."

"No, no one's here now." She tried to push past them but they each grabbed an arm. "Is that your purse on the table? Get it and we'll drive you with us. And bring your cell phone so you can call someone on the way to come be with you. You can't be alone."

※

Most of the flames were down by the time they turned into Dogwood Lane but the black smoke was still rising and the smell was terrible. The crowd of people parted when they saw the flashers on the police car. Katie jumped out of the back seat and one of the officers ran and grabbed her arm just as she reached the top of the steep hill that leads down to the pond. "No. You can't go down there, ma'am. It's too dangerous. And there's nothing to see."

But she did see. She saw the smoldering ruins of the seaplane. Just broken charred pieces. The officers were right. Nothing much that was recognizable was left.

She turned and buried her face in the officer's chest and wept. He was still holding her when a woman came through the crowd and touched his shoulder.

"I'm Joe Fallon's niece. His wife said if Kate Vinerelli came here I was to take her to their house. A doctor is there right now. He's given Maria, Joe's wife, something to help calm her. He could take care of Ms. Vinerelli too."

The policeman helped Katie into the woman's car. "But I have to go back home," she said. "I called my mom and I called Matthew's sons. They're all coming. I have to be home when they get there. Mom's coming from Gloucester. She's on her way already."

"I'll drive you there after you let the doctor have a look at you and I'll stay with you until your mother arrives. I'm Marylou, by the way," the young woman said.

Marylou, as good as her word, was there with Katie when Nell and Tom arrived. Although the doctor had given Katie some pills to help calm her, she only took one and it barely took the edge off her grief. But sobbing into her mother's ample bosom did help and eventually Katie agreed to take one more valium and she fell into an exhausted sleep.

– *Chapter 46* –

THE BOYS AND NICK ARRIVED while Katie slept and spent the night trying to make some sense out of what happened and in the morning she arose and refused any attempt anyone made to sedate her.

Although she spent most of the time looking out the windows, staring into space, she told herself she was at least aware and was helping make decisions about making "the arrangements," the term she had always hated.

She passed along names and phone numbers of people she felt should be notified but she let the others do the calling. She did talk to Matthew's parents, however, when Luke and Jason called them to tell them what had happened and agreed to travel with Matthew's closed casket down to Princeton for burial in the family plot. The small group of them left a few days later following the hearse, trying not to lose it in I-95 traffic.

They were somberly greeted by Mr. Gruber at the Hyatt where they'd stayed when Jonas was honored by Princeton only months earlier. And, for Katie and Nell, they were shocked to learn that Matthew would be buried in the same cemetery on Witherspoon Street where Jonas's ashes were interred with his wife's.

Matthew's parents met them at the gravesite and embraced Katie, letting her cry in their embrace as their grandsons put their arms around them all. It was a small gathering of loved ones and the service was short. Just before the final prayer of committal a limo pulled up and Annaliese and William emerged and went to stand by Luke and Jason surprising everyone by standing quietly, heads bowed, and then placing a flower on the casket before returning to the limo and being driven off.

❀

It was late the following morning when the group from Cape Cod bid goodbye to those from Princeton. Matthew's brother was driving his parents to catch an afternoon flight back to Florida. They promised to keep in touch. And Nick and the boys reminded Katie they'd all be coming to Cape Cod to spend Christmas with her in just a couple of months.

Katie and Nell got into the car with Tom and before leaving Princeton they drove to the cemetery for one last visit to the gravesite. It was raining and they didn't get out of the car and as they drove away Katie kept her eyes on the grave until the car turned the bend. Then Nell drew her close to her ample bosom and kissed her brow tenderly. "It's okay, Katie, m'girl, cry all you need to," she said as her tears spiraled down into Katie's springy red curls.

– Epilogue –

"ARE YOU SURE YOU WANT to do this, Kate?" Nell sat down next to Kate on the couch and brushed her hand over the soft downy head of the baby Kate held at her breast. "John Nadeau said he'd do it if you want him to."

"Yea, Ma, it won't be easy, but I want to do it," Kate said, putting the burp cloth over her shoulder and gently patting her daughter's back. "This story was so important to Matthew and me and I want to be the one to put it to rest where it should be."

Nell got up and walked over to the window. "They're here," she said. "I'll let them in."

Nick, Jason, and Luke had driven up from Princeton and stopped to pick up John Nadeau on the way. Watching them get out of the car and walk toward the house, Nell couldn't help but notice how Matthew's sons had grown and matured in the year since his death. They came wearing dress shirts and ties, blazers and chinos for this occasion and had an air of approaching adulthood about them even though they were still only seventeen and eighteen.

There'd been no hesitation when, weeks after the fiery crash, they learned they'd inherited their father's manuscript along with all his other possessions. They'd been told of their father's wish to donate the manuscript to the Wellfleet Library and that was what they wanted to do. Encouraged by Sam Madden who had been their father's agent, they had the book self published, got a small run of copies—just enough for John Nadeau, Katie and her mom, Nick, Liz in Concord, and a few copies for the library. And when the library contacted them to say they wanted to have a public acknowledgement of the gift and to have a segment of the manuscript read, they quickly agreed and asked Kate if she felt up to doing it.

Nell swung the door open wide for them and they went right over to the couch to hug Katie and to see their little sister.

"So is she walking yet?" Luke teased. "Three months old and all she's doing is rolling over and chewing her toes?"

Jason reached over for the baby and Katie put her in his arms. "Hey, Nancy-babes, how're ya doing kid?" he said, smiling tenderly down at her. Katie stood up and gave John Nadeau a tender kiss on the cheek. "Thanks for coming, John. And don't let me forget to give you the box of Davy's journals when you leave. I've kept them long enough."

Then she turned to Nick and when he opened his arms to her, she went into them, put her cheek against his chest and struggled to hold back the tears. Matthew's closest friend. He'd loved Matthew even before she had and had helped him through some difficult times. "I'm glad you're here, Nick. Thank you," she said quietly.

Nell had made lunch for the group and while she and Tom were putting it all out on the table, while baby Nancy was being passed from lap to lap, and while everyone else was playing catch up, Katie slipped away, unnoticed by everyone except Nell, and went over to what she still called Matthew's place across the back yard.

It was exactly a year now since the plane crash that took his life so suddenly and still most of his belongings were just as he'd left them that day when he went down to New York to put an end to the negotiations about the manuscript.

The boys had asked if they and Nick could come up and spend Christmas with her again as they did last year so close after the crash had happened. Nick would go back to Princeton, but the boys would stay the month they had off from school. And Jason was now accepted at Boston College and asked if he could use the cottage as his weekend getaway once he started school.

Shortly after their dad was killed, the boys had come and taken a few of his things they wanted to keep. Their mother had wanted to rifle through to see if there was anything of value, but they and Nick stood their ground against that. Luke had taken some old photograph albums to give to Matthew's parents in Florida and he'd chosen a favorite seascape to hang in his room. Jason asked if he could have his dad's journals and sketchpads and, even though she would have loved to have kept them herself, Katie said of course he could have them.

She didn't need tangibles, she told herself. She had so many tender memories of their time together. And she had the little cabin in the woods. Katie sat now on the edge of Matthew's bed fingering the opal ring she'd found on the mantle behind the wedding picture of Nancy and Davy the day after Matthew's death. She knew he'd planned it as her engagement ring and to surprise her with it that night.

She'd worn it ever since. Even during delivery of their little girl, Nancy Callahan Vinerelli, eight months later.

She heard a gentle knocking on the door and when she looked up Nick had come in. "It's time for us to go," he said. "You all right?" He took her hand as she stood up from the bed and as they walked to the door he put his arm around her shoulder. "I think it's pretty brave of you to want to do this reading," he said. He helped her into the back seat of his car next to baby Nancy's infant seat and waited to follow the others as they drove down Singer Lane through the woods. Katie clasped her little daughter's hand as they passed the place along the road where she and Matthew first met the early spring day and when she looked out through the windshield of Nick's car, she saw her mother in Tom's car ahead turn to look back at her with eyes that said, "Yes, Katie, m'girl, I remember too."

– End –

Printed in the United States
205798BV00001B/37-42/P